MW00364135

Other Novels by Randall Beth Platt

Honor Bright
Out of a Forest Clearing
The Four Arrows Fe-As-Ko

THE

ROYALSCOPE FE-AS-KO

A Novel by

Randall Beth Platt

CATBIRD PRESS

CATBIRD PRESS
16 Windsor Road, North Haven, CT 06473
800-360-2391; catbird@pipeline.com

Our books are distributed by
Independent Publishers Group

First Edition

This is a work of fiction, and the characters and events
in this book are fictitious. Although the character of
William S. Hart and of other Hollywood figures are based on
people with the same names, the author does not intend that their
words or actions be taken as having actually occurred.

Library of Congress Cataloging-in-Publication Data

Platt, Randall Beth, 1948-
The Royalscope fe-as-ko / by Randall Beth Platt. — 1st ed.
ISBN 0-945774-35-4 (cloth : alk. paper)
I. Title
PS3566.L293R68 1997
813'.54—dc21 96-54506 CIP

To Ollie
From Stan

Welcome Back

Well, I'll be damned if it ain't my favorite writer. Welcome back, son. Set down. You know, I kinda had a idea you'd be back for that silver cigarette case you forgot last week. I'll tell you something else you musta forgot: there's a depression going on, and if ol' FDR cancels this here writing situation for you, I reckon you could sell that case and get five dollars for it, so you hadn't oughta go leaving it places. You could live like a king for a week on five bucks.

You got time for some coffee? Good. — You know, son, since you left I been thinking. I been reading some too. Factually, I read a lot these days. Oh, I know you'd never think it to listen to me. But like you know, the way a man speaks don't say nothing 'bout who he's known, what he's done, or what he's read. So don't think this ol' gentleman ain't been to Verona, 'cause he has. Besides, nothing like reading on the past to make that ol' mem'ry gland start gushing.

It says here in this 1935 almanac that in the year 1900 a feller wasn't expected to live longer than forty-seven point three years. Let's see now, I'm seventy point . . . March, April, May, June . . . I'm seventy point four years old and hell, this rangy cow waddie's beat ol' Scratch outa twenty-three point one years already. I reckon he'll be mighty roiled about that when we do meet up, which, I'm telling you, won't be for many a more year if I have my way.

Nope, I'm feeling right good. Look at that hand. Steady as a prize cow pony pulling a calf line. And look at these eyes . . . blue and clear as they was twenty years ago.

Twenty years ago . . . let's see, that'd be 1915. I was fifty years old. Old enough to know that no matter how strong you think you are in the intellectuals, when you're offa your own range you're still nothing more'n a greenhorn. And you know how greenhorns spend their mornings hunting out mares' nests, their afternoons chasing wild geese, and their nights, burlap bag in hand, calling out, "Hey snipe snipe snipe!" and wondering why the hell the snipe ain't just marching hisself into the bag. I guess that, over the bunkhouse boys' guffawing, the snipes just can't hear you calling 'em. Yup, I shoulda known better. Royal was the greenhorn and Hollywood was his snipe.

Say, I got a idea! Since you was kind enough to set back and write up my Four Arrows episode, maybe ol' FDR won't mind if you hang 'round a spell longer and write down what happened to poor ol' Royal R. Leckner in the year of our Lord 1915.

Put a jolt of hooch in your coffee whilst I draw a bead on those days.

PART 1

one

I hate telegrams. Always have. Reckon I always will. Take firinstance this telegram I got in June of 1915:

> DEARESTDADDY stop (*which I shoulda right there*) MOMMAARRESTED stop SEND FIVE THOUSAND FOR BAIL stop ALSO NEED FIVE THOUSAND FOR LAWYER IN CARE WESTERN UNION SAN FRANCISCO stop MOMMA AND ME SEND LOVE AND REMIND TO FEED OUR HOUSE CATS stop YOUR LOVING DAUGHTER, ELSIE MAUDE stop

Not one 'please, thank you, or may I' in the whole dang thing.

If you think you're confused, think how I felt. My blood pressure still takes a leap when I think on that summer and that telegram that brought my solitude to a screeching halt.

Okay, I'll take a breath and back me up some.

You know, it's funny how things go along real easy-like for a coupla years and a man gets set in his ways, pretty much knowing what the next day will bring. Some folks call it general day-to-day living, some call it rut-riding, and me, I reckon I call it a dang blessed relief from the hoopla that usually follows ol' Royal Leckner. So when things go the smooth trail, I generally don't like to stir the dust up too much. For usually, WHOA! outa the blue, without any encouragement from me, life catches up and that smooth trail of mine gets buried in a sandstorm of one fe-as-ko firing hell-bent for election after the other. So, I shoulda taken more notice of the quiet.

Like you know, the year was 1915. Europe was at war with itself, the *Lusitania* got herself sunk by Germans, ol' Woody Wilson was trying like hell to keep us outa war, and some cranked-up Washington politicians had just saddled us hard-working U.S. citizens with a income tax, of all treacheries! All these worldly warnings I chose to ignore. Nope, war, taxes, and politicians I could reckon with. Universal misery was one thing—domestic treason was another.

Hell, I hate making a major confession before you've had a chance to finish off your first drink, but I reckon you'll be more sympathetic to my plight if I just come out and tell you: E.M., my wife of over twenty years, and me was going over some rocky territories. She'd landed me in more'n one rough spot in our long, fascinating relationship, and I reckon ol' E.M. had herself one of the longest teenager--hoods in history. So when she finally commences to pull the corner on mid-life, well you can be damn sure things got rough. She and me had us alota arguments over this'n'that—mostly little things would send her off, like fir-instance 'who the hell left the cream pitcher out' and 'why can't you just go out and ride some fence for a coupla days like you used to when you was younger and leave me some quiet.' Or onct she flew into a flurry 'bout someone, probably her own daughter, leaving her saddle with one stirrup longer'n the other. Sweartagod, just pitched a fit about her not having anything to herownself anymore.

'Course, I pitched me a fit nowanthen, too. You shoulda heard our flare-up when that peddler came through selling kitchen doohickeys. I saw the whole thing from atopt the windmill where I used to go to hide'n'spy'n'think on things. This peddler was young and handsome and probably hadn't had hisself a sale all day. You shoulda seen how E.M. was flattered by his talk. Why, from clear acrost the barnyard I could see her eyelashes a-batting and her figure a-swirling and her stack of purchases a-growing. I just sat there agitating whilst my wife flirted, yes *flirted*, with a man young enough to be . . . well, a damn sight younger'n her, that's sure. Onct he'd left and I come down all riled and heated up, E.M. hands me this story, she knew all along I was up there watching and she was just trying to make me jealous and here's the bill, serves me right, Ha! Alota credit she gave my knowledge of women. I saw the whole thing. But she just airs herself with a fan he'd given her, touting some new kinda wash soap, and looks dream-like off into the distance into which he'd disappeared, and insteada taking her into my arms and exploiting my own romantical ways, I say probably the stupidest thing to my wife I ever did say: I say, "When you gonna grow up, E.M.?" Then I started to walk away and WANG! that new cast-iron skillet just missed my ear by a inch. I kept walking like I'd just stood down Billy the Kid and halfa the Quantrill boys. 'Course, what I was really telling my wife was—"Be old." But I can only tell you that because now *I'm* old and all those days past are clear as spring water. Now. But then—hell, was I stupid.

So that very same year, 1915, when E.M. announced to me she was taking our daughter, 16-year-old Elsie Maude of the telegram, to San Francisco on an extended annual shopping spree, I said, "You go on ahead, E.M. The change'll do us both good. We been needing some time from each other anyhow." Hell, I just as well mighta said, "Go ahead. Leave me. I don't care less, E.M."

'Course, with the wisdom all these years and this here brandy is providing, I can tell you this is what I shoulda said: "You know, E.M., let's just you and me do the spree together this time. You and me been needing some time together—no horses, no wild-cat children, no books to balance, no peddlers." Then I shoulda swept her up in my arms, which was still pretty dang strong if I say so myownself, and took her away to that San Francisco town and wined her and dined her and lavished love and gifts and attention on her and not come back till we was our old selfs onct again.

But contrary to what you mighta heard, I ain't perfect, so oft I sends 'em both, my wife and my daughter, to San Francisco on what *was* to be a business trip and shopping spree.

Now, stop your cringing, son. I know the words women, business, and spree shouldn't oughta be uttered in the same breath. I can see as how they might be enough to scare the spurs offa some men. But there ain't nothing wrong with two women doing a little trading and a little shopping. It's just I wisht they'd kept their spending on clothes, gifts, household dofunnys, and vineyards like they was supposed to. But I told you how E.M. was getting herself distracted again, which she was then famous for—whether it was campaigning for new ear bobs or squawking about hen's rights or flirting with young peddlers, you could always rely on E.M. getting distracted about something two, three times a year.

Like firinstance back in ought-8, E.M. got herself real lathered up 'bout politics and voting and women's rights and all, and well, dang it! I'll just come out with it plain and simple: E.M. didn't much care for the way our home state of Oregon was handling things, so she got real insistent we move up to Washington State, where it looked like they was taking women a whole lot more serious. Looked like they was gonna give women the vote a mite sooner'n Oregon was, and that was all E.M. needed to pack her bags. Sweartagod, picked up our two baby boys under her arms and daughter Elsie in tow and announced we was moving. We had lotsa money, so I couldn't stand too tall on the we-cain't-afford-it platform. And since I'd been me too long off the range, too long in the 'companiment of streetcars, too long listed in big city phone directories, and too long away from the sweet smella cattle, I quickly agreed.

Oh, I know what you're thinking, but it wasn't *me* handed women all them rights. All I did was move a few miles northwards. Hell, the land she found outside Walla Walla Wash she damn near stole. (Come to think of it, I don't recollect ever seeing a billa sale.)

Well, if there's one thing I'm famous for it's I just wanna keep folks happy, and moving to Washington so's E.M. could do her suffer-aging didn't seem like too much in the way of a sacrifice for me. Hell, since she always told me who to vote for anyhow, I reckoned she might as well be doing it for herownself. E.M.'s pushed, pulled, and convoluted me real hard over the years, but my manhood's always been intact. Yep.

So, off to Walla Walla Wash goes us five Leckners—me to my first-owned spread, three younguns to the good life, and E.M. to her latest distraction.

'Course, E.M. was right about Washington, for that

very year, 1909 it was, she got her wish when we men finally saw the light or caved in (whichever reason you prefer) and gave women the right to vote in Washington. Oregon held out till '12, but like I said, none of it was *my* doing.

So you see, ol' E.M., never too far offa the intellectual altar, was a mighty proud and savvy woman-voter. And just so long she didn't get distracted again and take that temperance thing too serious, we got along real good. I told her, time and time over, "E.M., suffer-aging's one thing, temperancing's another. Stay the hell outa my drinking rights." But I reckon it wasn't E.M.'s fault that our Washington State was working real hard to take away those drinking rights.

So up we went to Walla Walla Wash, and oh was we high-arrival! I thought we had more money'n God, maybe even the Pope, what with E.M.'s inheritance and good accounting sense and a few lucky turns I myownself made. And E.M., well she knew just what to do with all that money. And now's as good a time as any to tell you something. No laughing, cause sweartagod it's true. First off, I was always attracted to E.M.'s nose. It was long and fine and seemed to work real good. And it had, well, a special feature. Seems it would start a ferocious sorta itching when E.M. got 'round what looked like a good investment. You know how some folks say their palms itch when they're 'bout to get some money? Well, E.M. always claimed her nose would itch, and maybe even get a little sniffly, when a good investment was at hand. 'Course, I'd usually just humor her onaccounta she was quite a money-handler. I mostly kept outa things, and it didn't bother me much she was more mystical at times than logical.

So, she invested our money here and there. Additional to her itchy nose, she was a damn good accountant, onct she conquered long division and decimal points. I knew she followed the who's-sick-and-who's-visiting-onaccounta-who's-sick-colum ns of the local papers. That way she had a bead on who was being measured for a funeral sermon a few days before the obituary column came out, and that way she got herself a jump on estate windfalls. Looking back, I guess I hafta admit that bean-counting nose of hers did more'n charm the daylights outa me and hold up her pinch specs.

But all the money in the world can't buy a smooth trail if you're married to a rocky woman like E.M., especially when one of her distractions set in. Oh, you can buy graders and pavers and the smoothest crushed gravel available to build a easy road, but E.M., she'd barrel through a mountain nose-first insteada taking the easy road 'round. To make matters worst, we had us a daughter cast in her momma's exact image. Looking so much alike I reckon can't be helped, not that E.M.'s qualities wasn't worth duplicating. It's just looking, acting, and thinking so much alike is downright scary, and I always did wonder where God's head was that day He handed us our Elsie Maude.

But hell, since I had me two spunky sons to play with, I mostly just gave E.M. and Elsie their imperial-like heads. You know, my cackles still salute on instinct when I look back at how them two women was together. Then I have to grin when I think how I was, more bewildered by 'em both than a hog-tied calf.

So now that you get the picture of who we was, I guess I can get on with where I was, which was a-setting on the front porch of my Royal Bar-L ranch house that slap-bang, slickery summer of 1915.

We had us a swing-like affair hanging from our porch. I can hear it now, creaking back and forth whilst I rocked. I was trying not to get too dozy, but you know how porch swings is. It was a warm morning in late of June and I'd been just feather-bedding around, cleaning my newest Winchester, looking out over my spread. Anyhow, I remember thinking on how good things was going and how quiet things was, since E.M. and Elsie was off on their Annual Spree in Frisco. Hell, I'd even forgot all about the peddlerman.

My sons, Charles (but we called him Chick) and Brian (but we called him Tad, making 'em both together the teama Chick'n'Tad) was never more All-American than they was that summer. Even though they was two years' worth of second thoughts apart, they was almost as alike as was their momma and sister, making me the only spare part. They was fair-faced and had brick-toppish hair, and all you ever heard 'bout redheads is true: give 'em their heads or they'll take yours. They freckled up real good and their eyebrows got all white in the summer sun, and with their blue eyes, well, I just gotta say they was red, white, and blue as the Fourtha July.

Chick'n'Tad spent their summer like all boys should: barefoot, half-naked, tan as allgetout, and riding the shoes offa their horses. Oh sure, they had chores and all, but mostly I let 'em run wild from the moment E.M. left to when she got home. Yessir, the Annual Spree was a vacation for alla us menfolk too.

So things couldn'ta been more peaceful that morning —which shoulda been my first warning. Like I said, when things is that tranquil-like, I'm sure to be heading for a big she-bang. (Ever notice the word ain't *he*-bang?) But even when I saw the dust a-rising off the winding road and I heard the put-pouie of the motorcar, I reckoned I was safe, what with the ladies being so far away and all.

Chick'n'Tad was riding bareback, escorting the automobile, a-whooping and a-hollering like they was Indians a-raiding a chuck wagon. "Pa! Pa! Company!" they shouts, like I was deaf and blind. It would look good to say that I rose careful-like and snapped my Winchester closed like I was ready for a showdown. But hell, we hadn't had us anything in the way of a rustler for nigh onto six years, and even then rustlers hardly ever drove a Model T with "Western Union" written on the door.

two

So there I am walking out to greet the messenger, when the dang fool made a dangerous move: he dangled the telegram outa the window—which, of course, was too great a temptation for my two young rowdies. Chick snatched it clean outa the driver's hand and Tad charged his pony past Chick, snatching the wire clean outa *his* hand. Well, you know how that set. I was lucky to make it back to the safety of the porch without being run over by my own flesh'n'blood.

By the time the telegram was delivered to me, it was in two halfs and my boys was each blaming the other for it. The messenger, calculating the dangers of leaving the sanctuary of his motorcar whilst my boys was on horseback, scratched gravel without so much as 'Howdy, Royal.' I waved anyway, then pieced together my telegram. I wisht the boys had torn it clear to shreds, onaccounta maybe ignorance of certain things is right blissful after all.

Which brings me back to me hating telegrams. Don't know why I bothered to save the dang thing. Lookit that. "Please feed our house cats." I still tell myself, for ten thousand dollars I sure as hell *will* feed their damn house cats . . . to the yard dogs! But you can see for yourownself right there . . . only a Gallucci-Leckner woman can send a 38-word telegram, daytime rates no less, and go from arrestment to ten thousand dollars to feeding cats! Nothing 'bout why E.M. was arrested. No 'Daddy come help!' And for cryinoutloud, everyone on the whole west coast knew how I felt about lawyers! And here's Elsie not batting a eyelash and asking me to send five thousand dollars for some fast-talking, slicky-dressed, tricky Philadelphia lawyer! Ha! Like hell I'd feed their cats!

Anyway, there I stood on the porch, halfa telegram in each hand, chin 'round my boots, staring out on the horizon and remembering all the times E.M. and I laughed ourselfs sick whenever she extorted money from her own daddy, even though he asked for it from time to time, being as how he was hisownself quite the extorter. Since ten thousand was such a hearty amount, I was thinking: Uh oh, now she was doing it to me! Me! Royal, the love of her life, who never got the hanga saying no to her, who'd let her go here and go there and who'd stand in the line of fire when she'd say this and say that, and who'd never give a damn who laughed at me for not keeping my own wife's reins from flapping in the breeze.

I reckon my face was saying, 'Oh God, help us all,' for Chick'n'Tad rode over and asked me who died.

"Huh?" says I. "No one. Not yet."

Then Tad, the youngest, looked at his pa, his sweet face going all serious-like, and said, "Is it from Momma?"

"What's she gone and done this time?" Chick, the realist, asked me, setting sidewise on his horse.

To which Tad fires to his brother, "She might be dying, you dirty ol' shit-ass poop!"

Well, Tad had been calling Chick a dirty ol' shit-ass poop all summer long and I reckon, momma dying or not, he'd taken just about enough. Chick leapt from his horse and pulled Tad clean offa his—and that horse was, as I recollect, smiling a little. So I thought I'd just let 'em discuss the issue right there on the ground whilst I went inside the house to consider the situation.

I kicked the door closed on their discussion and set at my desk, planning my first maneuver. I hardly looked up when Chick, followed closely by Tad, came charging through, going like sixty and each one holding a bloody nose, swearing a streaka black and blue.

I remember how I envied the boys not having one iota what was going through my mind just then. I guess now's as good a time as any to confess some more things: E.M. had invested in vineyards in the valleys 'round San Francisco, and each year she'd go check up on things and usually buy up more land. Well, she'd done right well for us and so I always sent her down with two things: lotsa cash and my power of attorney. Additional, E.M. and I always kept a goodly sum of money in California banks in those days . . . for vineyard business, shopping sprees, and to make things easier for our bankers and stockbrokers.

So just what the hell E.M. needed another ten thousand for scardt the bejesus outa me. Ten thousand for bail and a lawyer! Why, even gangsters and assassins never ran up legal bills like that. Least back then they didn't. Like hell she was setting in jail. No, I imagined E.M. setting high up in the stirrups in that fifty-a-night St. Francis Hotel suite, fanning herself with something like a jaywalking arrest ticket and awaiting my ten-thousand-dollar carte blanche.

Well, I knew I had me some investigating to do. Ol' Alex Bell had been able to work things so's you could call all over the land in those days, but I'll tell you, you'd turn gray, lose your teeth, and develop saddle sores waiting for the operators to get all their wires connected. So I wasn't gonna try and call 'way down to California. Not yet. Instead, I rode into the Western Union office in Walla Walla Wash and I sent my beloved womenfolk at the St. Francis Hotel, San Francisco, the following telegram:

> MY DEARS E.M. AND ELSIE stop WHAT THE stop ARE YOU DOING stop UNABLE TO ARRANGE TEN THOUSAND DOLLARS FOR BAIL AND LAWYER stop I DON'T CARE IF LAWYER IS CLARENCE DARROW stop FIRE HIM stop WHATEVER YOU ARE UP TO STOP stop GET YOUR BUSTLES UP HOME OR ELSE stop

There was no way in hell I was gonna blindly send them two women ten thousand dollars. I didn't give a damn what E.M. had done and I was hellbent on catching her doing it.

I'd been waiting 'round the Western Union office up to a hour when the operator comes and gives me the news that my two women wasn't no longer putting up at that fine hotel. No sir. They'd moved theirselfs to a place called the Ming's Palace Hotel in the Chinatown parta San Francisco.

I can still hear the voice of the Western Union man—Ollie we called him. "You okay, Royal?"

I was just staring acrost the street.

"Royal? Need any more telegrams sent?" Ollie prodded.

"Huh?" I think I finally muttered.

"Sounds like your gals are having themselves quite a spree, eh Royal?" Ollie says. "My missus's been yapping about going to California for years now. Ever since your womenfolk showed up at the lake in those swim get-ups they brought back from. . ."

I didn't need no reminding. I took him by the arm and escorted him back into the office, set him down, and started dictating a telegram to the Police.

This is the telegram I got back:

> MRS. ROYAL LECKNER. CASE NUMBER 35357, RELEASED TWO DAYS AGO stop ALL CHARGES DROPPED stop FINES PAID BY RESPONSIBLE PARTY stop THIS OFFICE SUGGESTS YOU KEEP YOUR WOMEN WHERE THEY BELONG AND STOP SENDING THEM TO SAN FRANCISCO stop WE HAVE ENOUGH PROBLEMS stop

It was signed by the Chief of Police hisownself.

I watched as Ollie interpreted the clicks into those words. When he was done, he looked up at me and asked, "Now, what'ya supposed they did?"

"Thought you wasn't supposed to read folks' telegrams," I grumbled, going through some calling cards I had stuffed in my pocket-book.

"Well, Royal, one can hardly. . ."

"Could you just let me think, Ollie?" I asked, cutting him off. I knew I was gonna hafta tip him plenty to keep his mouth shut.

What the hell was that E.M. up to? Whatever it was, I knew it musta been a lollapaloosa. I'll tell you honest, my biggest fear was that I, Royal R. Leckner, overnight, had become the biggest contributor to the Woman's Suffer-age Movement that which was doing its damnedest to go national. I'd heard how San Francisco was getting plumb tuckered out with women marching up and down streets, in fronta God, the federal building and everyone, spouting their suffer-age.

What made me think my own dear wife would try to out-fox her husband outa ten thousand dollars? Well, by the end of that fateful day, setting in that stuffy Western Union office, I'd learnt that the total sum of alla my California bank accounts was a whole, big, fat zero. Ol' Royal was at low tide.

I made me a call to the Southern Pacific and booked me a ticket for San Francisco . . . next one leaving.

Pass that bottle, son. Think I'll have a shot myownself.

three

I reckon both E.M. and me got what we deserved with our two encumbrances, Chick'n'Tad. In 1915 Chick was ten, which'd make Tad eight, giving 'em a total of eighteen years, alla which wore real heavy on us. It's not that we was spoiling 'em—well maybe we was—it's just that they was boys, plain and simple. Boys born to devilment and one Cowboys-and-Indians chase after another. 'Course, giving 'em want after need after whimsy didn't help much. One minute they'd fight like Trojans, then next they'd be closer'n Chang'n'Eng. But I'll tell you this, they was both my prides and my joys. E.M. had her Elsie and I had my Chick'n'Tad, and I don't know as there ever was, or ever will be, a more troublesome, loving, swearing, or altogether ballihooical fivesome as us Leckners was at times.

I plopped Chick'n'Tad on ponies before they was outa diapers and they was probably the best horse handlers I had on the place by the time they was in school. They just had the touch . . . some folks have a way with critters and some don't. Nothing made my flesh prouder'n when I watched my boys work stock in the corral or correct my calf tally or put a extra shine on their prize bull for the county fair.

Onct, when he was only about eight, Chick hauled in a orphaned calf one snowy day. I'll never forget how he looked: riding in with that scrawny, half-froze calf acrost his saddle-lap. How the hell he got that baby up in the saddle shall remain a mystery forever, I suppose. Anyhow, the boys built up a roaring fire in the old smoke house and together they spent one cold night rubbing some life into that baby and feeding it bottled milk they stole from the pantry.

Well, it wasn't long before Elsie, who was approaching the sophisticated age of fourteen or thereabouts, came sneaking in, all bundled up and hell-bent to help out her brothers. Now you gotta remember that Elsie didn't usually have much to do with ranch work, beyond riding for leisure. She passed up the cow jane business when she was about twelve, at which time she opened up a storefront and went into the boy business. But on that cold night Elsie helped the boys out best she could, and when that calf came 'round I thought we'd hafta declare a ranch holiday. I don't recollect ever being more swolt with pride as when my three youn-guns came outa that smokehouse, all tousled, sleepy-eyed, and weary, but grinning and emptier'n a zealot fresh offa a hunger strike. Speaking of zealots, that calf became Chick'n' Tad's prize bull. Took second in the state as I recollect, but the boys didn't have the heart to sell that bull for steaks like alota prize bulls ended up. Yep, there was alota me in Chick'n'Tad.

But even as I look back, with love, grins, and the feara God on how we was alla us together, it still don't gloss over how mad I was setting in that Western Union office. I thanked Ollie for rushing my telegrams through and I was hoping the fin I slipped him would encourage his tongue to take a rest for a while. Also, in light of all my financial woes that day, I wanted him to think that, hell, a fiver for a tip was nothing to me. After all, I still had lotsa money. Somewheres. All I had to do was get E.M. to tell me where.

When I got back home, I called in my foreman and told him how I wanted things done in my absence which, knowing E.M., could run into a considerable amount of time.

Our housekeeper back then was a loving old sort by the name of Ida. I also instructed her that should E.M. or Elsie or the Chief of Police or anybody else ring up looking for me, to tell 'em you don't know where I went and you don't expect me home for you don't know how long. Well, you shoulda seen how Ida looked at me. She'd been with us for six years, so she knew something was up. But I think I convinced her we was playing us a rounda fiduciary hide'n' seek and she wasn't to be too concerned about it at all. She just shrugged her shoulders like it was business as usual, and allowed as how I oughta take the boys and give her a vacation. I know blackmail when I see it, so I booked two more seats aboard the Southern Pacific and Ida, near as I recollect, had herself a real fine summer.

Hell, I thought, so long as I had Chick'n'Tad with me, it would be the three of us males against those two women, and I had a feeling I was gonna need all the sway I could get. So the boys was packed up too, spouting few complaints.

* * *

So there we was, the boys and me, standing at the train depot, our plunder stacked all 'round us. E.M. and Elsie took all the good luggage, so we looked like real carpet-baggers, right outa the sixties. And the boys looked like they was Huck Finn and Tom Sawyer running away from home, onaccounta their nice traveling togs was just plain too small. So Ida put 'em up in their best play clothes which, by the time we got to town, was all mussed up anyhow.

Well, so much for tipping Ollie to encourage him to keep his quiet, I thought when a man approaches me and calls out, "Say, Royal!" 'cause it weren't *any* man that said it. I stopped and turned 'round, probably looking a little chop-fallen. "Howdy, Wilton," I said back, but I was thinking, *anyone* but Wilton.

"Taking a little trip, eh?" he asked.

"Yep," I explained.

"Need a lawyer?" he asks, reaching into his vest pocket for his card, like trips'n'lawyers just naturally go together like guns'n'ammo.

"You can keep your damn card, Wilton. I know who you are and I know what you do." In those days we had one motor car ambulance in Walla Walla Wash and sweartagod, ol' Wilton chased it with such a earnest sensa commitment, they just commenced to let him ride along with his prospective customer. So, everyone knew ol' Wilton and usually about-faced when he approached.

Anyway, the last thing I needed that day was the sympathy of a lawyer, so I tipped my hat like as to leave. Then he said something which I've never come to figure out.

"Need some money?" he asked me. Well, I stopped dead in my tracks and turned real careful-like.

He was smiling kindly to me, like he wanted me to know he was sincere. Then he takes me by the arm and whispers, "Look, Royal, I know what you're going through. Why, my wife's in Seattle right now, even as we speak. Helping to organize a West Coast march."

"Marcha what?"

"Suffrage, of course!" he said, looking at me like I'd been living under a rock lately. "Ain't it enough we let women vote around here, but now they want it so's they can *all* vote. Even *southern* women!"

"Look, my going to California has nothing to do with. . ." I tried, but I reckon my deep-dark fears was coming true.

"Royal, Royal, you can level with me. My own wife told me why your women went to San Francisco."

"Shopping," I defended.

Ol' Wilton started to gurgle a little laugh of sympathy. "Royal, Royal, Royal," says he, tragic-like and shaking his head.

It was at that moment Chick comes running up to me with Tad trailing. "Pa! Pa!" he calls out, pulling at my coat tail. "Can we have us a candied apple?"

As I was reaching into my pocket for a nickel, Wilton beats me to it and hands Chick a dime. "Here, son. My treat," he says.

"Royal," Wilton continued to me, "I'm speaking now as your friend, a fellow comrade-in-arms. It's all over town you're at trouble's doorstep and it's your wife who's delivered you there." Then he sorta tells me up close, "I even heard about that peddler incident."

I looked him hard and growled, "What'd you hear about what peddler?"

"Look, Royal, we all know E.M.'s got a strong head."

I couldn't argue. Then he says, "Now here, take this." He re-hands me his card and continues, "It has my office number. I'm afraid you wife's reputation might have preceded her."

"I told you, I don't need. . ." I said, getting a little hot. But then his words set in and I stopped. "What reputation?"

"No charge, Royal. No charge." And for the third time he slaps his card into my hand.

"Excuse me, you said 'no charge'?" I asked. I looked at the card to make sure he was still working as a lawyer.

"No charge."

I pocketed his card and thanked him, muttering, I think, something about he was wrong but it was nice to have him in my corner.

"Just in case," he added, giving me a brotherly handshake.

Well, it's amazing how clear things is when you look back on 'em. I know now the value of those three little words, 'Just in case.'

four

The first leg of the journey was mighty viewish, being as how we was running alongside that mighty Columbia River. And I'm here to tell you that river and the gorge that held it in was nothing shorta gorgeous. Maybe that's where they got the word. 'Course that was long before ol' FDR and his damming ideas for the river, and it sure ran wild and frothy at places back then. I wonder what it'll look like onct they get the Grand Coulee finished. Every time I'm privileged to rest my eyes on that river and the velvet hills that run down to it, I wonder how the same One that created the forests coulda done such a fine job on the rivers too. Betwixt you and me, I think it took a mite longer'n a week.

When we got to Portland, we jumped tracks and boarded the Southern Pacific, and I splurged on a sleeping car. This I did as a favor to the rest of the passengers, onaccounta Chick'n'Tad. It was always damn prudent to have somewheres to corral 'em up and settle 'em down.

Yessir, my two hell-pups had theirselfs a regular holiday, taking over the train the way they did. By the second day they'd charmed the ladies, made a dozen friends, and held a porter hostage. And I, seeing the porter was in such good hands, found the bar car and set there awaiting the train's entry into the liquor-legal State of California.

You see, just the year previous, 1914, a buncha bible-backing, pulpit-pounding, temperance-toting folks (alota them men, too) took it upon theirselfs to vote booze out and sobriety in. But hell, I knew all along the minute we allowed women into those dang voting booths they'd pull something like this. I knew they'd rant, rave, lobby, march, whine, and moan my favorite whiskey right outa my hands and into the hands of purse-leeching moonshiners, who I'd then be forced to buy from at twice the price. And that's just what happened. Washington and Oregon too, so's it wasn't like I could sneak down acrost the state line and stock up. Now, to be fair, ol' E.M. enjoyed a short-snorter just as much as me nowanthen, so even though she was a suffer-agette she wasn't no Temperance Tilly, for which I was mighty glad.

Nope, she set that road good and even. Maybe that was something she got from me. You see, I always did ride real even in the saddle. I don't put too much weight in my left stirrup, don't put too much weight in my right stirrup. That way I'm more likely to stay atopt the horse, no matter what the terrain.

But anyway, since temperance came in and logic went out, I'd been a pretty dry cowpoke, so the bar car, with its assortment of liquors, was a oasis in a desert, and onct we was outa Oregon things got more relaxed. There I was setting with four fingers of whiskey, looking out over that beautiful northern California countryside.

Now don't go getting the idea I was a big drinker. Sluicing the worries ain't no shortcut to reducing the worries. I was just captive. Additional, from the very get-go I always thought a shot or two helped me to ponder through a vexing situation, like the one I was traveling, fifty miles per hour, toward.

I remember setting back, closing my eyes, and using the steady click-clack underneath to relax me. My first vision was of, wouldn't you know it, E.M. I had five years on her, so in 1915 she was forty-five, when most women had already won the porcelain hairnet and was crankier'n she-bears short on their hibernations. But not my wife. No, ol' E.M. took forty-five right smart-like. I still found her damn good looking. Well okay, maybe she did have a few streaks of gray, but mostly her hair was the same sleek black it was when I met her back in '92. Long and thick and black. Her I-talian face was wearing real good and her brown eyes was just as snappy at me as they always was. She was still right fetching, even though she was fast approaching her allotted forty-seven point three years.

The trip took just under three days, all tolled. We pulled into San Francisco late on a Monday afternoon in the last week of June. They set the steps down for us before the train had even come to a halt-to, and it was real handy having all our bags packed for us and tossed first onto the train platform. That way, we was able to get a head start on Frisco, not having to wait in the baggage line and all.

Well, you shoulda heard the oohs and aahs from Chick'n'Tad as we walked out onto the street. I'd done my best to prepare 'em for the sights they'd see. Being as I'd been to Frisco before, I could tell 'em 'bout the skyscrapers, the Snob Hills, fog horns, Alcatrazes and all.

Well, there just ain't no preparing any cowpoke —young, old, or middling—for the sights of any big city, specially Frisco. Chick'n'Tad craned their necks back and looked skyward, shaded their eyes and whistled in amazement. San Francisco wasn't no New York City, but it did wear a mighty shawl of commerce. And the shawl that day was a mystical-like fog.

Getting a cab was easy enough, being as they just set there outside the train station awaiting your pleasure. Naturally, I chose a horse-drove one over a motorcar, and the boys wasn't too happy 'bout that, but I reminded 'em four legs was far trustier'n four wheels any day. 'Course the driver takes one gander at ol' Royal in his mail-order travel duds, cowboy boots, and Stetson and takes me for a hayseed.

"Where to, cowboy?" he asks.

'Course hayseed is exactly what I felt like when he glares back at me and says, "You mean to tell me you're taking those two young boys to the Ming's Palace Hotel?"

"You know a reason why I shouldn't?" I asked back, feeling my heart thunk some.

"Well, that's in Chinatown, you know . . . it's going to be dark soon," he says, like he hisself was feeling a little on the anxious seat.

"So light yer lamps," I suggested, and I commenced to pile our things on board.

He did just that and when some of that light cast itself down on me, the driver does the dangest thing. His face goes all smiles and he says, "Say, where do I know you from?"

I allowed as how he ain't never seen me before onaccounta I ain't never seen him.

He turned back 'round, swearing he knew me. But I frankly had my mind in a thicker jam that day, for I was about to meet up with E.M. and Elsie. Now, it'd been three days since we left home and that means I had two sleepless nights a-pondering what treason my wife coulda hatched up in the three weeks she'd been in Frisco. But over the years, I've learnt not to get too hopped up 'bout things . . . you know, don't go twisting the lion's tail till you've heard the content of her roar.

The fog was falling 'round us in the 'companiment of

nightfall and the driver slowed up some—or maybe it was his horse who slowed up as we entered the Chinatown district. The boys had stopped their oohing and aaahing and I could feel 'em sidle up closer to my either sides. There was a eerie fogbow 'round the gaslights. I swear the horse started to tiptoe. Now don't laugh. If you'd been around horses long as I have you'd know it's true. They know when to keep their arrivals to a minimum. They know spooky territory when they enter it and reckon we alla us, the driver, the boys, me, and the horse all knew we was stepping careful through Chinatown.

There was those puffy paper lanterns swinging low over the streets, which woulda scared the shoes offa any horse of mine, and folks on the corners wasn't looking much like ol' Mainstreet USA. They was as Chinese as they was back in Shanghai—all silks and satins and pigtails and talk no one West of Ulysses S. Grant could understand.

"You know," the driver says down to me, "folks think this part of town's a real hellhole."

"Then you best make sure we don't fall in it," advises me, seeing he was close to knocking over some peddler's food cart. We got us swore at in Chinese, a first I reckon for alla us.

"So, what sorta place is this Ming's Palace Hotel?" I asked, leaning in closer to the driver.

"Well, the folks that stay there . . . well, they've been known to be a bit, oh, what's the word? . . . eccentric."

Eck-cen-trick. Three short syllables which pretty much described my wife. Ol' E.M.'d feel right at home there all right the way she'd been acting of late. But I asked, "Eccentric in what way?" although I think I had a pretty good notion what way they was—I had visions of this Ming's Palace Hotel being the hotbed for all that woman's suffer-age stuff that E.M. got herself so worked up over. Like maybe they'd taken over the joint, like revolutionaries is wont to do.

So when he answered me with, "Why, everyone knows that's where those movie people hang out," my mouth opened, my tongue flapped some, but nothing immortal fell out.

Eventually I managed, "Movie people?"

"You know, actors," the driver said.

Ohmigod, ACK-tors! I thought, setting back down. What the hell was E.M. and Elsie doing in the midst of ACK-tors? Dope fiends! High livers! Then all them stories of white slavery began to gallop full chisel into my mind. That was it! They'd been kidnapped by white slavers and the ten thousand Elsie wired me for was ransom money! Ohmigod! My two gorgeous womenfolk, dressed in see-through lace and hoochie-cooing in opium dens and calling it acting!

Well, if you think my neck veins is bulging now, you shoulda seen 'em then.

Anyhow, it took a few deep breaths to get me settled down. Chick'n'Tad looked up at their daddy and asked me what was wrong, and when was we gonna see Momma? I composed myself, set their heads at ease, and asked the driver to speed it up, even if the hill we was attacking was a real challenge to the horse.

We was alla us quiet the rest of the journey through Chinatown. 'Course you know what I was expecting in the way of a Ming's Palace Hotel . . . dark, leery, maybe a blind Chinaman fortune teller on the corner warning us to turn back. So when the driver announced we was there, I was mighty reliefed. The place sure looked normal enough.

The driver musta read my mind, 'cause he just grinned more and said, "Filled to the top floor with nuts."

Well, I knew all there was to know about nuts, I reckoned, including picking 'em, cracking 'em, and letting 'em grow. Some of the friendliest smiles outa my past came offa the faces of certified nuts. Plus, I did pull off the reknownst Four Arrows Fe-as-ko of 1893, for which I was then famous, at least somewheres back North of God. Mentally outa-sorts folks didn't and still don't scare me none. You always know where you stand with a half-brain, onaccounta the half the Man Above lets 'em keep is the trusting, loving half—not the half us so-called 'regulars' have to juggle about . . . good to evil, evil to good.

The horse gave a snort like as to say, hurry up, get out and let me outa here, which I was only too happy to take as a omen. But I have to tell you, that Ming's place looked right pretty. It had layers of balconies and nice red brick, like some place ol' Queen Vic mighta stayed in herownself. So, my heart settled a bit and I doubted there was even one opium bowl in Ming's Palace Hotel.

Walking through that hotel lobby, I gotta be honest, I didn't see me one nut setting around. All I saw was nice-dressed ladies and a few gents, all setting at tables sipping tea. Hell, I thought I was back in London for all the fineries I saw. Who in the Sam Hill put this genteel place here in this seedy parta town, I was wondering.

Trying not to look so westernish, I took off my Stetson before opening my mouth to the desk man. But I got a chilled voice when he asked, barely glancing at me, "May I help you?" I think maybe they teach them at Desk Man School to act sorta uppity-like.

"Yes," I replied. "I would like the room number for Mrs. Leckner."

It was then he looked me serious, and the same smile of recognition that was on the cab man's face was now on this feller's face. "Say, aren't you. . ." he began, pointing his pen at me.

"Royal Leckner," I replied. I didn't want to be rude, I just wanted to get to E.M. "Would you look for my wife?"

He looked a little disappointed whilst he said, "Leckner, Leckner, Leckner." He flipped through the register. "I'm sorry, I have no Leckner. Would you like to try someone else?"

"What the hell you mean, try someone else?" asks me, not mad, just confused.

"Please, sir. The tearoom," he said. He pointed his pen toward the folks sipping and nibbling and being, in general, quite sedate. "What I meant is, many of our guests and residents prefer to use their marquee names. Does your Mrs. Leckner go by another name?"

Well, the only mar-kee I knew about was that one of Queensberry, and I wondered if ol' E.M. had found herself another boxing man to train. "Mar-kee names?" asks me, wondering what satchel I'd tucked my old friends Mr. Smith and Wesson into.

"Yes, stage names," the clerk replied, like that was something I just oughta have known.

I was thinking of all the names I'd silently called my wife in the last coupla days, but in trying to keep the famous Leckner cool I said, "Mrs. Leckner is not a ACK-tor. She is my wife. Now look again in that book. If I have to tear this here place apart from its tearoom to its mar-kees fulla nuts, I'm gonna find her!" I then realized I was clutching the desk man by his tie and speaking nose to nose. So much for the famous Leckner cool. I apologized and set him down.

Well, as he wasn't too manly about my treatment and I think I even saw some tears in his eye, I figures, huh oh, I've riled me a light-stepper. He whirled the register 'round and said, "There! Look for yourself!"

I looked and didn't recognize any name there. I apologized onct again and, I gotta be honest, I was damn near close to tears myownself.

"Pa?" Chick said, tugging at my sleeve.

"Not now, Chick," I said, setting my mind to what I was gonna do next.

"Hey Pa!" Tad joins in, tugging at my other sleeve.

"I said not now!"

Then Chick'n'Tad said together and most insistent-like, "Pa-aaaa!"

I looked down at 'em to chew 'em out, then followed their points towards the gaggle of tea drinkers. "You stay here," I commanded, and they knew by my voice they oughta.

I took a few strides toward the tearoom and stared, not wanting to believe what my own two eyes insisted I see. There, centered in a group of well-dressed men, was a woman of a most striking and familiar nature. She was chatting gay-like. She held onto a long holder which had a lit cigarette on the end and, sweartagod, she put her lips to it and tugged in a breathful and let the smoke back out in dainty little puffs. No coughing or nothing. I walked smack-dab though sets of chatting people and didn't give a damn about manners. I stopped a good ten-foot shooting distance from her crowd, and I knew then how a gunslinger feels at a showdown.

My instincts wanted me to grab her up and tell her what for, but I realized I was in a whole other world, so I just stood there in fronta her and said, "Howdy, E.M."

Now, any other woman woulda dropped her tea cup, maybe even fainted, but my E.M. wasn't like any other woman. She looked up at me, smiled me her famous I-talian smile, set her cigarette holder down, exhaled some smoke, and said, cool as Custer, "Oh hello, Royal. What kept you, darling?"

five

Geemanee Christmas, just when you think you got the drop on a woman, she can look you over cool, smile half-crooked up at you and, just with her eyes, suggest it's all your fault.

E.M. rises and says, "Gentlemen, please excuse me." And, of course, they all, everyone of 'em, stands up just onaccounta she might stub her toe, I guess. Well, I had news for 'em: she coulda fallen flat on that nose of hers and I woulda tripped the first yap to rush to her rescue. I reckon that gives you the ideas that was rushing through my brainpan that day. Anyway, E.M. made it acrost the tea-room without so much as a titter or anything. In fact, I recollect she walked real regal-like, adding to my fury. No meekness, no nothing.

And so right past me she struts and, seeing Chick'n'Tad, calls to 'em with outstretched arms, "Charles! Brian! My darlings!"

'Course, being younguns they fell for it. They both

gushed right into her arms and, like all scenes betwixt mommas and sons reuniting, it was touching.

But not into ol' Royal's arms did that woman fall and I reckon I was crushed flatter'n a rabbit on a racetrack. Yeah, and with reflexes to match, onaccounta I was thinking but I wasn't saying nothing and I wasn't doing nothing but watching, until I finally got out, "E.M., you better start talking and it better be good!" I took her by the arm and started to escort her to the elevator. "We're going to your room."

"Oh, Royal," says she, "how romantic. But what about the boys?" I could tell by the tone of her voice she was trying to joke me outa my rage, which, dead to rights, was building right fine.

"Anything we got to say to each other they got a perfect right to be privy to," I said, stopping in fronta the elevator. "What floor?"

"Three," she said, kinda low-like. I guess she was finally acknowledging the corn and seeing the trouble she was in. That smile of hers was vanished and right there I was telling myself that I wasn't gonna let any of her tears, should she have the desperation to shed 'em, steal my thunder.

Even Chick'n'Tad knew we was all in for a brouhaha, for they was quiet and each one a-gripping their momma's hands. Well, there goes my male majority, I remember thinking.

Onct the grate on the elevator closed, I had the presence of mind to ask, "And just where is our daughter?"

"She's out for the evening," E.M. answered, kinda curt-like and looking straight ahead.

To which I asked, like fathers gotta right to, "And just who in this Chinatown hellhole is her chaperone?" I was bellowing, and I reckon half the passing second floor musta heard me.

"Oh Royal, this is 1915! It's perfectly all right for girls to. . ." She stopped when she saw my eyes, which we both knew was a damn prudent move.

The doors opened on the third floor and I looked into the hallway. My mouth musta dropped back down to the first floor when I saw them nude paintings on the walls.

'Course Chick'n'Tad, being All-American boys and maybe a tetch more evil'n most, drops their momma's hands and runs to the paintings.

"Saaaaaaaaay," Chick marvels, "wouldja lookit that!"

Ol' Tad, being not quite as sophisticated, just drops his chops and mutters, "Hot damn!" I acted fast, covered their eyes and, real aghast-like, demanded of my wife, "E.M.!"

Well, she was scrambling through her tiny beaded purse for her room key and pulled it out real fast. I escorted my protesting sons inside and slammed the door shut with my boot.

I never in my life ever saw a room like the one E.M. had for herself in that Ming's Palace Hotel. All I can say is this: take one wall from a palm reader's parlor, one wall from a Roman Senate, one wall from a gilded whorehouse, and the last wall from the 'Don't Do This' column in a decorating magazine and there you had my wife's hotel room.

I tossed my hat down hard to the floor and began with, "What the hell are you up to, woman?" She always hated it when I called her 'woman,' and I reckon she knew she ain't heard nothing yet.

"Royal, please, not in front of the boys," she says demur-like, which, she shoulda known, I saw right through.

So I asked, "You gotta bathroom here?"

To which E.M. replied, "For heaven's sake, Royal, this is 1915! Of course we have a bathroom here. Through that door."

"Gotta bathtub in it?"

"Of course, Royal. This *is* San Francisco, you know."

"Boys," says me, "get on in there and take yourselfs a bath."

"Ah Pa, do we hafta?" moans they, identical.

Well, like I said, I was generally real easy-going with 'em, but I'll give 'em credit: they knew by my eyes when I was roiled. They both slunk away toward the bathroom.

That made us alone, face to face and eye to eye. She looked at me and I looked at her. I walked around her, taking in her get-up. She held tight.

Then I set down on some kinda brocaded affair, crost my legs, and just demanded, "Well?"

Well, I knew better'n to think she'd fly to her knees and wrap her arms 'round my legs, begging my manly forgiveness, but I did think something in the way of a apologetic explanation was in order. Instead, she looks down at me and asks, "Well what?"

I closed my eyes to pull back my anger and then answered, "You have exactly five minutes to explain, Genesis to Revelation, what the hell you've done with all our California money."

The least she coulda done was to look surprised I knew about the zero balances. But she just held her ground, put her hands on her hips, and asked back, "Don't you even want to hear about my arrest? It was awful, Royal, just awful!" Then I saw the chute she was planning on prodding me through.

I said, "E.M., like you and I both recollect, it ain't the first time you been arrested. No matter what, I've seen you take worst. I also happen to know you was let off and given into the charge of a responsible party. Now who the hell you know besides *me* is a responsible party, may I be so bold to ask?"

I guess I was hollering by then.

But ol' E.M. held tight and said, "Yes, but Royal, don't you even *care* what happened?" At that, she sounded a little weepy, but I just dug my heels in. She set in the chair acrost from me. She took a big sniff but was yet to produce the waterworks. Then she continued with, "There I was, minding my own business. . ."

"Now hold it right there, E.M.," I interrupts, onaccounta I knew she musta been lying already.

She knew perfectly well why I'd stopped her, and she backed right up with, "All right, there I was, holding that torch. . . "

"Torch!" I hollered.

"Now Royal, I don't think I can get through this if you start screaming," she said, reaching, of course, for a hankie. She produced another sniff, this time in the 'companiment of a shaky lower lip.

So I re-asked, gritting my teeth, "Torch? And why was you holding a torch this time?"

"It was a torch-light parade!" she said a little snappish-like. And her eyes added a 'you dope!' to her reply. Then the hankie rose delicately to her eyes, which she was casting downward, maybe to encourage the deluge.

"I suppose this has something to do with that suffer-age thing of yours," I said, casting my arms about the room to make my point.

"Well, it started out that way. Just a nice, simple little rally. Why, you know how important suffrage is to me, Royal. So, when I heard there was going to be a rally, you just *know* I'm going to be there! Well anyway, things got out of control and. . ."

"For God's sake, E.M., quit wringing your hands! It ain't becoming of you!"

"Well all right, damn it, Royal!" she snaps right back at me. "They said I laid fire to the courthouse!"

I swallered. Now setting fire to the courthouse in a town the size of Walla Walla Wash might be one thing, but the courthouse in San Francisco! So, careful-like, I asked, "And did you?"

"Only a little," she says, defending herself with a straight back and a proud nose.

"Yes or no, E.M.!"

"Yes, my torch started the flag burning. . ."

"The flag of these United States of America?" I hollered. Burning courthouses is one thing. Burning the flag's another.

"Royal, it was an accident!" she hollers back. "Anyway, things settled down and they got the fire out. You know, since the earthquake they've really improved their fire department. . ." She stopped when she felt the fire in my eyes.

"So the courthouse is still standing?" I asked.

"Oh, the damn courthouse is fine, Royal! A new coat of paint up the front and. . ."

"Then are we getting to the part about the money?" I asked.

"In a roundabout way."

"Never mind the scenic route, E.M.!" I growled.

So then she looks at me head-on and states, "You know, Royal, half that money is *mine*."

At that point I couldn't take it anymore. I stood up, eyeballed her hard, and yelled, "For cryinoutloud E.M.! Tell me what you've done with all our money!"

E.M. looked around and said, "Please don't shout, Royal. Countess Arellia is conducting a seance!" She indicated the hallway outside, then gave her nose a unladylike tootning.

"I don't care if Catherine the Great is plucking her nosehairs! I don't care if you burned down alla San Francisco and halfa Oakland! What the hell did you do with all our money?"

"All right, all right, all right," E.M. says, more hankie waving, more tears welling forth. "It goes like this: I got arrested for the torch thing. Really, Royal, I was just standing under the flags outside, holding my torch. . ."

"Get to the improvement, E.M.!"

"Okay, okay. So they arrest me anyway. Some trumped-up arson charge or something. Anyway, I'm in jail. Well, you never take money to a rally in San Francisco, especially at night. It just isn't done. Pickpockets, you know. So I'm in jail and I turned to Elsie and. . ."

I turned slow and burnt her with, "Turned? Like she was right there in that jail with you?" My eyes was firing shotsa steel.

"Well, yes, you see Elsie was . . . well, mothers and daughters alike are all sisters in these matters. . ."

Some explanation. "You mean you got my daughter arrested too?"

"Well, she just was sort of swept along by the, well, the enthusiasm. Besides, she spoke real eloquent when we went before the night judge. Oh, sit down, Royal, and let me finish. So, there was this man in the courtroom. Our savior, really. He'd been shooting pictures of the rally and so he saw the whole thing and. . ."

"You mean like a newspaper man or something?" I asked.

"Well, not exactly, but that's not important. So, he told the judge what he saw and even offered to have the film done up so we'd have proof the fire was an accident. Well, the next day when that film came back, there it was, plain and simple, an accident. Not only that, he was the man who arranged for Elsie and I to move hotels so the press wouldn't hound us. You know, those pressmen are getting real pushy these days."

"The *money*, E.M." I reminded her before she got distracted by the boldness of the fourth estate.

"Oh, by the way, don't be alarmed by any articles you might happen to read about this. I've told you, plain and simple and true, exactly what happened. The court records show it."

But they didn't mention the money, so I asked her would she kindly explain to me about Elsie's telegram.

On that one her face goes all blank and I reckoned I had her. I reminded her of the content: bail, lawyers, ten thousand dollars, and I think I added something to the effect that someone had let out one of her cats, that prized Persian one I think, and it was gonna be a barn cat momma by August.

"Oh, Elsie's telegram. Wasn't that silly? I guess she wasn't herself for awhile. She must have panicked. We're working on it. Nothing like city living to teach a young woman straight thinking," E.M. continued, trying to pull me down another trail.

Sweartagod, I can't recollect if I was stymied or stupid or stubborn or just plain stinging. "E.M., how come you needed another ten thousand dollars when you've already gone through damn near everything we had here in California?"

"Well, there was this wonderful opportunity and, of course, we did owe Marco a huge favor."

"Marco?" I asked.

"Yes, Marco Magellan, the filmmaker, the man who got us off. Haven't you been listening?"

By then I was walking 'round her like a interrogator or something and I told her she better hadn't say another word other than a plain and simple answer to, "Where . . . is . . . our . . ." I pulled out a slip of calculations from my vest pocket and read the total to her ". . . our fifteen thousand, six-hundred and forty-three dollars?" I shoved the paper in fronta her nose and awaited her reply.

She took my paper of financial demise and said, "Well, actually, Royal, it's more like an even twenty thousand. I was able to mortgage one of the vineyards and I. . ."

"Mrs. Leckner," I says, holding in my voice best I could, "what have you done with our money?"

Her reply was a slow walk to a desk drawer, a pulling out of some contract-looking papers, and these words: "Congratulations, Royal! You own the controlling interest in a brand new moving pictures company!"

I took the papers, glared down at my wife, and demanded, "Huh?"

Well, E.M. hadn't spent too many of her days smiling meek-like, but you better believe that smile she cast me that fateful day was fulla inherited earth.

I was then wondering if the State of California hung or shot its wife-murderers, but you know how God interferes with evil-thinking nowanthen. As it so happens, the door to the bathroom opened just then, and there stood Chick'n'Tad dripping wet with one towel 'round 'em both. Water was gushing through the door like they was the last ones through the departed Red Sea.

"Hey, Momma!" Chick hollers, his hands on his hips and holding a back brush. "How the heck you turn off the water in this hellhole?"

Yep, it's true. We get just what we deserve in this life. Probably the one hereafter, too.

six

Now if that wasn't a scene, I'd like to know what was: E.M. and me, nose to nose in mortal combat, water gushing through the bathroom door, and my boys, one of 'em toting a back brush. We was alla us screaming, not a one of us listening to the other.

I got the water turned off and I'll tell you, it took a mighty tug against the knob. How Chick'n'Tad got it on so tight, I prefer not to know. Well, we was slipping and yelling and sopping towels around, and Tad was laughing at how slickery my boots was on that tiled bathroom floor. E.M. was holding up her lace-hems so's not to ruin 'em, and I know she was yelling just to keep from laughing at me. On my third skate through I was a goner, and maybe I did look a little on the comical side, setting nose to nose with the commode. But hell, I wasn't done chewing E.M. out, or grilling her for that matter, so the last thing I wanted to do just then, sprawled out on the bathroom floor, was start laughing myownself.

But I guess we alla us needed that laugh. Anyway, just as I was looking my most foolish—soaking wet, hair all undone, and face still red from everything—there comes a knock on the door 'companied by a "Mother! Mother! Open up, Mother!"

E.M. goes and opens the door on my a-wandering daughter, Miss Elsie Maude Leckner. She comes rushing in, saying, "Mother, I heard screaming clear down the hall. Is everything all . . . right?"

She looked over and saw me, her beloved Daddy, standing in a pool of water. Did she fly into my arms? Nope. Did she say a nice welcome? Nope. Did she offer me a towel? Nope. Instead, she looks at E.M. and says a most un-elegant, "Uh oh."

Whereupon E.M. says, and most prudently I'll add, "Oh look, Elsie, look who's come to surprise us."

Well, no telling what them women said to each other with their eyes, but Elsie allows me a cordial-like hello and with it barely a hug, onaccounta I was so wet, I think. Then she looks down at the river flowing from the bathroom and she adds, "Oh, and I see you brought the boys."

She careful-like stepped toward the bathroom and pushed the door open. 'Course, she knew enough not to give the boys a clear shot at her. So instead she said a sugary, "Hello, Charles and Brian."

To which they sang out their welcome, kinda a tradition for 'em, which was a hair-pulling verse from "She May Have Seen Better Days." All I can remember is the end part:

> Tho by the wayside she fell,
> She may yet mend her ways.

Some poor ol' mother is waiting for her
Who has seen better days!

Well, nothing made ol' Elsie madder'n when Chick' n'Tad sang her that song. But Elsie knew there was bigger tempests brewing.

E.M. always knew when to step in, being so experienced in things of this nature, and she picked it up by saying, "Elsie dear, you're back early."

Then, like I wasn't there, let alone dripping wet, Elsie takes off her gloves and says, real dreamy and dramatical, "Oh, that gorgeous, sweet, wonderful man! Do you know what that Chesley Warwick did? He *insisted* he get me back early, for my 'beauty sleep'."

'Course, it was the word 'man' and not them adjectives that riled me most, and so I inquired, "And just who or what the hell is a Chesley Warwick?"

Elsie looked at me and blinked those big eyes of hers and explained, "Only the actor hailed to be the Bushman of 1916!"

Don't recollect what scardt me most—the ACK-tor part, the aborigine part, or the fact that I'd somehow lost a year. Cautious, I asked, "Ain't this 1915?"

E.M. jumped in with, "What she means is, Chesley Warwick is a new, up-and-coming face and by this time next year he'll be a star as big as Francis X. Bushman."

"Who is?"

"Only the man voted by the slicks as America's Favorite Male Movie Lead." She goes on to inform me I oughta be lucky I got Chesley Warwick in what she called a 'exclusive' contract.

'Course I'm still leaking water all over, and the boys, a-splashing in the tub, was finishing up another rowdy chorus, when into the midst of this heart-rendering scene of family close-knitness comes another knock on the door, and in waltzes a woman who I immediately guessed, by her fringe and her spangles and her to-do, was the so-called Countess Arellia from down the hall, fresh outa her seance.

"A pox! A pox upon you all!" she screams, waving her arms 'bout the room, her bracelets a-jingling in the breeze.

"Countess! Whatever is wrong?" E.M. asked.

"A pox, I tell you! I had him! I had him! Right there, he was all around us!" Her eyes was black as coal and about as far away as Wichita. No doubt this was one of them eccentrics of which the driver had foretold.

"Then we heard the voices of angels, singing from on high," the Countess continued, her eyes widening and looking 'round the room.

Angels on high. Ha! Them was Chick'n'Tad.

Then the Countess continues with, "Then voices of anger . . . *your* voices . . . and he was gone! Gone, I tell you! A pox upon you all!"

With that she swirled her way out the door, although she was so spooky-like, I wouldn'ta flinched none if she'd gone right through the wall.

After the Countess had left, E.M. closed the door, glowered at me, and said, "Well, now you've done it. You have no idea what her poxes are like!"

That was it! Wetning all about me or not, I'd had it. I took my stance in the middle of the room, shot my cuffs, and got ready to do me some man-work.

"E.M., set down! Elsie, set down!"

And I'll be damned if they didn't. All was quiet, incept for the boys, who was still singing and laughing and splashing. I leant my head into the bathroom and said, "It may interest you two yahoos to know you both got a pox on you! So slap shut or else." Well, I knew that'd keep 'em worried. Besides, when my voice went scrabbly like that, they knew I was serious and they both sobered up.

Ol' Royal didn't climb the pulpit too often and I knew I best take advantage of it. "So let me get this straight," I began, taking those papers of incorporation offa the desk. "You two women burnt a courthouse *and* the American flag, got arrested and got acquitted, which logically led to hocking a vineyard and emptying our bank accounts, which concludes in buying a moving picture company?"

They just nodded.

"All that and in just three weeks," states Royal. "My God, E.M., I'm surprised you found the time to learn how to smoke."

"Well, having your power of attorney helped speed things up. . ." E.M. stopped cold, put down the salt shaker, and then just smiled me a weak one.

I took a long pause, the kind I'm famous for. I was flipping through the corporation pages like I was inspecting 'em, but all I was thinking was "twenty years to life, twenty years to life." I breathed deep and finally said, "So you two bought us a moving picture company. Tell me, E.M., who the hell saddled you with this?"

"It says right there, Royal," said E.M., pointing to the party of the first part.

"Marco Magellan?" I asked. "You gave all our money to some shyster with a handle like Marco Magellan?"

"He's a perfectly honorable gentleman, Royal! After all, he did get me off the arson charge," E.M. says.

"Get the money back, E.M. You can't have a damn moving picture company," I continued, handing her the papers.

"Royal, it's not like sending back a shipment of moldy hay," E.M. defends.

"I can't believe you'd do this without consulting me," I went on. Admit it, Royal, you were downright hurt.

"But Royal, I've always invested our money for us. Why, you said yourself, thousands of times, what a nose I have for business! I tell you, Royal, the minute I met Mr. Marco Magellan my nose started to itch like poison ivy!"

She smiles at me like that grin holding up her nose was gonna make things Jake-E-Dory with me, but I was damned if I was gonna let her nose take the credit for a twenty-thousand-dollar gouge in my bank accounts.

So I said, "You and your nose! When you gonna see a doctor about that, E.M.? I tell you that nose-itch of yours is nothing more'n Rose Fever!"

To which she comes back with, "The hell it is! Face it, Royal" (and she points to the tip of her nose) "I have the gift! Just as surely as you can carve up some stupid willow twig, run it over the ground, and find water, I can estimate the return of an investment by the degree of itch on my nose! And if I sneeze, all the better!"

Well, I didn't like arguing like this in fronta Elsie, but I was too far into the quicksand to pull out then. So I yelped, "Burro milk!" and flashed the contract close to her face. "I tell you, E.M., this time you went out for wool and come back shorn! You got allergies, and twenty thousand ain't nothing to sneeze at! So get it back!"

No sooner did that contract pass under her nose than it began to twitch like a sneeze was about to stampede through. E.M. snatched the contract, itched her nose, and said, "There! See theth. . . see theth. . ." Well, if it was a pretend sneeze, it was a damn good one, and Elsie handed her a hankie right on cue, then set back down.

Onct she recovered and blew her nose, she continued, "Honestly, Royal, I don't see as how this is any different from the time I bankrolled ol' One-Eye Jack Claiborn back in '99."

"Now, that was a damn risky longshot, and you know it! Only you and that nose of yours would take a seventy-year-old, half-baked, half-blind, sun-crazed crankpot, give him ten thousand cash, and send him off to the gold fields in Alaska!"

I didn't like the way the conversation was going, for like I knew she would, she gazed me over cool-like and reminded me that ol' Smitty came back a seventy-two-year-old millionaire with a six-hundred-percent return on our investment.

I looked at Elsie to see if she was buying that and, of course, she was smiling just like her momma, coy and confident all at the same time. Women. But I kept it up and said, "Face it, E.M., Smitty was plain dumb-duck-luck and no way that nose of yours can take credit for a mother lode strike a thousand miles away!"

So then E.M. tries, "You know, Royal, you have such little faith! You wouldn't risk a dime even if. . . if. . . J.D. Rockefeller himself guaranteed results! Signed in his own blood!"

Now I was getting steamed again. "Oh, it's back to *him* again! Well, you just keep Rockerfeller outa this! He asked your advice onct, *onct!* and you been dropping his name ever since!"

She just turned a little, gazed out the window and, pretending I was outa earshot, but knew I wasn't, said, "You can't go wrong with oil, Rocky." You can guara-damn-tee I'd heard that one a coupla thousand times before.

Time for Royal to try another trail. So I suggested E.M. come off the grass long enough to remember that flickers was a boondoggle, a fad, and I thumped this angle by reminding her that if I had a dollar for every time she'd told the boys they couldn't waste money seeing a flicker then I reckon twenty thousand wouldn't seem like such a loss.

"Yes, but that was in Walla Walla, Royal," E.M. says, like maybe pictures was somehow different there than in San Francisco.

"All right, E.M., go ahead and explain that," I said, folding my arms. "Go ahead and explain how you yourownself never allowed the boys a flicker nowanthen. And you, Elsie! How many times have I heard you say pictures wasn't no elegant way to spend time? Huh? Go ahead, ladies. I'm awaiting." I sure as hell thought I had 'em on that account.

E.M. said, logical-like, "Well, maybe I was wrong, Royal. . ."

To which I had to interject something on the line of that was refreshing to hear.

Then Elsie chimes in with how they'd been spending time studying the movie business and they both thought there was lots of futures in it.

E.M. backs this up with, "It's true, Royal. I can see the future of pictures now. Well, how can I describe a sunset . . . a rainbow, to someone who's color blind?"

"I don't know, Mrs. Astorbilt, twenty thousand dollars oughta buy alota words, so you best start thinking of a way to undo that legal mumbo jumbo you wrote up!"

I knew mother-daughter tears was gonna enter into it, so I was prepared. 'Course I wasn't prepared for what E.M. might have to say that came in 'companiment with those tears.

"Well, all right, Royal Leckner!" she began. "If you don't care about your own daughter's career. . ."

"Career? What career? She don't have a career! She's

sixteen years old, for crissakes! No daughter of mine has any business having a career at sixteen!" How one thing had to do with another, I couldn't even guess.

'Course E.M. knew, and wasted no time in enlightning me. She rose, queenly-like, and announced, "For your information, sir, Maude Miles has been proclaimed to be the next Mary Pickford." She pulled Elsie up to her side in a fine show of 'united-we-stand.'

"Who the hell's Maude Miles?" I hollered, my level of exasperation about to crest.

"I, Father!" Elsie elocuted back, like I shoulda known.

"Then who the hell's Mary Pickford?"

"Show him, Elsie," E.M. said in a tone I'd learnt to cringe at.

Elsie undid her hat, and what escaped was not the lovely black hair I'd grown so accustomed to seeing. She billowed the concoction out some . . . and concoction was just the word for it: long, tangled, curliewurlied, and *blond!*

I was stunned. Said nothing. Just stared.

"And I'll have you know," Elsie continued, taking a give-me-liberty-or-give-me-death stance, "Mother has been proclaimed to be the next Theda Bara! Show him, Momma!"

At that, E.M. took off her swooping chapeau and unhooked some pins hither and yon. Then, with a mighty gesture of 'take that!' she pulls away her long black tresses and slaps 'em down on the table betwixt us. I looked at her and there she stood, my forty-five-year-old wife, wearing her hair bobbed to the corę and earlobe short!

"Meet Rosa Montenegro!" Elsie announced with a flourish I'd only heretofore seen in a burlesque hall.

It was then, of course, I was wishting maybe the courthouse *had* burnt down.

seven

Like you might recollect, I ain't no crepehanger, but I am the sorta man who's gotta set back and recalculate just how things stand and take a study of things. I reckon now's the time, for even though I know how all this turns out, it still gets mighty vexing and you might need a little review:

Number one: I owned 75% of a moving picture company, the privilege of which lightened me by almost twenty thousand dollars.

Number two: Elsie was now a blond and was gonna pose for pictures under the name of Maude Miles.

Number three: E.M. was now a bob-tail and was likewise gonna pose for pictures, under the name of Rosa Montenegro.

Number four: Someone by the name of Marco Magellan was almost twenty thousand dollars richer and probably taking French leave on a steamer to Samoa.

Number five: My sixteen-year-old daughter, from a town the size of Walla Walla Wash, mind you, was being squired about San Francisco by a Bushman called CHES-ley Warwick, for cryinoutloud.

And Number six: As though the Jokester Upstairs hadn't pulled enough fast ones on ol' Royal that miserable day, we now had a pox on us!

So what'd I do? Wax me something elegant on the sins of such behavior? Nope. Lay me down the law to my womenfolk? Nope. Change outa my wet clothes? Nope. I just walked past America's two newest ACK-tors and asked, "There a bar downstairs?"

"Yes, but Royal. . ." E.M. says.

"I'm in it," growls me back as I walk out. 'Course, onct I was in the hall I had to unstick my wet pants from my backside. I then took myself downstairs, not caring how the hell I looked in that Ming's Palace Hotel.

I found the bar and I took me inside. I set on a stool and bent my elbow with two fingers of rye, which bootleggers couldn't even come close to imitating back home.

I looked 'round the room and yep, the cabbie was right, it was fulla nuts, one sort or the other. Never in my whole life did I ever see such a assortment of get-ups . . . Now, I know Walla Walla Wash ain't exactly the hub of fashion, but sweartagod, what those folks wore couldn'ta been the rage. Nor does ol' Royal generally judge folks by what they is wearing. Cripes, I told you how folks was judging me just onaccounta my dang hat. But at first glance 'round and with a head fulla concerns all of a sudden, all I saw in there was eccentrics, fringes, nuts, monkey furs, wackos, and ACK-tors. And now, here was Royal R. Leckner, generally just a cowpoke, smack dab in the midst of their bohemianess . . . with two more (all his very own) just like 'em upstairs.

As I was letting the rye do its job, thinking it was one of the best shots I ever throwed a lip over, a feller comes a-sauntering up to me and asks, "Say, aren't you Bill Hart?"

Now I want you to know I didn't then or do I now have nothing personal against light-steppers. They ride one side of the fence and I ride the other. It don't matter to me which hand they hold their reins in. Hell, even Indians left lizzie-boys to theirownselfs and didn't much care they was different breeds. But I was already heated, one finger into my rye, and damn tired of being mistaken for someone else. So when I replied, "You got the wrong man, mister," I know my voice sounded a little rough.

"My, you certainly bear a sparkling resemblance to Bill," he continued, stepping back a little cautious-like. "Oh, Mr. Magellan, look here. Doesn't this person look like Bill Hart?"

Magellan? There could be only two of 'em . . . the one who plotted a course around this world and the one who plotted a course around mine.

So, naturally, I looked over to this Magellan character. Even though it was dark, I picked him outa the smoky room. Now, normally I don't go 'round describing folks, being as how my eyes ain't your eyes. But in the case of this Magellan, I shall make a exception onaccounta I'd never, then or since, seen one like him. To start off, he had roundy shoulders making his neck stick out real turtle-like. He had deep dimples alongst his long, narrowish face, which was supported by the most generous set of chins I ever did see on one man. He wore sideburns and a pencil-thin lip-fern on topa real fulsome lips. His hair was black and slicked back, he wore a undertaker-black suit and, get this, a ascot instead of a tie! 'Round his neck was a black ribbon and at the end of it was one of them monocle doohickeys that I thought only royalty could pull off wearing. Then this yap rises, comes toward me, and screws this monocle in his eye socket like as to size me up.

"Remarkable resemblance," he says, looking me over like livestock. Then he offers his hand and smiles. Whilst we shook, he said, "But no doubt you've been told that before."

It's hard to thumb-down just what was going through my head. But the moment he smiled and spoke, I remember feeling sorta strange . . . like I'd lost something. Well, that don't sound like Royal R. Leckner, but that Marco Magellan had a quality 'bout him that made you want to look behind you to see if your shadow was still following. He was far from handsome, like I said, but when he smiled at me and shook my hand, I sure wanted to count my fingers. But here's the funny part: I smiled him back. Couldn't help myself. That's the sorta man Magellan was. And I reckoned E.M. and me was in trouble deep.

Then he stepped back, held out his monocle like as to use it for a magnifier, and said, "I know this might sound strange, but would you stand up, please?"

I looked at the barkeep, then at the light-stepper, then back at this Magellan. "What for?" I asked, thinking maybe I hadn't oughta be too cooperative.

"Oh, it was only a notion. I wanted to see how much of the screen you'd fill up."

I had no wit of what he was talking about, but I stood up, thinking, just in case, he'd know I was tall and still in my fighting prime.

"Oh, that's spooky," says the light-stepper. "All we need is some chaps, gauntlets, and guns and he's our man!"

"You might be right, Armando," Magellan said. Then to me he says, "Have you ever considered acting in cinemas?"

"Sin a mas?" asks me.

"Yes, motion pictures."

Oh, so *this* is how he does it, thinks me. So I was gonna play along and see how long it would take him to mention how I could own the whole damn industry, providing of course I had enough money. But like mosta my plans, they was spoilt just then by, you guessed it, E.M., who'd just crested the door.

She took one look at me talking to Magellan and her face went mighty pale.

Magellan followed my eye, saw her, and called out, "Rosa! Darling! Come here. Look at this man." He took her by the arm and I think I grew a inch taller. "Who does he remind you of?"

"My husband," E.M. replied, sorta faint-like.

"I beg your pardon, my dear?" Magellan said, blinking polite-like.

Then a smile comes to E.M. and with that recovery she said, "Oh, I see you two have met."

"You know this man?" Magellan asked. "And you never told me about him? Why, you know I've been combing the west coast for this rustic type for months."

I guess E.M. had spotted the hair in the butter and saw no other way 'cept to just say, "Royal Leckner, this is Marco Magellan. Marco Magellan, this is Royal Leckner. My husband."

Now, most men woulda felt like they'd been caught with their mustache drooping, but not a parlor-snake like Marco Magellan. Insteada dropping E.M.'s hand, he placed it in mine. He looked at us both together and said, "Beautiful. Just beautiful. Aren't they a complement, Armando?"

Smooth as calf ears, eh?

Armando stood back, took us in, and agreed, which was, I think, what he was paid to do. Upon Magellan's introduction, I learned this man was Armando Cato, Artistic Interpretator.

E.M. then reminds me it was Marco and his filmmaking genius that proved to the judge that she was no arsonist. Well, I knew I owed him one on that account, so I thanked him.

"Anything to avoid a lawyer, I always say. Besides, your beautiful wife has thanked me quite enough already."

I took my glare over to E.M., who was quick to say he meant the investment.

"Well, about that investment," I started, hoping my voice wasn't gonna go scrabbly like sometimes money matters made it go.

"Oh, this is no time to talk business. You and Rosa must have other things to discuss," Marco gushes, like E.M. was fresh offa the Titanic. "So many wonderful plans to make."

"Her name is E.M., but you can call her Mrs. Leckner," I said, a little fulla manhood.

"Of course," Marco said, almost with a little dip. Then he said to his assistant, "Armando, what time is our dinner with the bankers?"

Slipperier'n slick, Armando said, "Oh yes, I'm afraid we're a bit late already."

"Well, my dear, you know how I feel about punctuality." Then he looks at me, shakes my hand onct again, and says, "I'll look forward to getting to know you, sir." Then to E.M. he adds, "You should have mentioned your husband to me, Mrs. Leckner."

E.M. looked at me, then back to Marco, and said, "Well now, I believe I did. . ."

But Marco cut her off with, "I mean, of course, his remarkable resemblance to William S. Hart."

Then he takes a five-dollar gold piece outa his pocket and hands it to the barkeep. "Champagne for these lovely people." You can be damn sure I was keeping a eye on my wife whilst she looked at Marco Magellan and whilst he looked back at her.

He and Armando bid us good night and started for the door. Then Armando added, "Now Rosa, sweet, don't forget, henna tomorrow at ten." But Magellan had him outa the door before E.M. could reply.

I instructed E.M. to set whilst I followed them out. I pulled Magellan by the arm and he turned, elegant-like, and smiled.

"Look, Mr. Magellan. . ."

"Call me Marco, please."

"Look, Maar-koooo, I know I owe you a favor or two for getting my wife and daughter outa jail, but putting my name to some fad-monger flickers outfit ain't exactly what I call a fair exchange."

Marco sorta cocked his head and looked at me like I was talking another language. He had a real way of making me feel like I was dry-as-dust dumb. Then he asked, "Is that what you think I am? A fad-monger?"

"I'm a cowman and nothing else my wife has put my name to. Now, you being a gentleman, I'm sure you'll understand I want my money back."

It was like I was asking him to cut off a leg so's I could use it to beat his best friend, so I followed it up with a more sympathetic voice and something to the effect I meant I didn't have no business being in film business.

"I see," Marco said, using his monocle to fidget with. "I hate to bring lawyers into this."

"Now, I'm sure we can break a contract without the use of. . ."

Then he interrupts me and starts talking all dreamlike about other things broken: like promises, dreams, hearts, and I wanted to throw in ribs, but he kept orating till I thought his little friend Armando might faint with the tragedy of it all. I was commencing to feel a little low, but I was resolved not to cave in. I held tight until he agreed to meet me the next day at noon to dissolve the partnership and arrange for the money exchange. I allowed as how, being as I still owed him about the arson, I would pay all fees and such. We even shook hands on it.

I returned to E.M. in the bar. She'd opened the champagne, which I was sorry to see onaccounta she wasn't gonna have much to celebrate when I told her the curtain was about to fall.

"Here, Royal, have some bubbly," she said. Remember now, prior to now my wife never drank wine and now here she was referring to one by a nickname. I refused the glass.

"E.M., you *did* tell Magellan you was married, didn't you?" I thought I'd get her on the defense first thing.

"Just what are you suggesting?" she comes back at me.

"You know damn good and well what I'm suggesting! I'm recollecting all them pots'n'pans you bought from a peddler not so long ago. Some man flirts you some and you gotta go buy his lock, his stock *and* his barrel!"

E.M. stared at me, and I felt my blood chill. She iced me sarcastical and said, "Yes, I've always been a meal-headed saphead for an attentive man."

I shoulda considered that line some before I jumped in with, "You look me in the eye and tell me I don't got a right to be territorial about this."

"What's the diff? You'll be territorial about this anyway!"

There we was, nose to nose in a bar fulla strangers, talking 'bout matters mighty private, but doing it anyhow.

"You just tell me straight, E.M.: that Magellan cahooting you for more'n 75 percent?"

"Of course not!"

'Course, what I'd forgot was my own piece of advice that I'd so many times told my wife regarding our own sons, and that was if you was gonna accuse someone of rustling a steer, they might as well go out and rustle a steer. But I reckoned I spoke enough already, so I finally slapped shut. Maybe she did see nothing more in Marco than a opportunity. What Marco saw in E.M. was a whole other problem. One thing E.M. said I did believe: I was gonna be territorial about it anyway.

She set her jaw and asked me, "And just what did you tell him out there in the lobby? Challenge him to a gunfight or something?"

"Tomorrow at noon. Just him, me, his money man, and a banker for a witness. I'm getting us our money back. And you and the resta us're going back to Washington first train outa this hellhole." I didn't think that left too much in the way of speculation.

Only E.M. would have done what happened next. She stood up and announced to the whole bar, "Ladies and gentlemen, I am pleased to present my husband, Ebenezer Scrooge Leckner. The stingiest man in the west." Then she offered her champagne like as to toast me, and instead she pours the contents over my head.

She clomps out, the folks in the bar applauds, and I sets there, wet onct again.

eight

Like you might imagine, I got me a roomful of cold feminine shoulders that evening. I recollect it was in the dining room of that Ming's place that things come to a head. Elsie started up with her Father-How-Could-Yous and E.M. just pretty much ignored me. So I started things off with, "Now you all know good'n'well that this ain't no place for Leckners. Why, I reckon it's a damn sin even tainting our hard-earned money with something as laa-de-dah as flickers. I'll be damned if I can even see what you two women was thinking."

"Royal, this is a refined hotel, not a bunkhouse. Would you kindly refrain from swearing?" says E.M., not even looking at me.

I pointed my fork at her and replied, "There, you see? Right there. Back home you never onct blinked if I swore a lick. Look how different your momma is, boys."

But Elsie stands up, swishes her new blond billows back, defiant-like, and informs me, "Ye Gods, Father, if you interfere with my career then my life is over. Overoverover!"

"How do you want your epitaph to read?" I asked.

But she went right on with, "Very amusing, Father. But I'll tell you one thing, I'll not be going back to Walla Walla. If I'm to waste away into obscurity, I'll do it right here in San Francisco . . . where people are much more charitable to young women of reduced circumstances!"

It was a fine speech, and I looked over to E.M. and asked, "How much you been spending on her acting lessons, E.M.?"

"Joke if you must, Father," Elsie continued, "but I intend on being a star. Marco says I'm a natural. With or without your help!"

I reminded her that without my financial help, ol' Marco Magellan wasn't gonna make her anything but a embarrassed blond floozie, and without a ride back home.

She was still standing center-stage when she added, pointing a most dramatical finger God-wards, "Go ahead. Ruin my life! But I shall tell you this, as certain as there is a God above, I shall never forgive you for holding me back, Father!"

I looked up to where she was pointing and saw nothing but some cheesy murals on the ceiling. Then she takes her gloves and purse offa the table. "Mother, I would not be so insensitive as to ask you to take sides in this, the parting of our ways. I know when married to a (she points at me) *tyrant* such as this, you have no choice but to follow him to that hellhole back home. I shall mail you my address once I'm situated."

"Hey, I thought *this* was the hellhole!" Tad says to his brother.

"Slap shut!" Chick said, warning his brother with his steak knife. "Don't you see what's going on here?"

"Acting lessons?" Tad asked innocent-like.

"No, you dope! Elsie's staying here," Chick informed his brother with a wickedish smile.

"You staying here, Elsie?" Tad asked.

"Yes, Brian," Elsie said, swooping down on her brother. "Remember me often, won't you?"

But Tad didn't even make eye-contact with her. He

just grinned at Chick and asked, "How's about we flip for her room?"

I reckoned Sarah Bernhardt was preparing to take her exit. I looked at E.M. and said, "E.M., you make sure Elsie-Maude-Mary there is packed and on that train tomorrow. You got that?"

"Ha!" says the blond actress. "I'm afraid then it's au reservoir!"

That word made us all look 'round at each other. "What's that mean, Pa?" Chick asked.

Then Elsie knelt down betwixt Chick'n'Tad and whispered something in their ears, and whatever it was, it was a humdinger, for the boys set back with looks of scandal on their faces.

"What'd you tell 'em?" demands me.

Elsie smiles down at me and says, triumph-like, "Now you'll have something to remember me by!"

I looked at E.M. for help and asked her what the hell was going on. She shrugged and sorta smiled.

Then my daughter turned on her heel and took her exit with elegant clomp-clomp-clomps, which echoed real dramatic-like. I wouldn't of expected anything less from E.M.'s daughter.

Chick'n'Tad both put down their forks and clapped and whistled wild-like and called out "Ah reservoir!" Now, whether they was applauding her performance or exhibiting their pleasure of being ridda their sister for good, I suppose I'll never know.

I remember grabbing a passing waiter by the apron and demanding another rye . . . a double on the double. I cast me a glance over to E.M., who'd been suspiciously silent, and said, "Looks like you got your work cut out for you, E.M."

"My work was cut out for me the day I met you, Royal!" she snapped.

"I tell you, E.M., you've pulled some plumb crazy stunts in your day, but sweartagod, this flicker one frosts the cake!" My rye arrived, I grabbed it offa the tray, downed it, and slapped down the glass.

She made a reference that the cake wasn't the only thing getting frosted, and I jumped on her with: "How you have the spuzz to set there and criticize *me* after what *you* done! Time you lace up your boots, E.M. You two ladies had your fling. But I'll be damned if I'll see twenty thousand dollars go up the spout in flickers! There's no future in them things. Passing fancy is all! Just like everything else that comes on fast, drains your pocket, and moves on to make way for the next whig-ma-jigger!"

"But my nose!" E.M. counters, pointing to it.

"Oh, hang your nose!" That shut her up, along with a few close-by conversations.

But she was quick to regain some lost territory. "You know, Royal," she countered, logical-like, "I'm no dummy when it comes to contracts. Not only is that contract ironclad, it's damn good terms, if I do say so myself."

"Look, E.M., even if I have to get me a *lawyer*, I'm getting that money back," I said, remembering Wilton's card in my vest pocket.

Well, she knew if I threatened a lawyer, I was hell bent for leather, so she took down her mainsail and put up her jib. Her eyes started to get big with tears which, up to that day, she'd only used on real selective occasions, I might add. Even Chick'n'Tad took notice and stopped chewing as they watched their momma take me on.

"I suppose that's your way of saying our marriage means nothing to you," she said, this time making no effort to dab away her tears. Sweartagod, just let 'em fall right down into her crabcakes.

Chick'n'Tad looked at me for my reply, which was, "What's our marriage got to do with this dang fandango?"

Chick'n'Tad looked at their momma.

"That's all it is with you, isn't it? Money, money, money! You're so stingy sometimes you could skin a rock and sell the hide! How tragic, Royal. How truly tragic."

Chick'n'Tad looked at me.

"Tragic? Me? I've seen mules with better roached hair, E.M.!"

"Well, thank you very much, Marcelle of Paris! I happen to like my hair."

Now it was getting nasty and I changed my line. "Cripes, E.M., this ain't about hair. It's about. . ."

"Money, right?"

"No, not about money. It's more about well . . . changes, sorta."

Then, like in his innocent way Tad was trying to tell me something, he broke in and asked, "Pa? You gonna eat your pie?"

I handed it to him and tried to re-grasp my thoughts.

E.M. then handed me this one: "Maybe a woman needs a change now and then."

Then, like maybe he was trying to tell me something too, Chick asked E.M., "You gonna eat your pudding, Momma?"

She passed it to him and I thought a minute, then said, low-like, as though that'd keep my boys from hearing, "Is that what this is all about? *The* change, E.M.?"

E.M. just slapped her napkin down, looked at me like I was the dumbest thing since rocks, and said, "Oh good night nurse!"

She had all three of us menfolk confused, that's sure. Then she goes on with, "Too bad. You would have made millions."

Chick'n'Tad looked at me.

"Face it, E.M., some fast-talking slick comes around and applies hisself to your ego by promising you fame and fortune and youth and God knows what else. That Marco Magellan found your vanity vein, stuck it a good one, and nearly bled me to death. Same as that damn peddler-man. Lotsa women your age drop that same brick. It ain't nothing to be ashamed of." God, I wisht I'd kept my dang mouth shut. I musta been cutting her to the quick. Chick'n'Tad looked at their momma.

"My, Royal, you must think I've been acting pretty silly," she said. Wisht I looked at her and not my dinner roll. Wisht I hadn't replied something on the line of 'yep, pretty damn silly.'

It may only have been a butter knife, but it was a knife, and she was now pointing it at me whilst she growled, "Well, you're about as wrong as you could be, Royal R-for-Rat Leckner."

Chick'n'Tad looked at me.

I set down my own butter knife. Any time ol' E.M. used that R-for-Rat in my name, I knew things was getting big. But before I could say a word, E.M. got up and, just like Elsie, picked up her gloves and her purse.

Chick'n'Tad looked at their momma.

"Under the circumstances, Royal, you best get your own room for the night. After all, we'll be busy packing, and no doubt you'll be up all night thinking of other ways you can ruin our lives!"

Well, now the whole restaurant was staring.

Chick'n'Tad watched their momma clomp-clomp-clomp out, then they looked at me.

No doubt they was calculating their scorecards.

nine

Following my wife's advice, I got Chick'n'Tad and me a room for the night. I assured the boys that Momma and me was just having one of our discussions, and I reminded them how E.M. got when she was as distracted as she had been of late.

When the boys was asleep, I took myself back down to the bar, where I could continue to sort out my thoughts. Additional, I knew I was too tired to sleep for awhile. I was already feeling a little too far behind the cork, so I ordered a milk. I also knew I'd be needing a clear head. Maybe you know that God-awful feeling—you're halfway out on a frozen lake, confident as hell the ice is strong and thick. Then you hear a faraway snappling, which usually echoes real nice along the shores in the deada winter. You look down and watch the cracks locate your boots and, whilst you sink down slow-like, you know you ain't nearly as smart as you had thought previous. Well, that's how I felt just then: sinking slow-like.

So there I set in the bar, thinking back on simpler times when my most vexing issue on any given day was which horse to pull outa the remuda for a day's honest work . . . no women, no eccentrics, no thin ice, no ACK-tors, just horses, leather, and cow paddies.

Then comes a sound from a quiet, dark corner of the bar. Now, me being mostly a gentleman, I'm not real intimate with this sound, but I recognized it the minute I heard it. It was that stinging sound of a lady's hand acrost a man's face. If you ain't felt it yourownself then take my word for it, the sound echoes almost as deep as does the memory. There was no need for me to find the source of that sound, for it came clomping by me. She was a real looker. A young thing. Dressed all in furs and flourishes and reeking of her daddy's money. Her face was flushed and fulla that feminine righteousness I had myownself been treated to every day practically since I met E.M. I just watched her leave.

Then coming up next to me at the bar was the slap-ee. He was smiling and rubbing his cheek and, without saying nothing, the barkeep hands him a drink. He downs it, turns to me and, I hafta say, some folks is so damn beautiful that it sorta takes your breath away. I sweartagod, I never in my whole life ever saw a better looking man. What was God thinking, giving him those long black eyelashes when there was women out there reduced to applying fake ones? How come a man was blessed with that wavy coal-black hair when unblessed old maids was walking 'round with skinny brown-gray locks? How could teeth be so white and straight? How could a face be all that chiseled? And how could a smile be so damn arresting? All that good-lookingness wasted on a man. His only flaw, I reckoned, was he stood pretty short. Maybe five-three. Five-four including his tippy-toes.

He took a barstool, looked at me, raised his glass and the corners of his slick little mustache, and said, "To women everywhere." I lifted my glassa milk and agreed with his toast, incepting my own two upstairs, of course.

Then he turns his insulted cheek towards me and asks, "Think it'll bruise?"

I didn't even hafta look too closely onaccounta I could tell by the size of the slapper that she hadn't left no permanent damage. Plus I don't think anyone, women specially, feels too good about out-and-out destruction of such beauty. But I assured him with, "It ain't even red."

"Good. My face is my fortune, you know," he replies, like he'd been told that every day of his life.

"Why? You gonna be on the next dollar bill or something?" I asked back.

"Either that or a wanted poster," he ha-ha-ha'd. I ha-ha-ha'd him back. "My face is also my downfall."

You will notice beauty and humility ain't a double-humped camel.

Well, he was gonna expound whether or not I asked him to, so I ordered myself a shota brandy for my milk whilst the top-shelfer enlightened me. "Having good looks, well, face it, having beauty is a curse sometimes."

At first I thought he was English. Then I thought he was just affected. By the way he swayed, I reckoned he was also drunk. I mumbled, "Do tell?"

"Yes. The men you want to like you hate you for it and the men you don't want to like you love you for it. If you get my meaning."

"Well, as clear as I can tell, that was a woman that stomped outa here," I said.

"Then women. They're a whole other set of problems."

Now here I had to agree with him.

He goes on: "Women are just naturally jealous of a handsome man. You know?" Then he looks at me like waiting for me to agree and then he just says, "Well, take it from me."

"I can see where a woman don't take too kindly to a man getting more second looks than she does." I think he thought I was being sympathetic, but I was really ridiculing him and his smile and his gas-bag attitude.

He just nodded his head and said, almost evil-like, "It happens all the time. If you only knew the lengths I have to go for people—well, other men—to take me seriously."

"Maybe you oughta have someone break your nose or something," I suggested father-like, hiding my smile in my glass.

"Oh, many have tried, of that you can be sure." He took another drink offa the bartender, burped, and then goes on to tell me, with a face like his it looked like working on the silver screen was the best way a man of his talents could get hisself noticed. He wanted to build him some—what'd he call it?—credibility, that's it. Said someday folks was gonna take him and his face a little more serious. He tried to scowl me one, but it was no good—he was just too damn good looking and I think I mighta even understood a littla what he was talking about.

I recollect onct, back in the nineties, we had us a hand come through the Four Arrows Ranch looking for work. He was a damn handsome dude too. He finally left under a cloak of shame for the hounding he took from the boys who was, on a average, a pretty sore-looking bunch. Hell, even his horse didn't take him too serious. I heard he'd ended up selling Bibles in the South and got mixed up in running women and hooch and crime and . . . well, so that remembrance didn't make me any more fond of this feller at all.

So I saged him with, "Good looks is usually only temporary."

He then looks at me careful-like and says, "Yes, I can see you were once a handsome drake, in a rugged sort of way." Then he brings over one of those atmospherish bar candles and takes a longer look at me. He says, "You know, you look *very* familiar. It's almost as though I know you from somewhere."

"Everyone looks familiar in this town," I said.

"I wouldn't know about San Francisco. I'm from L.A., you know. My director-general and I are up here looking for new faces."

I said I wouldn't presume to speak for his commanding officer, but I didn't think he could get much better'n the face he already had.

I got three more ha-ha-has and a slap on the back and his reply, "Very droll, old man, very droll. No actually, we need rich, new talent for our filming venture."

I heard all his words, but only the word 'rich' sunk in. I played it safe with, "In that order?"

He leans into me and confides, "Well, we did find a couple of rich hot tamales, if you know what I mean." Wink, wink.

I knew who he was referring to and set me a snare with, "You know, I onct bilked a old widow-woman outa eighteen heada prize thoroughbreds." I could tell by his face he was impressed.

"No kidding?" he offers me a drink offa his credit, then adds, "Did you have to, you know, take her to dinner?" Wink wink.

"Took her to breakfast too."

I was about to wink wink him back and dig a little deeper when a bellhop comes into the bar, straight over to the One who Glitters, and hands him a folded note off of a little silver tray. He hangs around for a tip, which I noticed was of Mexican descent. The boy picks it up, grimaces some, and then says, "Oh gracias señor. Next time I'm vacationing in Acapulco I'll have some tipping money." My companion made a fast switch of coin, then excused hisself whilst he read his note, and it was sure queer watching all his handsomeness dissolve as he read. He quickly folded the note, stuffed it in a pocket, and downed his drink.

"Bad news?" I asked.

He said no, just urgent news, then smiled and left saying something like he'd enjoyed our little chat and good luck and all. He was outa the door in nothing flat. That left me and the bartender eye to eye.

"You by chance know that yap's name?" I asked.

The bartender sighed him some exasperation and said, "Klepelmeier. Herman. At least that's the name he's registered under."

"I suppose with a handle like that he has him one of those Mar-kee names," I said. Sure as hell that name wasn't gonna be much help.

At this the barkeep pulls out a ledger with two columns of names. He runs his finger down one column saying, "Klepelmeier, Klepelmeier. . ." Then he parallels that name to another name. "Yes, here it is. He also goes by the name of Warwick. Chesley Warwick."

'Course you coulda heard my heart hit my boots. Chesley Warwick. And to think my daughter, all five-foot-eighta her, had been seen publicly on the arm of that arrogant loath-ario.

The barkeep then pours hisself a drink, refills me, and says, "Klepelmeier. Warwick. He's a jerk-ass crook by any name. I'll be glad when him and his Magellan pal and all those other Happy-Hollywoods check out and let us get back to normal."

Naturally that was a topic I would of liked to of pursued, but I was interrupted by the same hotel-boy calling out my name for some reason.

The bellhop found me and told me I had a phone call at the front desk. The hour was next to midnight and I wondered who the hell was calling me.

The phone call went like this:

E.M.: Royal, it's me, E.M. Your wife.

ME: I know you're my wife, E.M. It's the name I ain't sure of. Why you calling me?

E.M.: To let you know that Elsie and me are at the train depot.

ME: Oh, any thoughts on where you're heading?

E.M.: Now look, Royal, I know you don't believe me, but Elsie at least is owed a chance at this movie business. I'm taking her to L.A. to try to set her up, and don't you dare think about stopping us.

ME: And just what're you planning on using for spondulicks?

Well, the simple little chuckle she gave me I would not like to hear ever again. But she said:

E.M.: Don't worry, Royal. Money isn't everything. We have talent. We'll manage.

ME: Sounds like you're leaving me, E.M.

E.M.: No more than you left me that time you went to the South Seas. Look, I got us into this, I'll get us out.

ME: Us? You-and-me us or you-and-Marco us?

E.M.: You know, Royal, I'm getting mighty tired of your stupid insinuations.

ME: Okay, okay. I'm sorry.

E.M.: Well, you oughta be. Now Royal, we still have

six more weeks of our spree and we're going to give Hollywood a try. So go home, count your cattle, and I'll call you when we get situated. Oh, that's our train. Bye, Royal. In spite of everything, I still love you. Kiss the boys for me. (*Click*)

I'm afraid only the desk clerk heard me utter into the phone, "All right, but I'm taking back my power of attorney!"

I stood there thinking whilst the desk man watched. "Is there anything else I can do for you?" he finally asked.

So I said yes, matter of fact, and was Marco Magellan still in residence? He hedged on that one, something 'bout insuring privacy. And I, knowing that money makes the mare move, held up a sawbuck and asked, "Does this cover the premium?"

Whereupon I quickly learnt Magellan'd already left.

"Where to?"

"South."

"How far?"

"That depends."

Another fiver. Thirty dollars later, this is what else I learnt from the deskman: Marco and his Artistic Interpretator, Armando Cato, along with that Klepelmeier-Warwick character was regular visitors, usually bilking rich eccentrics for movie money. I also learnt that Warwick spoke pretty damn good Spanish for a German pretending to be British and he onct talked big to a chambermaid 'bout none other'n Pancher Viller. And now they was all three heading to Hollywood on the same train as my wife, my daughter, and my fortune.

Mad? You wanna know if I was mad? Ever see the glare in the eye of a bull when you come at him with a nut-lopper? Ever smell the breath of a chute-cornered bronc?

Ever have rabies? Well, unless you've done alla those or been married yourownself, then I reckon you don't know how mad I really was.

I found the phone booth and called the train station. I was informed that the L.A. train was gonna leave at midnight and there wasn't gonna be another one till morning. I booked me and the boys passage and turned in.

Chick'n'Tad was glad we was outa Chinatown and heading south, and I promised 'em a better time onct we got to Los Angeles. I let 'em each pick out a magazine at the station, and I'll be damned if they didn't get *Photoplay* and *Motion Picture Story,* and I reckon I was too occupied to recognize the danger in that. On the train south I told 'em onct we got Momma and Elsie squared away and offa their high horses, we'd alla us go fishing in the Pacific Ocean and see us some sights. Well, they kept talking 'bout being in the movies too and said, hell, since that Mary Pickford could earn half a million dollars a year just making faces, then for sure they could clean up real good.

To occupy their times on the train, they stood in fronta mirrors practicing crying, laughing, and emoting. But pretty soon they tired with that and commenced to occupy the baggage car, and that bit of warfare seemed okay with the porters onaccounta they could lock the door from the outside and the boys promised not to play with the two coffined-up corpses traveling in there.

I was lucky enough to find myself setting next to a gentleman on the train who was from Los Angeles, and he filled me in on the territory. I said I was going there to look into the movie business and maybe even invest in it. Come to find out, he was some sorta accountant and knew all about the flickers and the money they made or didn't. He said I had to be real careful of shysters who set up shop and bilked folks for film money with nothing more'n promises and then left town with the cash. He also tells me that Hollywood wasn't no accident of providence. It was the film headquarters because the weather was good and the scenery was all built in beautiful and because it was about as far away from Edison as you could get and still be able to vote American.

"Edison?" asks me.

"Yes, as in Thomas, electricity, the moving picture camera," Archie, my companion, said. "He's trying to hang onto his monopolies on the equipment these movie men use. Well, you know what independent businessmen think of monopolies. Just go where they can't catch you. Since Edison's Patent Company is on the East Coast, then just take your camera and film out on the West Coast. Well, it's a moot point now. Looks like they're about to put the kibosh on Edison."

So there was Royal, learning something new at the turn of every bend on the way to Los Angeles, including a new word.

Archie was real helpful. I disclosed I was interested in finding me a man by the name of Marco Magellan. (I didn't tell him I was also on the trail of my wife and daughter. That's just not the sorta thing you confess to a stranger who works in numbers and percentages.) He said I oughta take on a place called the Beverly Hills Hotel onaccounta anyone who did anything to anyone in that film world did it at that place. He wrote down the name of some other places, restaurants and such. He was real helpful and I think he could sorta tell I was a man in trouble.

I was commencing to worry now that we'd been

warned Los Angeles was just a hour away. It was time for me to round up Chick'n'Tad and make sure they'd made good on their promises not to disturb the dead.

"We about to pounce on Momma?" Chick asked as we walked toward the baggage area onct we'd landed.

"Pounce may not be the word," I advised.

"We still just tracking?" Tad asked, thinking probably of happier times when the boys and me would go cougar hunting in the Blue Hills back home.

"I'm thinking we'll just us reconnoiter," says me, ushering them along aheada me.

Then Tad tells me, "Ah, reservoir! I thought we was going fishing."

Then ol' Chick took over and told his brother, "Shut up, squirt. Pa knows what he's doing. If he wants to reconnoit Momma, he can. Fishing don't have nothing to do with it!"

Tad looks up at me and, being the youngest, asks, "Pa, am I worried about Ma?"

I stopped and gave him my full attention. "No, Tadpole. Don't you worry. We'll find your momma and sister."

"Aw, I wasn't worried about *Elsie*," Tad corrects with that devil-sweet smile of his, "onaccounta I won the toss for her room."

This would be a good place to stop for tonight, son. Los Angeles is always a good place to stop, don't you agree?

PART 2

one

You know, every onct in a while I get me a whiff of something that sends me right back to Los Angeles in 1915. It must be some passing woman's perfume or corsage, but whatever it is, it's fulla the fragrance of orange blossoms 'cause that, my friend, is what Los Angeles smelt like back then. 'Course, I hear nowadays it smells more like Tacoma, which, in case you ain't been there, is right industrial smelling. Now there ain't nothing wrong with the smell of industry, 'cause with it you also get the smell of greenbacks, new boots, and dinner on the table. But oh, the smell of orange blossoms was surely the sweetest smell on earth to ol' Royal the day he stepped offa that train. I reckon I thought that any place with sky so blue and hill so golden and sea so green and smell so sweet just couldn't be all that bad, and at least I'd be tracking down my women in some mighty fine scenery.

Now, I don't know how much traveling you done, but even if you've done only a little local gadabouting, then you know how a building or two begins to represent a whole town? Firinstance, the Idlehour Glass Saloon in Idlehour, Oregon . . . you get the feeling for the whole town the minute you step inside and order a beer. (Chances are, you'll meet the whole town too.) Let me set you some other firinstances, ones that you might better know: Paris, France: Eiffel Tower; London, England: Big Ben; New York City: Statute of Liberty. All those edifices sorta set the tone for the whole city, right? Well, I think Los Angeles, California had its own tone-setter: The Beverly Hills Hotel.

The place was pink. Sweartagod. Not a sunset pink, not a blush pink, but a awful, baby pink! Now I can forgive a little mistake in the paint-mixing department, but pink? Well, you can guess how that set with my Chick'n'Tad. Tad allowed as how pink was for sissies and Chick, for onct, agreed with his brother. I think I gave 'em some don't judge the book by the cover routine before we marched inside.

What a layout! One look 'round and I thought so much for my book-judging lecture. There was high ceilings, Persian-like carpets, antiques, leather this'n'thats, bird cages, palm trees to the ceiling, and I don't know what other assortments. And I'll be damned if just about every dang person in that exotic lobby wasn't wearing whitish clothes. You know what I was expecting in the way of a greeting in my dark, westernish duds. So my loins was girded, but insteada getting the country-cousin-in-the-city treatment at this hotel, I was greeted with a great big smile.

"Well, Mr. Hart," says this clerk, "what can I do for you?"

"Name's Leckner," I says, a little vacant-like whilst I was looking 'round. "I'd like a room for me and my boys."

"Leckner?" he asks. I think he was frowning.

"Yeah, Leckner," I returns, taking him eye to eye.

Whoever this Hart was, I was determined to round him up and see what the hell he was doing with my face.

Well, the clerk had a hard time believing me, even

when I signed my name and my hometown. He finally called me Mr. Leckner, but I don't think he enjoyed that.

We was escorted through the lobby by a youngster in a snappy outfit, not much older'n Chick. Well, Chick was studying this bellhop's get-up and I just knew he was thinking something evil. But he knew I knew and so he kept his quiet. Other'n that, Chick'n'Tad was right impressed with all the cages in the lobby, which was filled with not just canaries but also monkeys and parrots and other such creatures, some of which I don't think I'd ever seen. Folks was setting in deep leather chairs, reading papers and peeping at us over the top and, like usual, there came whispers as we passed. I don't know if them head doctors had invented paranoia by then, but I think I was catching it anyhow.

So busy was Tad staring back (and probably making faces) at the lobby setters that he tripped on a fine Oriental rug and set up quite a ruckus. A gaggle of businessmen was interrupted as Chick walked through their group, and by the time we found the elevator I don't think there was a soul in that swank'n'posh hotel that didn't know we had arrived—boots, hats, carpetbags and all.

Me and the boys settled, and then I thought I'd like to snoop 'round a bit. After all, I'd settled a few hashes in my day; E.M. musta known I'd be hot on her trail. I needed to know where she was, but she didn't need to know where I was.

So I rang up the hotel phone operator and put in my reservation for a line northwards. When my call home to the Royal Bar-L finally came through, I asked our housekeeper, Ida, if there'd been any word from the missus. Well, you can imagine what poor Ida was thinking, me being in the very same state as my wife and having to call another state to find her. So I set her mind to rest and said E.M.

and me'd just missed connections, that's all. No use ruining Ida's summer.

Sad was I to learn that she hadn't heard from E.M. at all, but did I want to speak to the foreman onaccounta a fence had broke and a buncha my curious spring calfs had volunteered for my neighbor's herd? You got no idea how much I was wishting I was home, sorting out volunteers from enlisteds. I loved it when my spring calfs went curious.

After I worked out that problem, Ida comes back on the phone and asks me where could I be reached and was the boys being good? I told her I was in transit still and if Mrs. Leckner called to tell her you ain't got a clue of our whereabouts. "In fact," adds me, "as far as you know I may not even be in California at all. Tell her I'm in Timbuktu, for all you know." Well, so much for Ida's summer.

Well, should E.M. call home to corner Ida, I thought that lack of information would keep E.M. tossing awake nights and guessing what the hell I had up my sleeve, which I can tell you truthful I didn't even know myownself. I leant back on the bed and smiled up at the ceiling. But I soon felt Chick'n'Tad's eyeballs on me. 'Course, they'd heard all my lying to Ida on the telephone.

"What're you two looking at?" I asked.

"You sure swallered the Bible on that one, Pa," Chick the Bold said to me.

"Where'd you learn to say such a thing to your pa?" I asked him, trying to take the upper hand.

"Elsie," Chick answered me, simple and honest.

I mumbled, that figures, then thought I better explain things to my boys. Not the truth, of course, but I'd better put their minds to rest onct again. So I set up and said, "Now look, boys, I know what I told Ida wasn't exactly the whole truth."

"Not even half the truth," Tad said innocent-like.

And I said, "Nope, I reckon it wasn't even half. Anyhow, I think Momma and your sister, well, maybe they got theirselfs into some trouble. Nothing serious, now. But you know, maybe we menfolk needs to be a little deceiving so's we can help the ladies out."

Tad said, "Momma'd skin you royal if she heard you say that."

And Chick had to add, "That's sure, Pa. You know how she's always telling Elsie to stand her own stead."

So I just told 'em, "The trick is to help 'em, but not so's they catch on. Even better if they think they done it theirownselfs."

Chick'n'Tad exchanged their looks of puzzlement, then shot 'em back to me. "Pa, this one of them fe-as-kos you talk about nowanthen?" Chick asked, slicing to the meat of the matter.

Well, I had to smile some. "You might say that."

Then Tad exasperated heavy and fell back onto his pillow and said, "I don't get it."

What happened next makes me smile to this very day. Ol' Chick, alla ten years of age, goes over to his brother, touches his arm kind-like and, Sage o' the West, says, "You will, Tad. When you know about women. Ain't that so, Pa?"

That was indeed so, I told 'em both. Then I left 'em on their beds to catch some snooze. If you ever have sons, you'll know what I felt when I looked down on my Chick'n'Tad, sweetest reflections of the best of me and E.M., no matter how many fe-as-kos we was about to sail into.

two

The second day of our stay, I allowed Chick'n'Tad to explore their new surroundings, which mighta been a cheap trick to play on the Beverly Hills Hotel, but hell, for what I was paying I figured the boys could do what they pleased. And since the hotel boasted its own doctor and house detective, I reckoned most matters was covered and the rest would just have to be left to chance. Anyhow, I reckoned a place bold enough to be pink could damn well hold its own against Chick'n'Tad.

So, whilst Chick'n'Tad was staking their territories, I left to inspect this Los Angeles town.

Lord, the weather was beautiful. Whereas back home in Walla Walla Wash we'd be up to our armpits in dust and glazing heat, Los Angeles was nice'n warm, but not so's you'd cut a sweat. You could smell the salt air and I think that ocean worked to keep the heat from getting folks down. The palm trees held a fascination in me onaccounta I'd never seen such trees in the United States. 'Course, I'd been to the South Seas, so tropicals wasn't new to me, but there in Los Angeles they grew the trees so damn organized that it looked like a parta Eden itself. Long, lazy boulevards (most of 'em paved too) with palms lining up at attention, making you feel right important when you motored through.

The houses in that town were a strike different from

any other place I'd been to. Lotsa whitning, making the houses look sorta Mexican . . . you know, arch-type effects and that frosting-like finish which I later learnt was called stucco. And no one seemed too concerned about more'n one level. But the further out you'd drive, especially in my necka the woods, the houses got bigger and grander. Lawns was all kept nice and, I gotta be honest, it was a damn pretty town. Now, the downtown part was more normal, spread out hither and yon and with plenty of tall buildings so's that you knew this was a city to be reckoned with. I think the population had risen up past three hundred grand or so, and that's pretty serious.

Acting upon Archie-from-the-train's advice, my first reconnoiter was visiting the Courthouse. 'Course resting in the Suspicions Corner of my mind (which was something more'n a corner, the way things was commencing) was that Magellan and my twenty thousand was long gone . . . maybe in Mexico even. So there I was sifting through pages and pages of city, county, and state licensed businesses.

I looked under Marco.

I looked under Magellan.

I looked under Cato and Warwick.

I looked under Leckner, which was real wishful thinking.

I looked under Miles, Maude, E.M., Elsie, Rosa, Montenegro and, in a moment of desperation, I even looked under Arnold comma Benedict.

The number on the records room door indicated I was on the third floor, but I was feeling lower'n the undersides of the basement floor tiles.

Then, seeing my plight, the clerk takes pity on me (it was approaching lunch time) and asked when did I suppose such a outfit might of been chartered. A year ago? Two? Last century?

"What day is this?" I asked.

He points to the big calendar next to the big clock on the wall and says, "Tuesday."

So I replied, "Monday."

He gives me a scornful one, slams the book shut, and pulls out another, suggesting I take it to that table over there and look at yesterday's applications. Which I did.

I opened the book and put my finger-pointer down a column of the business licenses granted on Monday, wondering how many pesos there was in a dollar these days. The new businesses was pretty much what you might expect, only in alphabetical order:

Behring Moving Company
Corrigan's Compasses
Crane, Reamer and Donner Funeral Parlor
L and K Dog Training
Rob's Bookbinding
Royalscope Productions
Walton Excavating

My finger stopped, went up one line. Royalscope Productions? License #2388, Ref. Code: M. Hmmm. Royalscope. Catchy name. Musta been mine. Pursuing the cross reference code of "M", I pretty much confirmed things. I can't honest say if I was mad or glad. Glad Marco and his crew didn't hightail it to Mexico with my money or mad that he was proceeding through legal channels. After all, I'd rather use a shooting piece than a mouth piece any day. I rather me guns in Mexico than lawyers in Los Angeles, and the more legal-like Marco Magellan came off, the less chance I was gonna have getting that contract broke.

So I got the address of the so-called Royalscope Productions and found me a ride back to the Pink Palace, thinking this might take more time and money than I'd first reckoned.

I knew that the Pink Palace was gonna be no place for me and the boys to hold up for the long haul, so I thought I'd find us a boarding house from which I could operate. The more I watched that Golden City go by me, the more I knew I was a cowboy so far offa his range that probably even God had lost tracka him.

Back at the hotel I informed Chick'n'Tad to return the bellhop's uniform and pack their bags onaccounta we was gonna be moving to a boarding house, for we'd be needing more room and I'd be needing someone to look after 'em whilst I alone set out to reconnoit our womenfolk.

I stared at the phone, wondering if I shouldn't just call it a day and get the hell outa town . . . forget our almost twenty grand and take our babies back home where they was safe from eccentrics, ACK-tors the likes of Chesley Warwick, Magellans with monocles, and whatever other things might creep outa the tar pits in that state of California. Thought I'd just take the boys on home and leave E.M. to her own devises whilst she got this moving pictures streak outa her hair. What was left of it. I was damn deflated.

Well, I guess I was just staring at the phone for some while, 'cause little Tad comes up behind me, puts his sweet arms 'round my neck, and says, "Don't worry, Pa. Chick'n me'll help you. We menfolk gotta stick together."

Well, like you know, menfolk's way of sticking together generally ends up in a romp of some sorts, onaccounta honest and straight talk makes the throat go real scratchy. So me and the boys wrestled some on the beds, broke a lamp, and had us a good game of no-safties-tag. Looking at our room, the boys then felt safe in telling me we'd been asked to leave the Beverly Hills Hotel anyhow. It had something to do with letting some of the caged-up lobby creatures outa their confines.

Well, I wasn't sure if I was mad or proud. Can't stand me caged-up critters either. But I was the pa, so it was my duty to say, "I reckon I can't take you two hooligans anywheres."

"Sure you can, Pa," says Chick, pulling out my already packed-up satchel from the closet. "You can take us to the moving pictures."

"You can take us fishin'," joins up Tad.

"You can take us to Mexico. Sure would like to meet me up with ol' Pancher Viller." I stopped cold. I recollected that old outa-the-mouths-of-babes saying and reckoned Chick still qualified.

"Who you been talking to?" I asked, suspicious.

"No one, Pa. Swear."

I said, "Pancher Viller'd just as soon cut your liver out as look at you."

"Thought you said he was doing pee-ons some good, Pa," Tad jumps in.

"That was last year. This year he's nothin' more'n a outlaw holding a grudge, so get the idea of Mexico outa your head." I hated giving such younguns lessons in politics, but I had to set 'em straight on ol' Pancher. I then offered 'em first out the door. Well, like they always did when I was a little frothed up at 'em, they walked out with their backsides away from my boot. I settled up the hotel bill, which included the traumatization of a monkey belonging to Reese Somebody, whoever he was.

Onct we was back in the clutches of Los Angeles City, I began looking for boarding houses. The closer we got to that Hollywood place, where all the movie-making happened, the more houses we found. Some had signs that said, "No Children" or "No Pets," but mostly we saw signs that warned, "No Movies," which I think meant no movie people, you know, ACK-tors, and not that no movies was shown in that boarding house. Being as how the last thing Royal was was a "movie," I didn't pay those signs no mind.

I interviewed a few folks and well, toting two boys they interviewed us too. But I finally found a place that sported a "Well-Mannered Gentlemen Only" sign. I looked down at my boys and wondered if I could get 'em in on a technicality, onaccounta they was gonna be men someday and they was at least housebroke. We got interviewed by a nice little ol' lady who said she was game enough to take on our board and even the occasional overseeing of Chick'n'Tad. She said she'd raised her nine boys and Chick'n'Tad didn't look like they coulda been much trouble. We alla us slapped shut. Mrs. Taylor was a slip of a lady, but minuteness never seemed to stop most women. And the way she fawned over the boys, I thought we mighta found us a winner. The one hundred dollars cash up front damage deposit didn't hurt none either. I had to later explain to the boys that they wasn't under no obligation to meet or exceed that amount.

After we settled in, me and Chick'n'Tad took a walk and got our bearings. Mrs. Taylor's place set in a pretty neighborhood, for the city, that is. The streets was lined with nice trees called eucalyptus and the smell they offered was a real challenge to my nose. I couldn't describe it. I reckon you'll have to go out and smell one for yourownself.

* * *

Just down on the corner you could catch a streetcar to any place in the city. But sad was I to learn that you couldn't buy a glassa hooch in Hollywood. However, all I had to do was go a block the other way to the Los Angeles border and I could buy just about any type, local or domestic, that I wanted. They sported lots of wines in the stores back then too. I was strolling up one store aisle, just looking at all the brands, not that I generally knew one wine from another. Mostly what I did was see if maybe some of my own vineyards was supplying the grapes. No matter what E.M.'s nose had itched us into, I had to admire the woman's instinct for buying up land. I got to wondering why the hell she didn't go into the wine-making business, insteada just leasing the land to the vintners. I calculated plenty of money setting on the shelves of that store. 'Course, if them temper-ancers got their way, all the U.S. of A. would go dry and, face it, that was a real threat to alota us . . . not just imbibers, but growers as well. Like I said, it was a crazy time in the world back then.

I noticed whilst we was eating lunch at a place called the White Kitchen that my bankroll was looking a little scrawny. I'd had too many unexpected expenses and, for the life of me, I don't know why I hadn't learnt to pack extra cash when hot on the trail of my wife. It wasn't like I never had to take off after her before.

So after a few inquiries and being told "My pleasure, Bill," I found us the Bank of Italy, where I hoped I could transact some money-moving.

My Walla Walla Wash banker did like I asked and wired some money 'round, and I was allowed to set up a account to draw against right there in Los Angeles. Not only was I planning on using that account to draw against, I was also planning on using it to stash away my recovered almost twenty grand onct I got the Magellan matter settled. I reckoned the sooner I got that cash stashed, the better chance I had of hanging on to it. It might interest you to know, I did not include my wife's name to draw on that account. And I did that without guilt or a second thought. Besides, if I played my cards right, E.M. would never have to know.

I did feel a little ashamed when I also instructed my banker to take E.M.'s signature offa all our money for the time being. Back then, it was as simple as saying something like, "Well, you know how it is, Vernon. Some women just plow through money like it was grass and they was goats." He'd laugh with you and allow as how he had to cut his own wife off onct and we all go through it and it teaches 'em a lesson and whoever came up with the idea of charging to accounts and sending things out untried oughta be shot. Guess we had the telephone to blame for that. Nowadays it's harder to unattach your wife from your money, but back then all it took was a phone call. He said, as a bonus, he'd even walk over to Wilton's office and have E.M.'s name taken offa my power of attorney.

So it looked like we was digging in for a long summer's night. What had started out as a simple game of tag betwixt husband and wife had turned into a fe-as-ko of epic proportions . . . like one of 'em Greek episodes where lifes and fortunes, maybe alla civilization, was at stake . . . where men was men and to prove it they set around and expounded . . . where women used every weapon in the book, including lip rouge, to settle the score . . . where children was sometimes the smartest ones of all, and where cowpokes just generally stayed outa things.

'Cept this one.

three

Mrs. Taylor assigned our rooms and we alla us was pretty happy. The boys and me had a bathroom to share and we had nice views out our windows.

I leaned outa my window and saw that the feller in the room next to mine had hisself a balcony. And on it he set. I offered him a 'howdy' to bring his nose outa his book. He held his hand up, I guess to tell me just a second and he'd howdy me back. He finished what he was reading, took off his spectacles, and came toward my window.

He leant over the railing a little and offered me his hand. "Hello," he said, smiling shy-like at me.

I take his hand and offer him, "Royal Leckner."

He looks at me and replies, "William S. Hart!"

Now I knew this kid couldn'ta been the man everyone'd been mistaking me for, leastwise not in the last thirty-so years. So I set him straight on my name.

He put his glasses back on and said, "Oh, pardon me, it's just that you look so much like this. . ."

"So they tell me." I hated to cut off someone I just met, but I did it. "And you are?"

And he returned with, "Sailing O'Sullivan Strong."

Now, there was a mar-kee name if ever I'd heard one, and I think I pulled back my handshake a little early. "That's some name," I said.

"My mother thought so," he replied.

"No kidding? She hung that on you intentional?" asks me.

"It's a long, Irish story," he said. "Say, I'm sorry about mistaking you. I imagine it gets rather old hat." He was a nice-looking boy. Polite too. Maybe 20, 22. Dressed in a white sweater and slacks. I was noticing I was the only man in Los Angeles not dressing in some casual whitning. He had that roanish hair like Chick'n'Tad and nice blue eyes. Not too tall, but athletic anyhow.

"Reckon we're hitched to the same post," I said. He gave me a strange look, but I was getting used to such manners in Los Angeles. So then I asked, "Is Mrs. Taylor a good grub-spoiler?"

"Good grub-spoiler?"

To which I had to expound that a grub-spoiler was a cook, whether or not the grub was spoilt.

"Isn't that something of an oxymoron?" Sailing asked me.

I tried to get a fix on his face, see if maybe he was word-wrangling me some, but his eyes didn't give me a clue. So I saged him with, "Don't need to be no ox moron to be a grub-spoiler, but it helps."

He looks at me all flusticated and I just added, "It's a cowboy word. It don't have to make sense."

He took that in, then asked, "You're not a native, are you?" he asked.

"Everyone's a native, only from different places," I allowed.

Then he did a real curious thing. Insteada laughing sage-like, he picks up a pad and pencil and jots down what I'd just said.

"You writing a letter?" I asked, damn near half outa the window to see what he was writing.

His hair sorta fell down into his eyes as he looked over at me and said, "I'm sorry. What did you ask?"

"What's that you're writing?" I never minded being slandered, I just didn't like the idea of being libeled.

He showed me what he'd just written and maybe I was a little chopfallen when I saw he hadn't taken down my native wisdom, but had only the words 'hitched to the same post' and 'grub-spoiler.'

"You afraid you'll forget them words?" I asked.

He smiled me real nice, looking sorta sheepish and sly all at the same time, and informs me that, in addition to his Sailing O'Sullivan Strong name, he also had him three letters after it. They was P, H, and D. This kid was a doctor of the English Language, teaching over to USC, which even I'd heard of. He told me he was compiling hisself something he called a onomasticon, which at first I thought was something prehistoric. He informs me that was a book on speech mannerisms from yaps like me.

Over dinner I prodded Sailing into disclosing probably more about hisself than maybe even his Irish momma knew. He was so natural quiet and into hisself. You don't get no P. H. of D. by doing all the talking. 'Course, in strolls a walking, talking speech-mangler like me and you gotta figure ol' Sailing and me was destined for friendship.

Right from the get go, I got the idea he was real embarrassed for being so brainy. His face would blush like a blue dog when I pressed him into talking about his scholarly accomplishments, which included essays published in books even. He said he'd start off for school when he was a kid, but since he usually ended up getting bored, then teaching everybody including the teacher, he just started sneaking into the flicker shows insteada school.

Now, I would like to go on record, right here, before

I go a word further, that I, Royal R. Leckner, had never onct set foot in a moving picture palace. I reckoned I had better things to do with my time and money. Besides, everybody knew flickers was only a passing fancy anyhow. Why get to enjoying something you know ain't gonna be 'round next year?

But since I was now domiciling smack dab in the middle of the flicker colony, you gotta know my ears pricked up when Sailing said, "I've probably seen every Broncho Billy Anderson movie twenty times. Well, western pictures are my favorites. That's why, when I thought you might be the actor William S. Hart. . ."

I cut him off with, "You mean to tell me I'm sharing my face with a ACK-tor?" It was a double insult, thought me. Here I'd been laboring under the assumption I was a one uva kind in the facial department and now I learn my lookalike is just a ACK-tor!

But Sailing came right to his defense. He tells me he thought Hart was a fascinating man. A Broadway actor who was sorta new to Hollywood and the cinemas. He said he was quite a sensation and he had him a quality rare in most actors, which was his sense of good business and fair play. He ended his spiel by telling me Bill Hart was gonna be big. Really, really big. And he never missed one of his moving pictures.

I settled back down some, thinking oh well, at least I didn't have me no evil twin or anything. Nope, that woulda been too easy.

So then we just easy-talked some, each one of us sorta prodding the other—me prodding him on movies and such, and him prodding me to just keep me talking. At first it was sorta flattering, having him write down so mucha the way I talked. Then it got a little annoying onaccounta it sure slowed the conversation down some. But when I mentioned it, he smiled at me, said he was sorry, and put down his pencil. Somebody raised him real good, and I was hoping my own Chick'n'Tad was taking some notes theirownselfs.

Now, why couldn't my daughter find someone nice and smart like this here Doctor Strong, I was wondering. 'Course, looking back I think I was swayed extra toward Sailing onaccounta he seemed to hang on my words like they was gonna secure his future, which in a way they did.

Anyhow, I didn't spill too many beans that first night. I wasn't sure yet how far the pickle was gonna squirt and I sure as hell didn't want Mrs. Taylor or this Sailing feller to get the wrong idea of Royal and his family. And when Mrs. Taylor started plying the boys with questions regarding their momma and all, well I just said something cowboyish and Sailing finished the conversation off just fine.

Sailing Strong was a fine diversion for the evening. But you know where my head was. Now I never served in the cavalry or army or nothing, but I'd read about war-type strategies nowanthen. I realized a good general always knows his enemy, inside, outside, upside down, and sunny side up if needs be. Trouble was, I wasn't downright sure just who or what my enemy was. Well, I knew E.M., so I was covered on that account. I didn't know Magellan and didn't know if I wanted to. What little I'd discovered about that Chesley feller I didn't like, especially when I thought of him courting my own daughter. Then the flickers, thinks me . . . them flashes of light was the core to the whole problem, even if someone smart like Tommy Edison did have a hand inventing 'em.

When I told Sailing my plan, he shows me the paper where they advertise who was exhibiting what where and who to. He circles a few ones I might enjoy, one of which featured that Mary Pickford which my daughter was gonna be the next one of.

I asked Sailing if he'd like to see him this show, but he was teaching a night class at the YMCA.

Chick'n'Tad was happy to stay with Mrs. Taylor, who said she'd busy 'em with chores for cash, and my boys, any time they saw some money could be made, usually followed that trail till they was green-in-the-face sicka candy.

So that night, Royal, alone and unarmed, off into the enemy camp goes . . . start at the core and work your way out—works with damn near everything incept a apple.

The taxi-man dropped me off at the theater, which was called Talley's. The movie title was *Mistress Nell* and I took a pause—well, you know what mistresses was usually for.

I musta been a little late onaccounta the doors was closed and there weren't no people milling about. So I went to the window and knocked to get the attention of this man's back. He turned and, since I was looking toward the cushion-like entrance doors, he had to knock back at me saying they was full up.

When I gave him my full attention, he smiles and then opens his hatch up and says I could go right in, and it was nice to see me, Mr. Hart. Then he takes in my Royalish garb and says I musta come right offa the set. Seta what, I didn't know.

Well, if me looking like this Hart yap could get me through closed doors and for free, then I reckoned I could live with it.

Now I been to opera houses in pretty mighty partsa the world and I have to say, the lobby of that Talley's theater was right grand. I took myself upstairs, where I thought I wouldn't stand out so much, and found me a doorway to lean in whilst I commenced to witness my future.

Anyhow, the theater was about as pretty as anything. I noted there was a huge organ in the corner and I wondered if maybe we would be obliged to sing us some hymns before the flicker commenced to flickering. Well, I wasn't then or am I now a church-setter and I damn near walked out when the organ player walked in. Folks applauded the grinder and I went along with it.

Looking 'round at the feathers and satins and spangles of the folks around the theater, I commenced to run a quick tabulation of how many seats there was. I calculated that at ten cents per head, the ticket seller might do all right for hisself in this business.

The organist smiles nicely at us in the audience and then signals up to some person setting up above us. I looked up and there was the tiniest dang hole in the wall you ever did see. I wondered how the hell anyone would be stupid enough to buy a ticket for up there where they sure couldn't of seen much. Well, the lights disappeared in the room and then I realized the hole above us was where the flickers flickered outa.

Now I shall not bore you with the details of the movie onaccounta I disremember anything more'n thinking that Mary Pickford was right comeatable—looked alla ten years old and didn't to me look like anyone I didn't want my own daughter to be another one of. Even if it meant her hair was all blondie-locked. 'Course what struck me most was there was no way in heaven or, let's face it, hell that my Elsie Maude could ever be so sweet and childlike . . .

she could be the greatest ACK-tor in the world, but no one could pull off that kinda job.

I took myself downstairs before the ending so's I wouldn't be much noticed. I took me a quick swing 'round the lobby. There was lotsa photographs on the walls and my eyes was taken to one which advertised that Theda Bara person that ol' E.M. said she was sporting after.

The movie it taunted was called *A Fool There Was.* I reckoned that title pretty much just summed things up, and I knew E.M. was heading for disaster. The poster called Theda Bara a vamp, onaccounta she'd put out a sorta vampire-like spell over men, and I want to tell you, son, my eyes didn't need no glasses when I looked close at the pictures and saw that woman coming at me like she was gonna vamp me royal. Her hair was long and wild. Her eyes had darkning all 'round 'em like she was a zombie. And her get-up was about as forgiving in the foundations department as a piece of wet gauze. Like hell E.M.'d be the next Theda Bara! One of them vamps was quite enough for flickerdom. And I'll tell you this: E.M. could demand, "Kiss me, my fool!"—like it said under the picture—till the cows were blue in the face and I wasn't gonna let her, my own wife, vamp herself up on the screen for the whole damn world to see. Uh uh. Not ol' Royal R-for-Rescue Leckner.

I don't recollect what happened next. I think I just stood staring at the Theda Vamp, my mouth catchin' flies and my eyes desert-dry onaccounta I don't think I was able to blink much.

Then the movie musta let out, for the lobby starts to fill with people talking ooohs and aaahs and such like that. I ducked me into a door marked private 'cause privacy was just what I was looking for that night after I had stared direct into the face of mine enemy.

Insteada finding myself in a janitor's room or maybe accounting office, it seems I'd stepped into the theater manager's office or something. I shut the door, then leant against it and took in the plushness of it all. It had mahogany, velvets, and big portraits of dramatic-looking folks. It also had, amongst all this to-do, three men setting in it.

four

"Oh, pardon me," I tried, knowing I was about as outa place as a hog on ice.

Then it happens. I shoulda known it would. One of the three men in the room comes over to me, stands infronta me, places his arms acrost his chest, and says, "Well, well, well. William Shakespeare Hart. And just how did you get wind of this?" Then he turns to the other two men and asks them, "Which one of you two let the cat out of the bag?"

"Oh, take it easy, David. Come on in, Bill. Have a drink," said another man. He talked sorta slow and his voice was deep and opera-like. He hands me a drink and you know damn well I took it and downed it. Then just as I was about to set 'em all straight, the third man comes over to me, points sorta rude-like to my chin scar, and hollers at me, "Dammit to hell, Bill! Look at that scar! How many times have I told you I don't want you doing your own stunts!"

Well, I know I'd partook of their liquor and I was a

fish outa his own stream, but I don't take lightly to elevated voices and damnation all in the 'companimenta finger-pointing.

So I set down my glass and stated my name was not Bill Somebody Hart and if they'd excuse me I'd take my intrusion elsewhere.

By now all three of 'em was standing 'round me and I was feeling maybe like what a horse feels at a auction.

The first says, "Say, wait a minute. . ."

The second says, "You taken to wearing lifts?"

The third says, "This *isn't* Bill Hart."

I was about to agree, but the first then goes a little secret-like and says, "So if you're not Bill Hart, who are you and how'd you know about this meeting?"

I told 'em I walked in accidental and I was sorry and now I was gonna walk out intentional. I then passed under their noses the only thing I had in the way of identification —my brand registration for the Royal Bar-L.

"The name's Leckner, Royal R. I'm a rancher up to Walla Walla Wash. But it seems the longer my face stays in this town, the more my name's a lie."

The third man laughed at that and asked me to set down, have another drink, and he was sorry if there was a mix-up. He had him a southern accent and he was all manners and cigars.

"Then you don't know anything about why we're meeting here?" the first man asked.

"Nobody sent you?" the second asked.

They was now all three setting 'round me and I was thinking there musta been some sorta high talk-a-lorem going on.

I told 'em whatever it was they was afraid I knew about, they didn't have to worry onaccounta I didn't. I then told 'em under what treacherous circumstances I'd come to their town in the first place. I ended by indicating that up my way, three gentlemen didn't usually get this far into a discussion without introductions full-'round, unless a jury was involved.

So they introduced theirselfs as:

"David W. Griffith."

"Mack Sennett."

"Thomas Ince."

I reckoned by their expressions it had been some time since they met someone who wasn't already familiar with their names.

I had no idea, of course, who these fellers was in the cinema community. 'Course, I later found out: three of the biggest names in the business back then. But they got over it quick and I think my arcadian ignorance helped 'em open up a bit.

We poured ourselfs another drink and they showed some interest when I mentioned Marco Magellan, so I continued to untwist my lion's tail of woe.

"So," Mr. Sennett said, "that weasel is at it again."

"At what?" I asked back.

"Making another failure," replied Mr. Griffith, setting down his beer. He had nice, hooded blue eyes and I thought they looked a little sad just then. "It's people like Magellan that give our business a bad name."

Then they rattled off the names of his gone-bankrupt movie companies. Real winners, like: Goldie's Golden Auras (I wonder how much Goldie was taken for), Magellan's Masterpieces, Sarah-Graph.

"And what was that French one?" Mr. Ince asked, and they played around with frenchy words, then he remembered: "Fleurs de le Mageek! In short, Mr. Leckner, Magellan is a two-bit, no-talent chiseler of the first degree. He puts together money, he puts together a film. Talent is of little consequence to the likes of him."

Then I inquired about the names Herman Klepelmeier and/or Chesley Warwick.

Again, they exchanged tragic glances. The man with the cigar asked Mr. Ince, "Didn't you use him once, Tommy?"

"Once was enough. Haven't seen him since. But faces like his have a way of re-surfacing."

Like you know, I took my inquiry further and they told me Warwick was just too damn good looking for his own good, and his ego was so big it made up for his shortning, and if that wasn't bad enough, it was said he cahooted with nefarious types, whatever they were. They all agreed Hollywood had enough of its own problems in the vice department without adding a handsome face to it.

"You think maybe, on topt of everything else, they uses one of them infringer cameras?" I asked. If they did, then maybe I could bring the police into things and speed up my returns. Then, on the other hand, maybe my wife was then a accessory, or even me! So I wasn't sure which way I wanted 'em to reply.

They said he wouldn't have been the first filmer out west to shortchange Edison, and they said it in such a way I was wondering if maybe they theirownselfs was short-changers. Then they informed me Magellan was a sly one and as long as his movies was flops he didn't care, onaccounta it wasn't *his* money was lost. He just goes out, finds more money, makes more promises, and then films him another turkey. And all the while he was probably cooking hisself two setsa books.

"Well, you mean to tell me there ain't nothing anyone can do about him?" I asked.

Mr. Griffith summed it up for me in the 'companiment of the offer of a cigar: "Technically, Mr. Leckner, Magellan hasn't done anything illegal. Until someone can prove he's squirreling away his investors' money, he has full license to operate in this town. Even if we kicked his sort out, they'd just go somewhere else and start all over again."

"Tell me," Mack Sennett asked, looking about as trustable as a monk, "just how much money did he soak you for?"

I mentioned the sum and there was silence. The Inch fellow told me that was considerable hefty. That he'd been making films for some time and twenty grand could take him through several two-reelers. Then them three looked at each other like they was reading each others' minds and they said all together, "Russian Roulette!"

I allowed I was in a bind, but I wasn't about to play that game, to which Mr. Griffith was quick to inform me *Russian Roulette* was the name of Marco's last flop, for which he still musta owed money, onaccounta twenty thousand was more in the deMille department of film budgets.

Before I could get further confused, Mr. Ince says, "You know, I've always thought Magellan was on the wrong side of the camera. I don't know, he's hardly handsome, but talk about a persuasive style. Beguiling. I can see why women fall for his promises. After all, seduction is the key to our industry—if people weren't seduced by the fame, the money, the power, we'd all be shopkeepers and gin-slingers. And if *Magellan* can do that, pity the poor woman who falls for *Warwick*."

I was beginning to wonder if I should have a croaker see how my heart was holding up, for it'd been mighty active too sudden-like. I swallered and said, "So, what it boils down to is 'my money or my wife.'" I stood up to hear my sentence.

"Well, you might be out twenty thousand dollars," Mack Sennett said, "but I doubt Magellan will make a star out of your wife. He hasn't cast a talented person yet. No offense."

Well, at least that was good news.

Then the door opened a little and someone whispers into the room, "Mr. Ince, there's a reporter out here."

The boys looked at each other cautious-like.

"How'd he know we're here?" Mr. Ince asked.

"He doesn't," the man whispered in. "He said he followed Hart in and he was wondering. . ."

Mack Sennett pulled him in and closed the door. "You didn't tell him we're here, did you?"

"Absolutely not, Mr. Sennett."

Now there were four sets of eyes on me and I reckoned I knew what was coming next.

"He said all he wanted was a couple of photos with some starlets we hired for ushers tonight," the theater man explained, looking at me. "Would you mind, Mr. Hart?"

I put down my drink.

Then Mack Sennett said to me, "How would you like to help us out of a jam, Mr. Leckner? You see, we behind-the-camera boys shun publicity. If you'd just go out there and get rid of that reporter."

'Course I knew what a man in a jam looked like and I was looking at three of 'em—four, if there was a mirror in the room. I told the theater man to tell the reporter I'd be right out.

It was Mack Sennett who got him a big grin on his

face, and he said to his friends, "You know, gentlemen, I owe Bill Hart one for that Fatty Arbuckel episode."

Mr. Griffith seemed to get his drift and added, "Yes, and it seems Bill's kept more than one of my actresses out too late."

So the Inch fellow pulls me close to him and says, "Wouldn't you like to meet the man who's been causing you all this mix-up here in Los Angeles?"

"You mean, the one I'm about to go out there and be?"

"Yes. Did you know I'm his boss?"

"I didn't."

"You know what it's like to have one of your top hands try to tell you your business?"

"I do. Can't stand me a chesty cowpoke."

"Me either."

Thomas Ince, Mack Sennett, and D.W. Griffith all discussed things, and I think that was the first time I'd ever been referred to as a opportunity.

"I think we ought to teach him a lesson. Maybe let him know he can be replaced," Sennett said with an even bigger grin, and I could tell he was probably the Big Joker in Hollywood. They convinced me it was gonna be a hoot and I'd have a good get-even laugh on that Hart for him causing me so much trouble.

They didn't have to say anything more.

So I went into the theater lobby with the manager and had me my photograph taken with not one, not two, but *six* beautiful young things, and the pose was, get this, ol' Royal lounging lengthwise in eacha their arms, like they was totin' a beam to a barnraising.

I didn't put up too much of a fuss.

Then the reporter man left and so did the ladies, and

they was even giving me their names and phone numbers, and one even gave me her address, along with a seta winks. What a world it was becoming! Then I slipped back into the office, and the three movie men had things all worked out.

They had arranged for me to be driven up to a spread called Inceville, named after Tommy Ince, somewheres north of Los Angeles. It was there that Bill Hart worked on making his movies. The plan was for me to go up there with a letter from Thomas Ince and act like I was gonna be the next one of him, meaning Hart, of course.

Just as I was taking my Hart-like leave, I turned and looked at the three movie men. Mr. Griffith was leaning on the desk and the other two was setting on each side of him in chairs. I smiled and said, "You boys make quite a triangle settin' there."

"Just don't tell anybody," said Sennett.

And I haven't, till now.

Oh, you might want to make a note that the partnership them three was concocting in secret that summer eve in 1915 was to become Triangle Films, but I never onct saw anything in the way of a Royalty.

No matter, onaccounta I felt like I'd made me a few new friends, and I hafta admit, these movie people, the *real* movie people of 1915, was no more eccentric than me. They was nice and intelligent and business-like, so helping 'em play a joke on their friend was right up my alley. But even now, twenty years later, I can't say for sure just who the brunt of their little joke was.

five

I knew it was late, and I was tired. But one trail just seemed to lead to another. Sorta like hunting. Or looking words up in the dictionary. Anyhow, I was thinking maybe I oughta peek around this so-called Royalscope place, the address of which I'd copied down from my previous investigations, so I had a taxi man take me there. 'Course I had no idea if I was heads up or tails down, but I think the parta town we was in was sorta Bowery-ish, which you'd know if you'd ever been to New York City.

He lets me out and says the address oughta be somewheres in that block and if I wanted him to wait it'd be lots extra. I remembered I'd left my friends, Smitty and Wes, back at the boarding house, so I told him I'd pay the waiting charge.

Halfway down the block things was looking just like warehouses and such. Then, in the reflection of a streetlight, I see something move halfway up the side of a building. It's a man on a scaffolding and what's he doing? Putting up a sign. He was holding a sign that had one of my favorite words on it:

ROYAL

in great big, English-looking letters. And painted already on the building was the name Lutherscope Productions. Now I was confused, so I called up to the man what he was doing.

He barely gives me a glance, like putting up signs in the middle of the night was perfectly normal.

He says down to me, "The big spender who owns this joint is too stingy to replace the whole sign, so I'm putting up half a sign," he calls down, smearing his speech a little onaccounta the mouthful of nails he toted. Then he proceeds to hammer up the ROYAL sign right over the Luther, so it came to read Royalscope Productions. I wondered who the hell Luther was and if maybe he was getting any visitors at the poor house.

"Think I can go in and look around?" I asked, noticing that the front door was half open.

"I don't get paid to think. I get paid to replace signs in the middle of the night," he grumbles back down at me. Union man.

I took that as a yes.

It was dark and almost musty inside the warehouse. I reckoned the place hadn't seen much commerce of late. Onct my eyes got adjusted to the dark, I could make out a small stream of light coming from acrost the room. Naturally, I followed it.

Hell, if *my* twenty thousand dollars was paying the bills, then sure as hell I'm not paying all-night light bills. But a voice comes wafting and stops me cold. I slipped closer and hid so's I could hear and the talker couldn't see me. Eavesdropping is one of this cow waddie's best honed skills. Ask anyone. So I did it.

The voice was speaking in Spanish and I never learnt mucha that language. I just knew some general *vacarro* terms that drifted up north over the years from Mexican cowpokes. So here's the words I was able to pick outa the conversation: something that sounded like 'Mausers,' which threw me off onaccounta that was a German type of gun; 'pesos' which everyone knows; and then lotsa Spanish numbers.

Then the feller makes him another phone call, this time in English.

"Marco. Me. Chesley. I'm in the studio . . . Yeah, he's putting it up now . . . Looks just like the last four. At least we found a rube with a better name this time. . ."

I'd been called a rube a few times in my life, so I held tight and kept listening.

"I told you, I'm working as fast as I can. Look, I just finished going over the books . . . Well, I think you better be bothered. We need more money . . . what for? Past debts, current debts, and if you think you're going to be big in this town, then you better be prepared to spend some big bucks . . . So how's it going with that Rose or Rosa or whatever you're calling this one? . . . Look, that hick daughter tells me everything. Her old man's loaded. Twenty thousand is nothing to him . . . Yeah, some kind of cattle baron or something. So you keep working on the ol' lady and I'll keep working on the sweet thing."

I dared me a peek in through the door. Chesley was sitting on a rickety chair, his feet up on a turned-over box crate labeled "Explosives," which I was then wishting was maybe full and primed. Then he added in a nasty little English accent, "Tut tut, old man, not to worry. I told you, I have connections. So, best ring up Rosa. She and her lovely daughter are at Aunt Audie's Hollywood House. Well, just thought you'd like to know we have our phone hooked up again, old boy." And he hung the phone up.

I was outa there before he'd set upright. And I was mighty glad I'd sprung extra for the waiting taxi cab.

I was thinking hard the whole way back to Mrs.

Taylor's and halfway into the night. This is how I sorted it all out:

I was right about Magellan.

I was right about calling my banker.

But that Chesley had me confused. Why did a face fulla fortune have to talk like such a crook? If he had him 'connections,' why the hell was he wasting 'em and cahooting with the likes of Marco?

I'd had me enough unanswered questions for one day and I think I even looked forward to getting outa town the next.

Early next morning the boys and me was on the front porch awaiting our ride up to Inceville when Chick asks me, "Say again where we're heading now, Pa?" I reckon the boys was getting mighty confused 'bout things.

Tad says a "Hope it's fishin'. Ain't had us much fun since we been here, Pa."

To which Chick adds, "Yeah, we gonna fish or cut bait?"

Well, I knew who he'd heard that from and though I don't think he realized it, it was quite a question. I was gonna cut me some sizeable bait all right. But I said, "We're going to Inceville."

"Inchville?" Tad asked. "Momma up at Inchville?"

"No, your momma's here in town."

"Then why we going there?" Chick asked.

I looked at my boys and I wondered if they knew what desperation looked like on the face of their pa. All I said was, "'Cause I gotta do something. Now get a smile on your mugs. This'll be big fun. I hear tell this here Inceville is just like home . . . cowboys and Indians and horses and cattle and movie-makers to boot. I'm gonna meet us up with that Bill Hart."

"Who's Bill Hart? Sheriff or something?" Tad asked.

Then Chick, the practical one, says, "Yeah, this Bill Hart gonna get us our twenty thousand back?"

Lucky for me, a car comes 'round and honks for us. Lord, what a vehicle. It was black and long and with a yeller hind end sorta. Well, the boys was right impressed, I'll tell you.

We got us first to Santa Monica, which set pretty as you like right on the shores of the Pacific Ocean. The driver informs us there was a Palisades or something there. He said it was all sortsa fun. But the best of all was a roller coaster, the likes of which I don't remember seeing anywheres, even that one up in Jantzen Beach in Portland. The boys spotted it before they spotted the ocean and well, after all the fun I hadn't let 'em have, you can bet your best saddlebags we alla us, driver included, took us a ride,

The boys fussed some when I told 'em we had to get on up north, onaccounta I had bigger fish to fry that day. Whilst we rode, I took a bead on the land which the driver called the Santa Ynez Canyon. The hills was beautiful and I knew why those movie folk, since they was in the business of re-creating, picked such a parcel of land. 'Course that was long before anyone thought about color in film, but even in black and white I figured that Tommy Ince bought him the right side of paradise. But I hoped to hell he never set foot in my own corner, up at Walla Walla Wash, for if he did he'd see what real scenery was and before long I'd be overrun with ACK-tors myownself.

Our car stopped at a long pier, which was held up good by commerce and buildings and such, and I asked the driver if we could maybe get out here and walk the resta the way. He said that was fine with him and when could he pick us back up. I picked a hour later that day and he turned 'round and left us there. I let the boys play on the beach whilst I poked 'round some. Onct more they griped when I called 'em up, for they'd been working right seriously at figuring out a way to get aboard this ship anchored off shore. Well, I'd read 'em plenty of Robert Louis Stevenson books and the ship looked downright Long John Silver-ish to me too.

Lunchtime was approaching and so I took the boys and me into this beanery setting on the wharf. The place looked real homey on the outside, but as soon as we walked in I knew maybe it wasn't the place for younguns. There was dock workers, cigarette smoke, and alota beer glasses about. But we was hungry and the food sure smelt good. Chick'n'Tad wanted to set at the counter, where they could spin their stools till they let go their lunches, but I made us set in a corner booth. Like always, I kept my back to the wall and my eyes on the crowd.

When we was deciding betwixt lemon or chocolate pies for dessert, in walks, sweartagod, a Indian. Well, Chick kicks Tad to get his attention and Tad pokes me to get mine.

"Look, Pa. What you reckon a Indian's doing in this necka the woods?" Tad asks.

"Hush," warns me. "Indians got rights to be anywheres they want. That one probably works up the hill on them Thomas Ince films. Now, keep your eyes low and respectful."

Well, maybe I shoulda said it louder, for no sooner did this Indian set hisself down at the counter when a couple of sea-going toughs come up to him and starts poking fun.

A big, ugly customer thunked the Indian's shoulder and said, "Hey, Chief, maybe you oughta go on back up the hill. This place is for white folks."

Well, the joint was death-quiet. Then another sailor slaps the Indian from the other side and adds, "Ug. You big ugly Injin. Git on outa here before the cavalry comes to herd you out."

It was that word—herd—and the way he said it that did it for me, and I reckon for Chick'n'Tad too, 'cause they looks at me with eyes big and hurt. 'Course, my blood hit boiling when I saw Indian injustice after all the years we'd worked for equality up our way.

The Indian was doing his best to ignore the men. Others in the joint was beginning to grow in courage with each unanswered insult they lay down on that man.

I walked me over to the counter and tapped one of the sailors on the shoulder. "Pardon me," I says, "but I reckon this here man don't want you breathing so close to his food."

"Well, I *reckon* you oughta mind your own business. We don't allow no Injins in this place," one growls me back.

The other adds, "Yeah, matter of fact, we're not real fond of *any* strangers here."

I looked 'round and figured I could take two, maybe three, before I got into real trouble. I looked back to Chick'n'Tad, who was spitting in their fists, but I told 'em, "You boys get on outa here. I'm just gonna settle the bill."

Hell, I'd been aching for a good fight for maybe nine, ten months, and I reckon I'd finally found a cause good enough to proceed. One sailor grabbed me by the arms and the other delivered a blow to my stomach. I nearly broke in half and wondered why I thought I was only twenty years old. Well, the Indian rises offa his stool and comes to my rescue. He was right big for a Indian. Hell, he almost took off a sailor's face with his fist and I was damn impressed.

He turned and gave me a quick look, and I turned and got the one sneaking up behind me.

Well, everyone seemed to have something to say on the matter. There was shouting, swearing, and alota fists swinging all about the place. Like I knew they would, Chick'n'Tad buckled a few legs and raised a few inseams right along with the resta us mature adults.

I don't think I ever enjoyed a fight more'n that one on the pier of Inceville. Seamen fight a whole lot different than cowboys do, and I think I learnt a few shots as well as taught a few myownself.

How did it end? Well, a whistle blew outside and that meant lunch was over and it was time for the sailors to get on back to work. The place emptied like nothing ever happened, 'cept you could tell with one glance that the joint got the worst of things. They all filed on outa there, slapping backs, comparing bumps and, get this, putting five-, ten-, and twenty-dollar bills into a jar marked RESTITUTION setting next to the door, and I then knew that beanery was gonna make out right equitable.

That was my first encounter with longshoremen. What a crowd.

That left me, Chick'n'Tad, the owner, and the Indian sizing up the damage. The owner counted the money and smiled. Then he pulled a coupla steaks outa the cooler and handed one to me and one to the Indian. Then, speaking not a word, he brought Chick'n'Tad out their pies and started to set the tables and chairs all back about, like it was all business as usual.

The steaks went to both our faces. Sure as hell felt good. I can feel the coolness now. I can even smell the rawness. Now, how do you reckon the first feller ever came up with the idea of applying fresh meat to a fresh-battered face? Beats me.

Anyway, I helped the Indian up and he said, "My place is up the hill." He sure had a deep and powerful voice, and I knew by the way he talked he musta been educated offa the reservation. Then he adds, "We might need some stitching up."

"You gonna do it yourownself?" Chick asked, face fulla pity and pie.

The Indian held the steak over the side of his face, but I could tell the other side was smiling down at the boys. "We have the best medicine man in the business," he says, leading us outside.

We musta looked right comical: a battered Indian, steak on his face, followed by a battered Royal, steak on his face, followed by Chick'n'Tad, pies on their faces. He led us to a tent and, like you know, I was expecting Indian things all about. I been in plenty of Indian lodges, tipis, and wickiups in my day, but those California Indians, now they was a different stroke. It was all white-man furnished, top to bottom. Desk, chair, rug, bed, wood stove, telephone. He set us down to his desk, which had a big mirror over it.

"You first," says me. He slowly took the steak off . . . sometimes it sticks a little and that sure smarts. Then he starts to wash his face off a bit and it looked real swolt and maybe in need of some stitchery.

It was then we all stared into the mirror. For along with the blood, off comes the redskin, too. I dropped my steak, the boys dropped their mouths, and the so-called Indian's face went about as blank as any face, fresh outa fighting, could. I was staring right smack dab back into my very own likeness. We looked at each other, then back into the mirror, then back at each other.

I stuck out my hand to shake his, smiled me a sore one, and just said, "Well, I reckon that makes two of us, Bill."

six

They say ('they' being the same ones who calculates how many years we're expected to live, I guess) we each and every one of us got a double setting somewheres in the world. Now I don't think it proves much by going out and looking for this so-called twinster, but I can tell you this: if you do ever bump into one another, it's downright scary.

Well, Bill and I each rose and compared our heights. Damn near equal, incept I was a touch taller. He took off his Indian wig and we saw our hairs was the same too, 'cept there wasn't much gray in his. Same builds, same hands, same everything.

"You know," Bill said, his face still fulla amazement, "If it weren't for that scar on your chin. . ."

"I reckon we could be twins," I finished for him.

"Say, Pa, there something you ain't been telling us?" Chick asked.

"Yeah, Pa, Momma's gonna be tickled pink when she sets a gander on this," Tad adds.

I thought it was about time I introduced myself, so I

did, then my boys, then we had us some real identical laughs.

"How old are you?" Bill asked me, taking off the rest of his film makeup.

"How old are you?" I asked back. Men got a right to be just as secretive as women regarding age, I reckon.

"Well, I'll tell you . . . I'm as old as my tongue. . ."

"But a little older'n your teeth?" I finished for him.

We laughed at that chestnut and then I asked, "Come on, Bill, how old?"

"Forty. . ." he begins, which was good enough for me, so I finished it for him, "five."

It might interest you to know we also stretched the leather identical.

"So why the Indian get-up?" I asked.

"For a film I'm thinking about. I made myself up and figured if those wharf rats fell for it, my audience would too. But I sure as heck wasn't expecting that sorta trouble from those sons of seacocks. I owe you one."

To which I replied, "Well, you'd think I'd learnt to mind my own business, but poking fun at a lesser, that really fires me up."

"Lesser?" he asked me back.

"You know, not someone who *is* lesser, someone who's *got* lesser . . . like Indians."

He smiled back at me and then noticed Chick'n'Tad was getting mighty fidgety a-setting on his bunk.

"Your boys like horses?" Bill asked. 'Course, I hadn't gotten 'round to telling him where we lived and what we did for a living. I told Bill my boys loved horses, and he said good, follow him, but don't get too close to the critters.

We walked over to a corral which was at the center of lotsa stables and what looked like a small western town, sorta. Yeah, small western town. It looked like Idlehour, the town that I earned my spurs in, 'round, and on. Only, sweartagod, it was only the fronta the town . . . like maybe the boys that was hired to set the place up joined one of them unions and walked out on strike halfway through the job. I later learnt this was the way they made movie sets and they hardly ever built a back side to the buildings. Sure looked queer to these eyes onaccounta I'm used to back doors too.

Well, seeing those horses in the remuda was all Chick'n'Tad needed to feel right at home. They climbed the fence and Bill looked a little nervous.

"Oh, don't mind them, Bill. Horses don't scare my boys none," says me.

"Well, these aren't pleasure ponies. This is the toughest herd of broncs in the west. There's a bellyful of bedsprings in each one! We had them brought in from from the 101 Wild West Show in Oklahoma. Guaranteed to buck better'n any." He looked at the critters like they was gold in the bank.

Well, I'd heard of that wild west show, but for the life of me I couldn't figure out why he'd be so proud his horses was buckers.

So I asked, "You boys do rodeo work up this way?"

"Oh, maybe once in a while to blow off steam. But never with these old snoozers. We only use them when we need to film a wild horse. Besides," he adds, looking at his horses, "there's just something very, I don't know, poetic about a wild horse . . . a horse no man can break."

Now, you may think you know about William S. Hart and you might even be a fan of his, but that was the real Bill Hart speaking . . . the one I got to know. Any man who could tell a perfect stranger, even if he was his double, that a wild horse was something poetic, well, I knew from that moment on we'd be friends.

"What brings you and your boys up here, anyway?" Bill finally asked me.

This reminds me of the Inch fellow's note in my hip pocket. I pulled it out and handed it to Bill, saying I was not much more'n a coincidence with a message.

He reads the note, which I later learnt warned him not to pull a Charlie Chaplin and ask for too much money or else he could be replaced by the reflection watching him read this note.

Bill laughed and said, "Ha! Without me, Ince would be washed up in a year. I'm cheap at twice the price." 'Course I had no way of knowing, but Bill and those other three names was about as close as loops on a noose, and betwixt the four of them practically owned Hollywood. Then Bill looks at me a little serious-like and asks, "Say, you don't *really* have any ideas about beating my time in films, do you?"

I guess if you use your face to make a living, nothing's more of a threat than some identical face coming into the picture.

"Hell no, Bill," I said, smiling him back, "I came up here to beat someone's time *outa* films."

Then he said, "Well, this sounds interesting. I never knew anyone who wanted *out* of the business."

"Well, she don't exactly know it yet," I admitted. "You married, Bill?"

Well, I reckon my question answered alota things, for he laughed hearty, slapped my back, and said no, but he had a feeling I was gonna remind him why.

* * *

He allowed as how Chick'n'Tad could stay around the horses, providing they didn't get too close, then Bill and I left for more touring of Inceville. All I remember thinking 'bout that first hour in the company of Bill Hart was, he was about as normal as me, and I was beginning to wonder if all I'd come to hear about ACK-tors was only rumors. Oh, Bill mighta been something of a brushpopper, but hell, a southwest cowboy was better'n nothing. He was right as rain, good as any cowboy I ever met, and a sight better'n alota folks I'd run into in my day. Hell, if he was one of them eccentrics, I'd eat my boots, spurs and all.

Well, he gave me the tour all right, as far as we could go on foot, that is. He shows me a Spanish mission, then a full Sioux camp complete with real Sioux. Hell, Bill even showed me the front half of a Dutch Windmill village, sweartagod. Turns out this Inceville place was thousands of acres and it'd take a good horse, several days, and alota cold beer to take us through it. I could tell by the way he talked he was right proud of the place. He showed me this and that about the film business. When we ran into another ACK-tor or a wrangler or someone, Bill'd introduce me as his double, which I later learnt was more'n two times one.

"So Marco Magellan's going to make your wife and daughter his new stars," Bill finally said, leaning, quite cowboy-like, against a fence. "Some people never give up."

I leant back some myownself and said, "Well, from what I hear he pees a tetch more'n he drinks, if you get my meaning."

Bill laughed and said, "Yeah, only down here we say, all his geese are swans. Yep, Marco Magellan's the turkey of the industry."

I wondered which fowl my E.M. was gonna end up being. I said, "Sweartagod, Bill, for the life of me I can't figure out what my wife's up to. She's usually so savvy herownself, you'd think she'd see that Magellan is nothing but a wagon fulla fence holes."

I then asked him about Chesley Warwick. Funny, all you had to do was mention his name and you'd get a face fulla winces. "You know," he says, "I held my breath when word got out that Marco and Warwick had teamed up." I held mine whilst he added, "Think of it as Attila the Hun meets Napoleon Bonaparte." But all I could see was ol' Royal meeting Waterloo.

Then Bill adds, "This business promises a lot, but seduces even more."

There was that word again: seduce.

"I feel a pity for you, friend. I wish there was something I could do."

There was my opening. "Well, Bill, maybe if you was to come on down to Los Angeles and tell my wife whose clutches she's in, she might be persuaded to give it up, you being such a big name and all." But even as I was talking, I knew E.M. probably wouldn't even believe it if God Hisself filled her in.

"I reckon that would break her heart," Bill said, like he knew E.M. better'n me. Sad thing was, I reckoned it would too.

"Look, what say we go on down to the screening tent and get our minds off Magellan? Maybe we ought to round up your boys. Think they'd like to see a couple of my latest pictures?"

I didn't confess they'd never ever seen a moving picture and I wasn't so sure I wanted to get 'em started with it. (I was still mad as hell someone'd introduced 'em to chewing gum.) So I said I'd call 'em, but to start without 'em if they didn't answer, which they hardly ever did. Sure enough, they was nowhere to be seen nor did they whistle me back.

"You know, Bill, this'll be only the second moving picture I've ever seen." I reckon I felt bad that I seemed to be the only person in California who hadn't heard of this ACK-tor, and I think I was a little embarrassed to admit it.

He looked at me like I was from another planet, then smiled, slapped my back, and said, "Then you'll be starting at the top, son."

Well, the tent was dark and cool and Bill got us some beers from the cooler. I put mine to my swolt eye and I'll be damned if I didn't look over and see Bill doing the same thing.

"We're building a permanent screening room down the hill a piece. But this tent works for now, and we get a good breeze through it."

I had no idea what I was in store for. 'Course there wasn't no organ playing. Just coolness and darkness. Bill says, "Go ahead, Sammy. Any time you're ready." Then I heard the flick flick flick of the machine, and I think I figured out then why they called the things "flickers."

The words that appeared on the screen called this film *Pinto Ben*, whatever that was. My first reaction was they left out the 'a', but then I wondered why they'd call a movie after a bean. It said it was written and directed by William S. Hart, so I knew I was in the company of several talents. Well, right away I liked the film onaccounta it sure looked like the old days when I was foreman of the Four Arrows Ranch. These men was driving cattle to the big city, Chicago I think it was. Anyhow, Bill played this cowboy who had a real feeling for his horse, which was the Pinto Ben of the title. The words was all in poetry and made for real fine reading. Then things turned for the worst and I, knowing cattle the way I do, saw that the men up on the screen was in for trouble from a stampeding herd.

I recollect looking up at that screen and seeing myownself, even if Bill Hart and me hadn'ta looked anything alike. I could do that, I kept on saying to myself. I could be myself up on the screen. That ain't being what you ain't.

"How much you get paid to do this?" I asked Bill after awhile.

But Bill wasn't listening. He was stuck to the screen and shushed me. He was most taken in by his image on the screen, or so I thought. I looked closer and saw his eyes, big with wetning. I looked back up and saw more emoting and more riding and more cowboy work and more opportunity.

The big finish was about to come upon us. The cattle was stampeding through a long, narrow chute with Bill on his Pinto Ben trapped at the end. Well, this Pinto Ben takes the gate at the end of the squeeze-chute for all he was worth, just clears it, and lands on the other side. But his front leg goes out when he lands and I knew what that usually meant.

Then they showed Bill holding the head of his heroic pony, who had took a awful fall. Then came the last lines of the poem, which the Bill Hart next to me whispered out loud.

> Reckon some o that blood come out o my heart,
> This heart that Ben had won,
> So long Ben—all in a day's work,
> So long—you son-of-a-gun.

We sat in the darkness for a bit whilst the film flapped 'round the reel behind us. I was thunderstruck. I felt my heart in my throat as I recollected my own best pony back in the nineties. Out comes my hankie. I looked at Bill, who'd pulled out his sneezer, too. He blew his nose and blotted away some tears.

"Sorry," says Bill. "That always chokes me up. That was my own horse, Fritz."

I hollered, "You kilt your own horse for that?"

Bill laughed and said, "Take it easy, friend. Fritz was only stunt-acting."

I settled back down and stared at the blank screen. Well, all I can say is, as I set there in that tent, I think I had a revelation or something. Not angels or nothing God-like . . . I just kept staring, awestruck-like, at that blank screen and said, "Run me another one, Bill.

seven

"This next film is a bit easier on us horse lovers," Bill tells me whilst they was setting it up. Then I think, I'm in here crying over some cow pony I'd never even met and I didn't even know what ol' Chick'n'Tad might be up to. I took me outside and looked 'round. I got a breath of fresh sea air and it made me feel better, even though the boys still didn't answer my whistle.

The next film was called *Keno Bates, Liar,* and this time Bill was a gambler called, you guessed, Keno Bates, liar. No sooner did the movie commence when I surely did get caught up in it.

Well, whilst all that mellerdramer was unfolding, I'd occasionally glance me over to Bill and then back up to the screen. I knew by then not to interrupt Bill when he was watching hisself, but I sure do remember thinking, I can do that, I can do that. Here's a rundown of what we was watching:

As the story unraveled, this hero feller, Keno Bates, kills him a robber and lo and behold, he finds a sweet-faced picture in the robber's pocket. It's the picture of a girl—the robber's sister, coming that very next day to see her brother, who she didn't know, of course, was a robber, and a dead one at that.

So Keno Bates, Liar, tells the girl her brother was kilt in a mine accident and he hisownself gives the girl a nice cabin and such. Well, like you gotta figure, he falls for the sweet'n'innocent and, of course, there's a jealous dance hall girl who spills the beans and tells the sister her very own lover kilt her very own brother. Well, just as things is ripening to a real dramatical pitch, including Keno Bates, Liar, taking a gunshot wound, there comes from somewheres outside our tent quite a ruckus. But I don't think too much of it, the movie had me so snared thorough and throughout. Then I heard a crash and some rip-snorting, then some screaming and hollering. But ol' Royal was too caught up in the movie to think about his own two issues. Till I heard Tad a-hollering, "Go get him, Chick!"

I looked over to Bill, and he was looking a little concerned. It was then the side of the tent crashed in with the 'companiment of that telltale scream of a horse mentioning to the person on board he ain't about to be broke. The person on board was Chick, fanning the hell outa a bronc. They was ripping the place up worse'n we did the joint on the wharf. 'Course Bill sprung to his feet to avoid getting run over and I think I just set there trying to see 'round the horse and catch me the rest of the movie. I was a little more used to such pranks than Bill was. Well, the horse stopped bucking, then he snorted, breathed him a heavy sigh, and Chick, with the movie playing on his face, looks down at me and says, "Like hell these gizzard poppers can't be broke!"

To which I hollers, "Well, break him somewheres else!"

It was then, of course, the horse onct again swapped ends and Chick damn near went through the roof of the tent. Not that it much mattered, for the poles was beginning to sway, and by the time Chick got his cold-jawed, high-poling, man-eating, gut-twisting spinner outa the tent, it was just chaos all around us. Then, like that wasn't bad enough, in comes Tad, swearing a blue streak and telling me no fair onaccounta Chick didn't let him have a turn!

The tent was ruint. Bill Hart was a cross betwixt a-mazed and b-crazed. The rest of the camp had arrived just in time to see Chick ride his sunfisher, topped off gentle as any ladies' horse, right on outa the tent. I doubt that horse ever again wrinkled his spine, even for money.

And worst of all, I never did get to see if poor Keno Bates, Liar, got the girl or the dance hall floozie, or maybe just packed it in and died instead.

We followed the fuss outside and, when the dust had settled, Bill looked over to me and asked, "Where'd your son learn to ride like that?"

"Oh, didn't I tell you, Bill, what I do in Walla Walla Wash?" I said, holding back a smile. "We're ranchers."

Bill looked over to Chick'n'Tad, then at his so-called 'unbreakable.' "I'll be damned. Just like me when I was a kid," says he, his face fulla wonder.

We could tell Bill was right impressed with the whole

thing. Probably about as impressed as I was about all his movie acting. It was sorta like we was swapping fascinations—you know how that goes: each thinks the other is luckier or hell, maybe even better off, than the other.

Tad came up and asked Bill, "You was a cowboy too? Pa said you was a ACK-tor, one of them fly-catching scene-lifters. Ain't that what you called him, Pa?"

Chick adds, "Yep. Them was your very own words in the motorcar, Pa. You didn't say nothing about him being a wrangler."

I looked at Bill and he seemed to understand onaccounta he was head-back laughing, full chisel. He allowed as how we was maybe alla us right. But mostly his love was for his critters, and I'll be damned if he didn't even thank Chick'n'Tad for reminding him of who he was at heart: a humble, earthy farm boy.

Then Tad comes up with, "Ah reservoir, mister, I can ride better'n Chick!" Then to prove it he poked his finger into the ex-bronc's belly, which I recognized as a maneuver to get the horse started up again. But Chick held him tight.

Well, Bill gave Tad a real father-like hug, then he patted Chick's leg and said, "Cool him down real good, son."

"I'll break the resta the rough string if you want," Chick offers. I could tell by his face he knew he was outa the woods for the tent and horse breaking.

"Not today, son," Bill said. "But how'd you two lodge-wreckers like to come up some time and stay around a few days? I can always use two good wranglers." Bill winked at me, and I winked back, knowing the boys would like that.

Chick'n'Tad took the horse back on up the hill.

What Bill said to me next I never came to understand till some time later. He said, "I reckon you're the luckiest son of a gun in the world."

* * *

Onct the boys got back, we began walking down toward the wharf, where we was gonna meet up with our driver to head back south. Bill and me walked on ahead. Even though I offered to pay for the tent, even the bronc if he wanted, Bill allowed as how we was even-steven.

"You sure? Magellan mighta fleeced my wallet, but I still got a coin purse left," says me, grinning.

"I ought to pay you, Royal," Bill says.

"What for? Hell, you lost a day's work to boot."

"For reminding me of something I've come all too close to forgetting, all too often," he said, sorta looking out over the ocean. Then he looks me straight and reveals, "When you make your living pretending, it's good to get a reminder of the things in life that really count." He held up the note I'd given him. "Like good friends." He looks towards Chick'n'Tad and adds, "Good family, good fortune." Then he looks me straight in the eye and adds, "Good face."

"Ah, the four F's."

And you know, when I get too fulla myself I think back on those four F's and Bill's face when he recounted 'em, and that usually brings me 'round.

We said good bye and Bill said he'd be thinking on a way to help me outa my Magellan fix. I gave him my telephone number and said someday we had to set back and compare cowboy stories. He said he had a hundred of 'em and I said we was gonna hafta take turns spellbinding.

* * *

Whilst waiting for our ride back to town, me and the boys set on a bench overlooking the ocean. I started thinking on that second movie Bill ran for me—the sweet sister-lady and the saloon vamp. Naturally, those thoughts led me to my most present danger: E.M. and Elsie and the seductions they was facing.

So, when the driver came to pick us up and asked me where to, I instructed him to firstly drop the boys off at the boarding house, but then to take me to a Aunt Audie's Hollywood House.

I thought I was gonna get me my women back on track, without thinking I might end up getting de-railed myownself.

eight

The boys fell quick asleep in the comfort of that leather-plushed car seat and I myownself mighta drifted off. I was sorta daydreaming on the events of the day and worrying about the events of the evening to come. I reckon I dozed off and had me a small nightmare as to what Aunt Audie and that Hollywood House mighta been like. I pictured me a mean ol' Amazon in the form of Miss Audie, and I found my heroish self having to lie, cheat, steal, and finally break down a door or two to get me to my womenfolk. I snapped awake and had to shake the images by wondering what the hell I was doing, dreaming dreams so wicked.

So I pretty much was ready for anything as I stood

there on the sidewalk infronta Aunt Audie's Hollywood House. Like most places in that parta town, the house was about as sweet as it could be, especially in the streetlight. Two stories of niceness and green lawn and porch swing and roses and a intricate set of trellises going all up the side, and a big "Ladies Only" sign.

But when I knocked on the door, the Amazon of my imagination did not appear. This Aunt Audie was tiny, white-haired, and by her apron and her aroma I imagine she'd been doing nothing more evil'n burning cookies. She asked if she could help me and if I was the Fuller Brushman onaccounta one of her boarders was having a real bad time with her fuzzy hair. 'Course, I knew then I had the right place.

I took off my hat and asked, "I'd like to see my wife, please."

She looked a little like husbands was a new commodity in those parts and wondered which one my wife might be.

"E.M. Leckner. And then there's my daughter, Elsie Maude."

"There's no one here by those names," Aunt Audie nforms me.

I then recollected the mar-kee names and Aunt Audie allowed as those two was staying there, but since there was a no-man policy in effect I was gonna have to await in the setting room, being as my two women was both out. Sweartagod, out in a strange town fulla eccentrics at eight o'clock, and on a Saturday night no less.

Upon further inquiry, I learnt my daughter was out with 'that' Chesley Warwick, and any time a woman uses the word 'that' infronta a person's name, then you know you're in trouble. She didn't know who E.M. was with, but she said she'd seen him around before. 'Course, I knew.

I chose to wait on the front porch where the air could help keep my head clear. Aunt Audie brought me some lemonade and some fresh-outa-the-oven cookies.

It was Elsie who first comes home. Since it was dusky, I couldn't get a real close look at the man who—get this—just let her outa the car. Not so much as getting the door or escorting her up the walk or nothing. She thanks him for a charming evening and he drives off. I don't care if it was 1915 and we was in a civilized parta the world, manners was manners, and I reckon I just found me one more reason to break that Chesley Warwick's nose.

You shoulda seen the look on my daughter's face when I stepped into the porch light. She gave me a casual-like 'Oh hello, Father,' but she took a step back and smiled me a weak one. I could tell by her face she was damn shocked to see me there. For a actress relying on facials to get her movie work, I reckon she was gonna need a helluva lot more acting lessons.

"Looks like you're doing right well living on your 'reduced circumstances,'" I said, referring to Aunt Audie's house and the last scene me and my daughter had shared up to Frisco.

"A. . . a. . . How long have you been in town? Momma'll be so surprised when. . ." She gives me a peck on the cheek and smiles pretty up at me.

"Long enough," says me, trying to forget which finger she usually had me wrapped around.

She stammers some, and I knew she didn't know how much I knew and that she was far too much her mother's daughter to give out any damaging information as to her whereabouts and whatabouts. So she informs me Momma probably ain't gonna be too late and she was tired and welcome to L.A. and don't think for a minute that me showing up meant she was gonna go back home to Walla Walla now or never.

"Elsie," says me, trying not to raise my voice, "there's some things you oughta know."

"I know so much more than you think I do, Father," she informs me. These are words a father hopes he'll never hear from his sixteen-year-old daughter. She looks off into the distance, all imparadised and dream-like and further informs me, "For instance, I know I'm in love."

"No you ain't," I said stern-like. "You're just . . . distracted."

Elsie smiles at me and says, "And I've never felt so wonderful. Here I am in this beautiful city. A wonderful man who loves me. A movie director just awaiting to star me in a role. A career in movies at my feet. It's all so dead-oddles wonderful, Father. And as soon as Marco finds the perfect scenario to showcase me. . ."

"Scenario? What's that?" I asked, never liking words that end with that ee-ooo sound.

"Well, you can't make a film without a scenario," she informs me. "You know, a story. A script. Marco says he's interviewing some of the best in the business. So you see, Father, like it or not, Mother and I are about to enter a whole new universe." And here she plays with my lapel and adds, "And what's twenty thousand little ol' dollars compared to the happiness of your family?"

To which I chucked her under her chin and replied, just as sweet and southern-like, "Just every little ol' penny of your inheritance, sugar."

Well, that didn't set her back none. She just said maybe we could get together some time and good night and then left. Yep, a absolute tintype of her mother.

It was another hour on the porch awaiting part two of

my problem. And this part was gonna be a tad more difficult. This time the car, a real rattletrap, stops, a back door opens, and Marco Magellan comes sweeping 'round the front to assist my wife outa her side of the car, which, by the way, had the words ROYALCOPE PRODUCTIONS scrolled out on the door. Yes, Royal*cope*—to which someone then added a S squenched where it shoulda gone in the first place. And when I say Marco swept 'round the car, I mean it, onaccounta he was draped in a long, black, satiny cape—can you imagine—deada summer no less.

He allows E.M. out and takes her arm and starts walking her up the walk.

"My dear, I can't tell you how ecstatic I am on your progress," he gushes.

"Yes, but when do you think we'll start filming?" E.M. stops and asks.

To this Marco laughs to the moon. He says, "Patience, my dear, patience. We've only just begun. You saw the studio. There's so much to do. And Rosa, for the epic I'm planning I'll need a few more investors." Then he goes on with, "Rosa, there is something I have to tell you." And you can be damn sure my hearing just improved. "I would be nothing if it wasn't for you. Oh, it's not just the money, it's you—your spark, your faith, your. . ." I appeared outa the shadows. ". . . husband."

Ol' Marco hardly flinches. He'd make a fine gambler, I thought. He smiles, and I remember how white his teeth was under the street light—almost like a dog baring his fangs.

I bared my own as I came closer, and he said, "Ah, Mr. Monteneg . . . I mean, Mr. Leckner, how fortunate to run into you. Now, as you know, I was unable to make our little meeting in San Francisco regarding the refinancing.

But your wife told me you'd decided to keep your 75% and let us run with it."

"Oh, you ran with it all right," I mumbled whilst escorting him to his car. I opened the door for him, and he wrapped his cape around him, got in, and said, "You realize, of course, this is all very innocent."

"Seems to me my 75% oughta give me some exclusive rights, Magellan," I steamed.

"Oh it does, it does."

E.M.'s first Los Angeles words to me were, "Now, Royal, he's unarmed."

"Like hell he's unarmed, E.M. You just head on in whilst Mr. Magellan and me talk us some business," orders me. I'll be damned if she didn't do just like I said, but I think she turned back onct or twice and smiled a little. I guess I'll never know for sure.

This is what I told ol' Marco, with Armando as his driver and a witness: "Where I come from only one thing's of more value than a horse."

"Really? What's that?" Marco wasn't flinching here either, mind you; I think he was actually curious.

"A good woman."

"Ah yes."

"And if we hang us horse-rustlers up my way, you oughta see what we do to woman-rustlers. I'd tell you, but I don't think Armando there is up to hearing it. Comprendo, Marco?"

It was dark so I couldn't see their faces. Marco held his own though and replied, sorta conceited-like, "Well! I don't know whether to be insulted or flattered."

I told him I didn't care what he was so long as he was now informed.

"Of course," he replied. "After all, you do have controlling interest."

"And that's the next thing. I want my money back, Magellan."

Here his face goes all tragic-like. He did do good faces, I'll give him that. He says, "But every penny of that money has already gone into our operation. There's nothing to give back."

All I could see was that half-new sign, the warehouse fulla emptiness, and the memory of that Chesley setting on a explosive crate.

"You got receipts to back that up?" I asked him, talking down at him as he sat in the car.

"Of course. But you have to believe me, sir, as soon as we hire a writer of some repute we'll be on our way to success," he says.

To which Armando leans over and adds, "Everything hinges on the right story, Mr. Leckner."

Then, thinks me, hmmmm. I knew me a writer of some repute. After all, Ph.D.'s didn't come in Cracker Jacks, leastwise back then they didn't. So I informed Marco and Armando of the name and the phone number of their writer.

Marco looks at the name Sailing O'Sullivan Strong and then back at me. "What are his credentials?" he asked me.

I took a holda Marco's satiny cape, pulled him a little closer, and said, "Me."

Marco looked into my eyes, and if he was any judge of a fight or flight situation, his moment was now at hand. Then a big smile comes acrost his dimpled face and he says, handing the name and number to Armando, "Armando, call this man first thing in the morning. If our major investor says he's our writer, then he's our writer."

I added one more sealer: "Ever play Russian roulette?" I asked. Armando and Marco consulted each other's faces before answering. Then Marco nodded, but he wasn't about to tip his hand.

"Just wondering," I replied.

I stepped back from the car and left it at that. After all, I didn't want to waste all my spuzz onaccounta I still had E.M.'s hash to settle and I was commencing to get tired.

nine

I asked my wife if she would like to set a little on the porch and maybe have some lemonade, civil-like. I'd been planning this meeting for a while and still, like San Francisco, I wasn't at all sure what I was planning for. So we just set there and rocked some. I was awaiting for her to speak, and who knows what she was awaiting for. We hadn't been the besta friends of late—she embezzling money, running off, cutting her hair and such. And I may not be the type to hold any grudges, but I gotta tell you, I was feeling a little steamed. She didn't say nothing, just rocked and sipped some lemonade like we was Mr. and Mrs. Rebecca of Sunnybrook Farm.

Halfway through a cookie she mumbles, "How did you know where I was?"

Well, I was just awaiting for her to throw out the first pitch and I said I had my ways and like hell I was gonna go back home and leave her to her spree and who in the name of Aunt Martha did she think she was being seen in public with the likes of Marco Magellan and did I have news for her, and who knows what else I spouted for the whole neighborhood to hear. She just set and listened like she'd heard it all before, which, if you put all our discussions together, probably she had. I immediately felt better.

I leant back in the wicker rocker and, as I recollect, she looked right comeatable in the light. And the sound of night clickers in the background was right soothing. I took me some deep suspirations like I was regaining control. She handed me some lemonade and that helped. I ended my spiel by jumping to the heada the class and asking my wife—right out in the open—was she being seduced by that Marco Magellan?

"By Marco? Ha! I don't know whether to be flattered or insulted," she replies.

I mentioned, wasn't it curious Marco'd said the same dang thing, only the other way 'round. But I then reminded her maybe there was more'n one form of seduction. She looked over to me and I'll be damned if she didn't mention the sorta seduction betwixt a man and his wife, which wasn't exactly the one I'd climbed the pulpit to discuss —which I forgot anyhow when she next suggested she could sneak me upstairs, that this discussion weren't fit for front porches, even in Hollywood. Ain't that just like a cornered wife? I decided it wouldn'ta been gentlemanly of me not to let my poor wife explain further. I washed down my surprise with a last shot of lemonade and suggested she proceed, but what about Aunt Audie and the Ladies Only sign?

"There's a ladder in the bushes under my window," she seduces.

"Ain't that handy. And how the hell you know that?"

"Well, Royal, there *are* fifteen women living here. Aunt Audie finally put out the ladder. She got tired of replacing the trellis," E.M. explains, like Ladies Only ladders was logic and law in this here Hollywood.

So, she goes up to her room and gives me the signal, but I had to wait for another feller to finish his climb before moving the ladder to E.M.'s window. 'Course, him and me had to agree on times of departure so's neither of us would be without a ladder when we needed it.

It was a easy climb and I felt like a kid again.

Whilst lounging in each other's arms, we sometimes did us our best talking. 'Course from our honeymoon on out we'd agreed that during these glowish times one topic wasn't to crost our lips: money. So it was tricky for me to talk about Marco Magellan and the films and not mention any sum.

"E.M.," says me, whispering of course. "Now, about that seduction word."

"Oh, don't worry, you did just fine," she says, snuggling a bit closer to me.

"No, not that one. I mean how this whole town can seduce you. I mean, here you got total strangers courting your looks and mon . . . a . . . assets, and you see how beautiful those photographs can make you look and you see how the audience's. . ."

"Royal, what are you getting at?" she asked, looking at me direct.

"Well, a town like this wants youth—so if you ain't young when you hit town, then there's folks here to help you flap back the calendar some. And don't you think it's natural . . . maybe not wanting to grow . . . older maybe? You know, like trying to look younger, which is real good,

E.M., don't get me wrong. But don't you think this here Hollywood film foofaraw is for younguns?"

"Like Elsie?"

I stepped right into that one, grappling irons and all.

"Now, E.M., I gotta be honest. I just don't think Elsie's got the talent to pull this one off, which don't mean I don't worship the trail upon which she tromps."

"That's why Armando Cato gives acting lessons. To teach us, Royal."

"Now, E.M., can you look me direct in the eye-dots and tell me you think our daughter has any talent for such things? I mean, she ain't no Mary Pickford."

"How would you know? The closest thing you've seen to a moving picture is maybe those Hawaiian Squab peep shows they set up at the State Fair."

It was here I told her I knew a helluva lot more'n she give me credit for. I told her I'd done me some investigating and found out alota things, including ol' Marco's and Chesley's reputations around town. E.M., of course, didn't believe me, and I didn't think that was the moment to mention Marco ain't made him a star yet and he was already considered the Kinga Turkeys. Nor did I mention he was just honey-foggling her for her. . . my. . . well, our money. When egos was at stake, then money oughten not to come into the picture. No one likes to be informed it ain't your looks or your smile that brings someone a-courting. Now, I wasn't gonna be no mood spoiler. After all, E.M. and me had crost too many rivers that summer to try and paddle all the way back home in one evening. But I had to get Chesley Warwick in edgewise, which is probably all the room he deserved.

So I asked, "E.M., tell me what you know about this Chesley whatever his name is."

"Oh, Elsie's very smitten by him."

That I knew, so I muttered, "That don't make him a eligible candidate."

"Candidate? For what? Mayor?"

I told her she knew what I was referring to and asked what else she knew about him incept he's a short and handsome dog? She elucidates that she didn't think Elsie was too serious about him, but in this town it really matters who one is seen with and, face it, everyone notices Chesley in a crowd, so they can't help but notice her, too.

"You know, E.M., I been checking up on these characters you've hooked us up with. I'm afraid the general consensus ain't real flattering."

"Oh," she says, "Chesley's been perfectly honest about that. He told us everyone's jealous of him. Why, you know what that's like." (Which was pure apple butter and nothing but.)

"Stick to Warwick, E.M.," I said, ignoring her slicky compliment. "Fact is, I heard he's got hisself nee-farious connections."

"Nefarious?" E.M. asks back. She tells me nobody ever really uses that word and I must have been dreaming. "Nefarious!" And she laughs.

Hell, if she wasn't gonna believe that word, she wasn't gonna believe who issued it either. So I said, "E.M., I would think maybe you'd be a little more concerned about our daughter."

It was then she reminded me of the famous Walla Walla story of Princess Pea Vine. Walla Walla, in case you didn't know, is getting famous for its peas, and so there's this festival celebrating that fact. Each year, they pick out a buncha princesses and then they elect the Queen Pea and everyone has lotsa fun. Anyway, Elsie was a princess a coupla years ago and come to find out the brothers of one of the other girls was thought to be stacking the ballot boxes so they could claim royalty in their family. Plus, the Queen Pea gets a whole year's worth of peas, too. Well, when Elsie finds this out (Chick'n'Tad somehow figured into this part, but I was always too scardt to find out just how) she sets her a trap and I'll be damned if she didn't swoop down on the three brothers and catch 'em in the acta stuffing that ballot box.

Well, as E.M. reminded me, onct the doc got done sewing up the boys, with Elsie handing him the catgut and iodine, the whole election was over and the sister won, but Elsie was given a free year of sparring at the Walla Walla Gym.

I was smiling whilst E.M. reminded me of what our daughter was made of. "You think she's got a double-fisted heart too, E.M.?" I asked.

E.M. didn't answer right away and I knew that if she fell silent then she wasn't ignoring my question, she was ruminating. Finally she says, "We can teach her right from wrong, a right cross, and the right fork to use for dessert. The rest of it she has to learn for herself."

Now it was my turn to fall silent. Then finally I asked, "What does nee-farious mean?"

She rolls into me and says, "HelliflIknow. Whatever it is, we're above it."

HelliflIknew either. Anyway, I held quiet on the conversation I'd heard betwixt that Chesley and Marco. I knew that with E.M. I'd be needing a ace up my sleeve.

But she comes at me with a ace of her own: "You know, Royal, seems to me you more'n anybody else should understand just wanting a chance at something—no matter how many times you've been to bat and struck out—no matter what the handicappers say about you. No matter how disadvantaged or washed up you are—all people really need is a chance."

I took myself back a few years, recollecting how it had usually been me making that same speech to some other sayer of nay.

"So, all's you want is a chance, is that it?"

"*Elsie,* you nitwit!" she barks. "I'm talking about Elsie! Do you think I'm doing this for me, do you? *Her* chance, *her* future. My God, Royal, you're dense as dirt sometimes."

"But what about Rose Monte-whatever the hell that name is?"

"Would you have rathered I let her go off into this all alone?"

Well, no. Then I reminded her about that Theda Bara Vamp she was gonna be the next one of and that I seen some pictures of her and that woman oughta be run outa town, doing that act to innocent men.

"Miss Bara is not only a well-respected woman in this town, she is also one of the nicest, Royal. What people are on the screen and what they are in real life are two different things. Hmmmm, now let's see, where've I heard that sort of sentiment before? Oh, I remember: the day I met you, remember? You were trying to talk me into helping you and, what did you call them, four 'mentally outa-sorts,' win back the Four Arrows Ranch."

Well, I had to laugh. She was right there. I was a fine one to go 'round pointing fingers at 'seems' when 'seems' don't ever do reality justice.

I took a long pause and recollected my day with William S. Hart . . . farthest thing from what I'd heard a movie star was like. I reckon, in the passion of meeting up with my wife, I'd forgotten what a magical day it'd been

. . . the Inceville ranch and all it's doodaddy trappings. That movie, when I saw Bill cradle the head of his dying pony and I damn near bust in two for the tragedy of it all. And when I saw Bill emote whilst lying to a pretty girl, I damn near wanted to jump up and spout the truth myownself. If anyone, especially E.M., had told me I'd be moved to tears and rage by the emoting of someone I didn't even know, on a screen, in the dark, then I'da laughed myself sick. But there was a magic to some of it . . . it wasn't a real world, but it was magic.

"You know, E.M., I might understand things a bit more'n you'd suspect."

"How do you mean?"

"I mean . . . I met someone Hollywoody today. Why, he wasn't no ACK-tor, not the way I think of 'em. He was about as regular as me. It was William S. Hart." E.M. cast me a strange one. "You don't believe me, do you? Sweartagod, I spent the day with him up to Inceville, that film place he works at. Just call up my boarding house and ask the boys. They was with me. And he ain't all I met . . . what're you looking at?"

She was just a-staring at me, and the light from acrost the room musta been real favorable onaccounta she took a long gaze at my face. Then she jumps outa bed and pulls a magazine out from under her pillows. *Photoplay* it was. Then she starts to page through it real fast-like.

"Well carry me out and bury me proper, I thought you looked familiar!" she finally says, showing me a fairly good representation of Bill's face.

"You talking to me or that picture?" I asked back.

"Well, I'll be damned. You look just like him. I guess I never studied on it before. Sure, take away your chin scar and. . ."

I touched my chin scar and the memory that came with it. "Don't you ever take away this scar. First one you ever gave me and I come to liking it."

E.M. got back into bed and compared me and the magazine photograph. "You're nicer looking, Royal." What a cookie-pusher, I thought, a grin acrosting my face.

I allowed, "I'm a tetch taller too."

"And I'm sure you're a better horseman," she added, applying another layer of apple butter.

Well, I basked in that for awhile and I reckon in the heat of that bask my guard went down a bit, for when she said, "It says here Bill Hart is an overnight sensation in this town. He's already among one of the highest paid stars. Gosh, Royal, just think of what *you* could do. . ."

I remembered how handsome Bill looked up on that bigger'n'life screen and I got a little starry-eyed and said, "Yeah . . . just think. . ."

"Why, not only are you better looking, you're taller, a better horseman aaaaaannnd. . ."

Her 'aaaaannnds' was always the kickers.

"Aaaaaannnd you own a production company."

I looked at the photograph, then at E.M., then out over my imaginary public, which was hailing me far and wide and plunking down ten cents a seat just to look at my handsome face. All I said was, "That's a fact. . ."

We shortly fell to sleep, E.M. maybe with dreams of counting millions of profit and having a famous daughter and maybe even a famous cowboy-actor-husband, for all I know. I fell asleep dreaming of Pinto Bean ponies, quick-draws like I used to practice when I was a kid, cattle drives like in the old days, and sweet young things praising my actions.

Little did I think them sweet young things might also

be the ones that got me in trouble. It happened like this: We'd set us the alarm to get us awake good'n'early so's I could sneak me out of that Ladies Only house with most of my respect intact.

So I was dressing and getting ready to sneak me back down the ladder outside E.M.'s window when Elsie comes flying into the room. I was standing on the ladder and had me the window curtains betwixt me'n my womenfolk, but I surely did hear their talk. It had to do with the morning newspaper and a photograph contained therein. I was just getting ready to poke in my head to whisper good bye, when the curtains rip apart and there stands my wife, eyes a-blazing gunfire. She shows me the picture—it was the one I posed for in Talley's Theatre, with me and the six, count 'em, young beauties, each with a armload of me. I wasn't 'round long enough to read the caption under the photograph, for E.M. not only swatted me over the head with the paper, but she then gives the ladder a man-like shove away from the window and watched me crash to the bushes below. She looked down at me and hollered, "You six-timing sonuvabitch!"

I looked up at my wife sticking her mean head outa the window. It was then that visions of me being famous, and the publicity photographs that accompany it, quickly and most thankfully vanished.

ten

I let myself into my room and was glad that no one heard me coming in so early and in such a state of disrepair. I got to bed and tried to pull off some more sleep, but faces kept flashing in and outa my mind—like there was a big picture screen in there now. I saw E.M.'s face fulla anger. I saw the six giggly-wiggly starlets wading in a sea of twenty thousand George Washingtons, and each George was laughing at me. Every Hollywood face I'd met, including the taxi-driver, was all opinionating on my dilemma. I was sure one spun-about cowboy. Additional, I was also worried about that feller in the next room back at Aunt Audie's, for in my fall from grace I'd forgot all about moving the ladder over to the next room. Finally, the Critic Upstairs got tired of all my worry factors and let me drift off. My boys pulled me awake about a hour later.

The day was gonna be a hot one, that we all could tell upon first sniff. 'Course Chick'n'Tad, now they knew there was that Palisades place in Santa Monica, had their lifes all planned out.

Interested was I to hear the hellophone ring early that same morning. Mrs. Taylor called upstairs for Sailing to come to the phone.

"Who's calling?" Sailing asked from the landing.

"A Mr. Magellan."

He comes down, not fast and excited like most young

folks woulda, but slow-like, with his tablet of writing paper and his spectacles low on his nose.

He answered the phone, but only after finishing the sentence he was scribbling out. He put the pencil behind his ear like I'd seen E.M. do when I'd interrupted her doing those new-fangled income taxes.

He listens to the phone, then says, "I'm sorry, I think you must have the wrong man."

I grabbed Sailing's sleeve and said a big "no he don't."

"I don't write for the moving pictures," Sailing informed the caller.

"Yes you do," I corrected him, and he gave me a look which he probably shot his freshman students when they misspelt 'cat.'

"Oh? Whose recommendation?" Sailing asked, taking his glasses off and finally looking at me direct. "Hold the line, would you please?" Then he covered the phone up some and asked me, "What's all this about, Mr. Leckner?"

"You're a writer, ain't you?"

"Yes, but. . ."

"Ask the man how much," I suggested, recollecting that college professors usually got paid hardly enough to buy pencils, tablets, and reading glasses.

"Tell me, sir," Sailing spoke back into the phone, "Does this position offer any money?"

He nodded whilst Marco let go of more of my investment.

"I see," Sailing said. "Oh yes, that's quite interesting. And just to write a story to what . . . showcase? Oh yes, I see. Well, I still need to keep my USC position, you understand that, don't you? I can't just leave my students dangling."

Smart kid, I was thinking. Go a few steps down a trail before closing the gate on the one he just left.

He finally hung up the phone and turned to me. "Why would you think I'd be the man for that job?" he asked. A direct question, quite a novelty in that town, I noticed.

Well, I decided to depart with some of my woe. I first asked him the meaning of nee-farious and he gave me all the necessary adjectives. Words like wicked, evil, heinous, and so no matter what E.M. said, I was gonna hafta be nee-farious myownself to get us outa this fe-as-ko. When I explained to Sailing the fix I was in and how if someone I knew and trusted was involved in this scenario thing, then I might be able to leave town with these things: my wife, my daughter, my dignity, and my money—and those ain't necessarily in any order of importance.

"Well," Sailing said, having a cup of coffee, "it seems to me if you were all that concerned about this, you'd want to go oversee things there yourself."

I hated it when someone halfa my age was twice as logical. I hadn't even thought of that. If I was in their midst, I could watch E.M., Marco, Elsie, that Chesley, *and* my money, or any combination thereof.

So I was going to join the ranks along with Sailing, only I was thinking of me being more like a spy or something clever like that.

The next thing I did was inform my boys we was gonna head for Royalscope Productions.

Then Chick asked, that narrow suspicious look in his eyeball, "Royal's Hope? So what you hoping for, Pa?"

"Royal*scope*," I corrected, wondering if maybe Chick needed one of them hearing tests. "It's the name of that picture company your momma got us into. You boys wanted to be ACK-tors, remember? Well, I reckon you now got your chance." I thought sure that would make 'em backflip. Hell, might as well throw the whole fam damily into the pit, thinks me. Sink, swim, or cut bait, we was alla us in this together.

Then Tad asked, holding out his hand like a street peddler, "How much?"

"Someone as young and pretty as you," says I, "oughta think about working for the experience you'll likely get, if you keep your eyes open and your mouth shut."

"Hell, Pa, that ain't no fun. I heard movie actors get five bucks a day, and I reckon that'd do us just fine," Tad continues, a little more like E.M. than I think I woulda preferred.

So I used one of her approaches and said, "Tell you what, you can extract your five bucks a day from your momma."

To which Chick said, a looka hopeless forlornment on his face, "Well, now you done it, Tad. You know what Momma'll say: I'll be happy to invest your allowance for your college education. Ah reservoir, Pa, I ain't going to no college nohow, and Momma's already got it bought and paid for!"

Well, I wasn't gonna argue with Chick, just ten and some change, 'bout going to college. So I just said, "Well, son, without no college I reckon you oughta be thinking 'bout learning a trade. So come on, we're alla us gonna inspect the movie trade."

Chick looks at his daddy and puts his hands on his hips like I always did when I was getting fatherish with him. He says, "Pa, you already got yourself a trade. You're a rancher and do you reckon it'll serve you good to trade trades now, at your age?"

Well, he did all right with that spiel, but I said age don't have nothing to do with nothing.

Tad looked to Chick and asked, "What's he talking about?"

Then, like I wasn't there, Chick replied, "I think Pa's been put on a crosstown bus."

"And what the hell is that supposed to mean?" I asked, having a feeling I'd just been insulted.

"Well, like you and Momma always tells us, 'Don't go no place you can't afford to get back from.'"

Well, I got his meaning and I think I resented hearing so much logic from a ten-year-old, especially when he was quoting *me*. All I said was, "You two yaps coming with me or not?"

They allowed as how they didn't have nothing better to do, and since they was living on 'reduced circumstances' anyhow, like ol' Elsie, they might as well. So we alla us, Sailing included, climbed aboard a crosstown bus, like Chick had foretold, and ended up at the doorsteps of Royalscope Productions.

Disappointed was I to see that Royalscope wasn't much grander in the daylight than in the dark. The cheesy sign which announced my name and buried Luther's didn't do much to indicate a great future was at hand. We walked inside and all was dark and quiet. Chick'n'Tad knew at onct they'd found theirselfs a right interesting playland and was quick to disappear, nodding a 'OK' to my warning not to think, touch, or talk at nothing.

Like you knew I wouldn't, I didn't forewarn Marco that we was dropping by. Like I told Sailing (and he wrote it down), why the hell pass bullets before the showdown?

Well, I would not care to, nor could I, duplicate the expression ol' Magellan shot me when we walked into his office. But he was quick to recover, I'll give him that. He walks 'round a desk and gives me a big welcome. I made note that the chair and the explosive crate was replaced.

"This here is Mr. Strong," I said.

I didn't like the way Marco was looking at him. Sailing, like I told you, was fair and handsome onct he got his hair outa his eyes and the specs offa his nose.

"Ever do any theater?" Marco asked him, making a square outa his fingers and siting Sailing in the middle of it.

"Well," Sailing said, smiling a little shy-like, "now that you ask, I did improvise Hamlet my freshman year. Our Hamlet got the mumps and had to drop out."

Whilst I was curious about improvisational Hamlet, Marco said, "Hamlet? My, my." I reckoned the only Hamlet Marco knew was the one-horse, jerk-water one from which he sprang.

"And in my sophomore year I played Juliet," Sailing offered.

We alla us looked at him and he allowed as how it was a all-boys school and since he was only thirteen and his voice was still high up there, he was picked.

"Well, I can see you're going to be just the right man for our job. Now that your voice has changed, that is," Marco said, getting a laugh outa Armando and bringing some redning to Sailing's face.

We had one of them awkward silences when no one is sure what to say next, and I always held that the first one to break such a silence will lose seniority, so I just smiled at Marco till he could stand it no longer and thanked me for lining up such a esteemed scenariost and was there anything else he could do for me?

"Such as?" I asked, narrow-eyed and keeping my hands close to my pocket book.

"Well, see the place, meet the crew, inspect the books," he suggested.

"He can't do that, Marco," Armando the Artistic Interpretator said blunt-like.

"Of course he can," Marco said, laughing a little nervous-like.

"I mean, Chesley has the books." Now I didn't know Armando too good, so I couldn't say for sure, but the way he said 'Chesley' sounded like even he wasn't too fonda him.

"Well, the books are yours to peruse when they return," Marco allows.

The last thing I was expecting was him to be so agreeable. "Well, Magellan. . ."

"Oh, call me Marco, please. . ." he interrupts, squelching some of my steam.

So I then informed Marco and Armando that since they had my wife, my daughter, and my money, they now had me. "I can't fight you so I'm enlisting. I'm here to oversee my investment."

Slick as goose grease, Marco smiled and said, "Well, that would be wonderful. Just wonderful. Since you're new to the business, we'll make you a producer. Say, have you ever run a camera?" Sweartagod, just like he had his own movie story of what was about to happen to alla us and he had his lines memorized and everything. Sure as hell made him hard to second guess.

I allowed as how I could run just about anything, then

I saw a opening, so I asked him, "What sorta camera you using?"

"A brand, spanking new Bell & Howell. It cost me my last penny. I mean *our* last penny," Marco defends. "In fact, our camera is the reason I couldn't refund your investment even if I wanted to. Getting the new camera was your wife's suggestion. In case you hadn't noticed, Mr. Leckner, your wife is a woman of many talents. Now, what else would you like to know?"

I looked at Sailing and figured we'd better start talking 'bout the sorta story was gonna be filmed. So I asked that very question.

Then, like he'd been reading ahead too, Armando dives into another box and comes up with some more papers. Upon Marco's say-so, Armando handed me some typed-up pages with the title, sweartagod, *Rage in Bagdanistan*, whatand wherever that was. Marco said he thought they'd start with this story and work from there. I looked at Marco and asked him for a brief rundown of the story and, sad I am to report, it sounded to me like turkey dinner with all the fixings.

"Well, I was thinking something more in the line of a westernish picture," I said, handing the papers to Sailing for his disapproval.

"With all due respect, westerns will never catch on, Mr. Leckner," says Marco.

"I got knowledge to the contrary," I said, recollecting all those fifty-five square miles of Inceville.

"Do you know what I paid for *Rage in Bagdanistan*?" Marco asked me, his eyes going a little narrow, like if I didn't understand theatricals, then surely I must understand economics, which if I did I'd be on my Royal Bar-L branding calfs.

I turned to Sailing and asked if there was even such a place as Bagdanistan, and he said not in the last week or so.

Armando steps forward at this point, looked at me, turned to Marco, and said, "He wants to do a western. Have a *heart*, Marco."

Marco turned on his assistant and grumbled, "I *must* maintain my artistic indepe. . ." At which point something sank in and he turns back to me and says, "Ah, yes. *Hart.*" He then circles me some like he did up in San Francisco, and I got his meaning.

"Not so fast. *I* ain't doing any acting."

"Oh, you won't have to act," Marco informs me. "We will only feature you in the film in little places, you know, here and there."

"What the hell you talking about?" asked me.

"Well, do you know how terrific it'll look if people think we have the great William S. Hart making a guest-extra appearance in our film?" Then his eyes go all big and he looks to the rafters and mushes his hands all around like he's fingerpainting a movie in the air. "I can see it all now. We can work a whole promotion around this: Who is the mystery celebrity in this film?"

"No sir, anything Royal R. Leckner does he does onaccounta it's him doing it and no one else he happens to look like!"

To which Magellan comes outa his trance and asks, hopeful-like, "Does that mean you'll want a role more suited to you? Even better!" Again, the hands fashion him a scene. "William S. Hart, beware! Marco Magellan's new discovery will have you seeing double! Get it? Double?"

Someone had to stop him and quick.

"Climb offa your dream-cloud, Magellan, and listen here. I ain't exploiting my face for you or anyone else.

We'll do us a western piece onaccounta I know western things and Sailing here has been studying and writing westernish things and we all know you gotta write what you know, right? We can do us a western piece based on that and nothing else. Bill Hart's got nothing to do with it. So Sailing, you write up something along that line."

I could see Marco's wheels still a-turning as he said to Armando, "Mr. Leckner's right. We're canning *Rage in Bagdanistan.* We're going to shoot a western piece. Make up a list of the cast requirements."

Sailing was looking through the screen story pages. He looked at Marco and asked, "Is this all there is to a film story? Why, this is not much more than an outline with some dialogue here and there."

Marco looked at Armando and said, "He's going to be a natural, isn't he?" Then, back at Sailing, he said, "Just follow that format. But why am I telling this to you? A doctor of English doesn't need to be told any of this. All we'd like you to do is to find a part for. . ." he snaps his fingers and Armando places in his hand a list of actors who needed parts, ". . . these talented thespians."

I looked over Sailing's shoulder and saw a substantial list of female names, one of which immediately caught my eye. "Helena Troy?" I asked. "She still around?"

"Oh, then you've heard of her?" Marco gushed.

"Yeah, the Greek ship launcher."

Armando and Marco laughed at my drollness onct again and corrected my history. "No, no. Miss Helena Troy is one of our most enduring stage legends. It seems she's gotten wind of our venture and when Chesley told her . . . well, she insisted she and some other . . . seasoned ladies from the Curtain Call Home on Gower Street invest ten thousand dollars."

I tried to imagine that Chesley romancing several 'seasoned' old stage women ten thousand dollars' worth.

"What can I say? One hates to take money from someone with limited resources, yet one hates to turn down a chance at the future."

I wasn't going to get into how much future did he think anyone living at a place called the Curtain Call Home could have. Knowing Marco and his ilk was bilking little old ladies just made me more resolved to get us outa this.

I made comment to Sailing I reckoned he could build hisself a whole other doctorate on what he was about to accomplish. Then I added, "Oh, and whilst you're at it, Sailing, maybe you could find a coupla parts for my two sons." Sailing added Chick'n'Tad to the list and looked at me like that was gonna be easy as dammit. I then turned to Marco and asked, "By the way, what's a producer do?"

Marco and Armando unisoned, "Oh, nothing much."

It was then a buncha people came in, E.M. included, Elsie and Warwick not included, putting a end to our conversation. Marco came out and gathered his troops around him. He introduced me as the 'founding father' of the company, which sure as hell made me sound old. He also announced that they was gonna put up a western and not a desert movie like they'd previously planned. He then introduced the esteemed Ph.D. writer whose credentials preceded him.

He told his troops he was eternally grateful for their financial patience and that their multi-talented own Chesley Warwick was, even as he spoke, out securing more investors, and any day now they'd all be able to eat regular and pay the light bill.

Whilst Marco was talking, I gave my wife a little, pleased-with-myownself acknowledgment. You shoulda seen the look she shot back; I loved every minute of it.

After the announcements, E.M. corners me and growls out a What the hell you up to, Royal? sounding, I thought, a little like myownself when I was catching her at something shady.

I told her I was just making sure my money was being, oops, *our* money was being well spent. Then I took her by the arm to a dark corner and said, "You know, E.M., I twisted my ankle when I fell offa that ladder."

"You didn't fall, you were pushed," she reminds me. Then a smile comes acrost her face and she adds, "Um . . . Royal, I read the caption under the photo in the paper and, well, hee, hee, hee, I guess I should have known that picture was William S. Hart and not you. I mean, how would you . . . I guess I was blind with jealousy."

'Course, she had 20-20 backwards and forwards compared to me, I can now safely add.

I'm ready for another snort. How 'bout you?

PART 3

one

Now, this is how things stood: We had no story, two costumes hanging on a nail, a rap-rattled warehouse called a studio filled with unpaid 'Gunnibe Stars,' and Royal thinking he was in control of all this nothingness by way of the titular title: Producer. Sailing holed hisself up in his room at Mrs. Taylor's to concoct our picture story and, as far as I could tell, he was the only one working with any sensa mission. 'Course he was also the only one who was smart enough to insist Marco give him a cash (as in greenbacks) advance for the story. Pretty savvy for a professor, I remember thinking.

Well, whatever Chesley Warwick was up to in the fiduciary department, he was fast, I had to give him that. For it was only two days later, whilst we was setting 'round looking for direction, that Marco comes in a real hog in togs. He arrived in a fancier car and handed out 25-cent cigars, and Armando feathered hisself out real snappy, too. Then trucks started arriving, bringing in pictures of countryside painted on movable walls, lots more lights was being hung, and the wardrobe department was two rooms now—a men's and a women's—not just a coupla nails hammered into a wall. A whole movie studio was being built right in fronta my own eyes and in one afternoon.

The entire place was filling with a sensa excitement whilst our troop tried on costumes and ooed and awed and opened trunks and played with makeup and such. I hafta admit, it was sorta exciting watching all this come to life, like Christmas at the Starving ACK-tor's Home.

Even Chick'n'Tad, who'd been in real grumpy moods onaccounta they was getting so bored, springs to life. They'd disappeared for quite some time. About the time I noticed they'd been gone too long, they reappears with smiles on their faces, and when I asked 'em what the hell they been up to, they allowed as how they was building theirselfs a fort in a back room, onaccounta it had big, strong boxes for them to climb upon. I reminded 'em all this here movie stuff was just rented and they best not go breaking anything or else it'd be coming outa their pays.

All the while, I kept me a eye on the front door, awaiting the arrival of Chesley Warwick. You see, he hadn't yet laid eyes on me since our first encounter up at that Ming's Palace bar when he was in his cups and spilling the beans to the husband and father of his two rich, hot tamales. I recollect thinking I was looking forward to seeing what sorta ACK-tor he was when he laid eyes on me. I had me a whole buncha lines memorized for the occasion—lines like 'Just what the hell you after, anyhow?' and 'Just what's your real name?' and 'You courting my daughter for marriage or something else?'—you know, typical suspicion lines.

The wind comes outa my sails when my own daughter Elsie arrives with Chesley that afternoon. She was hanging onto him like hope hangs on a old maid. Whereas Elsie normally wore them two-inch heels, I made note her shoes was now flat as her first cake, and she was even still a coupla inches taller'n him, so she stood sorta stoop-shoulders next to him. But this Chesley comes right over to me and gushes something on the line how he'd looked forward to getting to know the next Bill Hart and wasn't it a small-world-coincidence that we met in San Francisco and would all end up working together.

Too smalla world, I think I mumbled.

Elsie takes my arm and says, "Oh, Daddy, my life's just the dead oodles!" She hooks up with Chesley's arm too, and the three of us stood there—me and Chesley looking at each other and Elsie betwixt. Never did I recollect my daughter's eyes so filled fulla admiration for a man other'n me. Seeing that look in her eyes, well, I saw I had me a whole new problem. I realized Elsie was fast approaching a time when she was gonna choose betwixt her father and husband-to-be anyhow and, I gotta be honest, Chesley was too damn smooth-looking for any of us to ignore. And just like her mother, if I put my foot down, ol' Elsie'd just step on it and over any line in the sand I'd drawn. So if I told Elsie I thought Chesley Warwick was a nee-farious, top-loftical sonuvabitch looking for fame, fortune, and fast floozies, and all at the expense of her broken heart and my broken bank account, well, you know how she'd take that bit of information. Probably be so mad she'd run off to Mexico with him and spend the resta her life selling tortillas just to getting even at her daddy.

And by the smile Chesley was casting me, I reckon he knew what I was thinking and that, as long as Elsie was standing betwixt us, he was almost dang near untouchable.

* * *

Now then, just when you think things can't get more interesting in the heart department, allow me to add this extension.

It was a day or two later, when Sailing had arrived at the studio with some newly-writ-up pages of our story. He'd been pretty much incommunicado and said most writers wrote in that state. So, he had yet to meet my daughter, and when he did it happened in this fashion:

Armando, our Artistic Interpretator, whatever that was, was doing a class on makeup and costuming and hair fashioning. Elsie was having herself quite a time applying a layer of old-lady makeup, you know, just sorta having some fun playing dress-up and maybe having herself something in the way of a preview of what she might end up looking like if she lived herself a evil life of sun-soaking and cigarette-smoking. She had drawn lines hither and yon for wrinkles and had pulled her hair back in a old-maid bun, then powdered it all white. I had to admit, watching her from acrost the room, she looked real threatning.

So in walks Sailing and he asks what I was smirking at. I asked him if he'd yet met my daughter and he said he'd heard plenty but so far had been spared the pleasure. So I whistled and Elsie looked up, having heard her daddy's I'm-a-whistling-so-you-best-come-a-running all her life. She comes over and, before she can open her mouth upon a coupla blacked-out teeth, I pulled Sailing through the door and said, "Thought you'd like to meet Dr. Sailing Strong, our story writer."

Sailing bowed some and said, "Why, Miss Helena Troy. I would have known you anywhere."

To which my Elsie drops open her mouth, Sailing and me start laughing, and Sailing gets him a slap acrost the face. He was shocked at first, then we both just laughed harder. I don't suppose I'll ever forget my daughter's face, looking like a insulted, baby Methuselah. Now whether it was her mouth half fulla teeth, her forehead lined like sheet music, her hair all powdered white, or the sting of his cheek that firstly made Sailing take interest in my Elsie, I cannot rightly say. But all I had to do was watch his eyes and I was wondering if maybe she'd slapped more'n a bruise into him.

Just when I was thinking the introduction had gone pretty good, Chesley comes waltzing into the studio all Hart, Schafner and Marxed from head to toe in elegant Hollywoody toggery. Elsie, forgetting her makeup and insult and all, says to me, "Ye Gawds, look at Chesley! He looks swell-a-gant! Daddy, doesn't Chesley look just wonderful? You ought to get yourself some togs like these. You'd look ten years younger if you got out of black." Cripes, when the Elsie Express derailed, she took the whole damn train with her.

Chesley looks at her old-lady face, walks over, and says, "Why, if it isn't Miss Helena Troy." And he sweeps him a long, low bow. Did a slap he receive for his comment? Nope. What he got was a high-pitched giggle that previously I'd only heard when I caught Elsie and some other girls a-spying on the 'Boys Only' portion of Prairie Lake back home.

Sailing saw the whole thing and just rubbed his face. He comes over to me and asks, "Don't tell me—that clenchpoop is the famous Chesley Warwick."

"Clenchpoop?" I asked, hearing me a new one and immediately liking it.

Sailing walked over and introduced hisself.

"Oh yes, Strong, the writer," Chesley says. I could tell they had them one of those handshakes where one is testing the strength of the other. 'Course, Sailing had maybe a whole ten inches on him, so guess whose corner I was gonna back. I stood there and was most interested in how my daughter was gonna referee things.

Then Chesley asked, "Say, is my story ready?"

Sailing replied, "*Your* story? *I'm* the one writing it."

Chesley smiled a faint one and said, "Of course, old man. Don't take on so. Is *our* story ready? There. How's that?" He winked at Elsie.

Elsie giggled and I just stood silent and watched. Hell, who needed moving pictures when real life was farcical as this?

Sailing held tight, eye-balling Chesley, and said, "Well, since you asked, *our* story isn't quite done yet. You see, I'm having a little trouble with your . . . character, Warwick. But now that I've actually met you, I think I can see what direction I need to take."

Chesley looked a little concerned, but not so's his face went any less handsome, and he said, "Need help? I've written a few stories in my day."

To which Elsie added, "He's really very good at characterization, Mr. Strong. Better write this down."

"Dr. Strong," he corrects her, not taking his eyes offa Chesley. "Oh, I think I have a handle on it. Now."

Chesley excused hisself, saying he'd better talk this over with Marco, that the idea of a writer having trouble with his character was a rather annoying one, and he didn't have all the time in the world, you know.

I was laughing to myself and I think Sailing was, too.

Elsie was not. She turned on Sailing like one of her cornered house cats and said, blacked-out teeth and all, "Some day you'll *brag* you were a writer for the great Chesley Warwick! If you don't get fired, that is! You *did* remember my father's the major investor in this film, didn't you? So this story of yours better be a humdinger or your whole career will be over! Overoverover!" Then she took herself one of 'em exits she learnt in acting lessons. Armando woulda been prouda her artistic interpretation.

I was never more disappointed in my daughter in all her life as I watched Royal's Highness disappear back into the makeup room.

I apologized to Sailing on her behalf and said she'd been acting a little phony of late, that nothing he saw—the hair, the clothes, the makeup, the attitude—was a honest reflection of what my daughter was really like, in her own element. When you use a bread ball for bait, I mentioned, you usually catch yourself a carp, and Elsie'd been a fly-caster all her life. I sorta changed the subject by asking, "So, what kinda ink you planning on slinging for that Chesley Warwick? You thinking what I'm thinking?"

Then he grins me big, sorta like I do when I gets hit with the kinda inspiration that might fall a tetch on the devil's downside. He starts ripping papers offa his clipboard and he tosses 'em into the nearest trash can. Then he takes his pencil offa his ear-ledge and commences to write at a real furious pace.

A coupla hours later we was alla us gathered on the outdoor stage. They looked real good, as actors do, setting 'round in the sun, which was diffused by screens of muslin. Marco looked a little more tweed-like than usual: jodhpurs, boots, loose silky shirt open at the neck to allow his chins some breathing space. Onct Armando got our attention, Magellan started to talk. This is how he started things:

"This won't take long, children (yes, he called us 'children') and then you can get back to your duties." (Duties? My only duty was setting around worrying.) "First of all, Dr. Strong has informed me the screen story will be done by Friday."

There was some polite clapping. But when I looked over to Sailing, he was faraway-lost in his writing. Off to the side, sorta hidden betwixt a scene of the Alps and a hacienda, I saw Chesley and one of our 'extra' girls whispering together. I see her hand him a envelope, which he kisses and pockets, and then I looked 'round to see if Elsie was looking at what I was looking at. I got her attention and pointed to Chesley, but when she looked his way, he was joining us on the stage just in time to wink and wave at Elsie.

Add this to his list of credibilities: two-timing skinch.

Then Marco goes on: "Once I have the complete story, I shall cast the roles. Chesley, you, of course, will have the male lead, as per your contract. I'm sure Dr. Strong has written you a role that will insure you the stardom you so well deserve."

I looked over to Sailing, who was now staring cool-like at Chesley and tapping his pencil on his front tooth. I'd seen him do this on several occasions of deep P. H. of D. thought and I couldn't wait to see what kind of role would come outa the pen of a just slapped, just snubbed, besmitten Doctor of English.

"And finally," Marco continued, "we will begin filming on Monday. Two weeks to film, two weeks for clean up, and on August 22nd our premier at the fabulous Oriental Gardens Theatre. That gives us exactly one month, children."

I don't know why, but my heart took a solid thunk when he said that. Now whether it was fear, excitement, or cowardice talking to me, I had no idea. I had to admit, I was real anxious to see just what kinda movie director this Marco was and what kinda ACK-tor Chesley was, but in the back of my mind I wondered if they was gonna vamoose and leave us all hanging. E.M. had told me I was wicked to think such thoughts about such obvious geniuses. I was holding my final call until the filming began and finished.

The meeting broke up and we alla us went about doing our various movie things, which was, like I told you, just mooncalfing. But you know me: I can't stand me to set around counting my thumbs.

So I thought I'd corner Chesley and see if I could rile him some. Him and Elsie had stayed setting under the light diffusers so's they could get the sun but not the tan. I insinuated myself to their conversation.

"So tell me, Mr. Warwick, where you from?" I asks.

"Oh, all over. I've been around," he replies, blowing out some irksome smoke from his gasper.

"Oh, when I first met you I thought you mighta been English, then I thought maybe you was Mexican when you pulled pesos outa your pants, and then there's that Klepelmeier handle—that's gotta be a little on the German side."

'Course I was watching his face for a reaction regarding my knowledge of his real name. He didn't even blink. Elsie did.

"Father! Just what are you implying?" Elsie demanded. She recognized my tone of voice from all the years of me interrogating her or the boys or her momma or a stray steer. Then, since it usually takes a few beats for some things to sink in, Elsie turns toward Chesley and asks, "Klepelmeier? Ye Gawds, Chesley!"

I watched Chesley Klepelmeier's face as he listened to Elsie laughing and looked at me looking at him. It was one of those times I wisht I was more worldly, onaccounta I sure as hell thought he was quite a conglomeration and I woulda loved to have been thinking the worst. He tells us his mother is from Mexico and his real handle is—you listening?—Herman Manuel Mendoza Klepelmeier. He informs Elsie that's where he gets his Latin looks. Then he asks for Elsie to please excuse us so we could talk man to man.

After she'd left, Chesley said he was wondering if that first meeting of ours in the San Francisco bar had left me with the wrong impression, and I said I thought I'd gotten me the right one and then finished by suggesting it was Elsie's impressions what worried me.

He smiled his handsome Latin smile and I knew my father-logic was gonna be no match for it in the eyes of a sixteen-year-old, star-struck girl. He stood up and, as far as I could tell, it didn't bother him none I was three hands taller. He gave the 'completely honorable intentions' line, which we alla used back when we was young, handsome, and had something on our minds.

So I eyeballed him a good one and said down to his chiseled nose, "I'm watching your every move, Señor Herman Manuel Chesley Mendoza Klepelmeier Warwick. And any combination of your handles so much as breathes off-kilter towards my daughter, I'm on you faster'n interest on debt. That clear?"

He looks me back sorta arrogant and says, "Perfectly. After all, it's *your* money." Then he winked at me, yes winked, and left. I saw Elsie grab him from behind and he grabbed her back. I heard them laughing too as they walked off, arm'n'arm.

My mouth was on the stage floor. I was standing alone. How come every time I went to draw fresh water from the well all I got was backwash? I needed outa there fast. What kinda world was this? I gathered me up

Chick'n'Tad and we split faster'n a new ax through old kindling.

On the street car ride home Chick'n'Tad asked me why my ears was so red, and I said sunburn, but Chick told me he didn't much like that Chesley Warwick either. When I asked him if he'd been hiding behind curtains again, he said only enough so's to ruin Chesley for Elsie in case whatever I was thinking didn't work out.

I thanked him.

Then, to make me feel better, the boys sang one of their favorites, and it was real nice to have the backa the street car all to ourselfs. Chick'n'Tad, sweet-voiced, serenaded me with their 'Dam 'Fino Song' and dam 'fino where they picked it up, but it went something like this:

There was Mr. Dam and Mrs. Dam,
The Dam kids, two or three.
With U.B. Dam and I.B. Dam and
The whole Dam family!

That was us all right, and ol' Royal was on his way to being the damnedest one of 'em all.

two

So Monday rolls 'round and there we all set, awaiting Marco Magellan to hand out the scripts that Sailing had labored over. Everyone was fulla excitement onaccounta they was each and every one of 'em sure that they was gonna be emoting things immortal in the movie show.

I was setting on some crates in the corner of the room, with Chick'n'Tad next to me. I think I set apart so's I could get me a better picture of what was happening . . . or maybe more like, if I was set apart I wasn't a real part of that character academy. How the hell did ol' Royal stray so far from home, I was thinking as I looked at the eccentrics and ACK-tors, alla which I was aiding and abetting.

Suddenly Marco comes flying outa his office with Armando in close pursuit, and behind them comes Sailing in his usual stroll. He gave me a big grin of wait'll-you-see-this! Marco handed out our scripts and I looked at the title.

It read: *Birth of a Badman.*

Chick looked up at me and asked, sorta outa the side of his mouth, "You reckon this here is something Momma'll let us act up in?" But I couldn't start a answer, for Marco clapped his hands and called out, "Children, children, please. Now, I know you all have questions. But first I'd like to introduce you to the newest members of our troop." He motioned to his office. "We are honored to have joining us today several distinguished ladies from the Curtain Call

Home. Fortunate are we these fine thespians are at liberty and available for our film."

Armando stood up and started a applause as these grand dames entered from Marco's office . . . and a grander seta dames I don't reckon I ever saw all in one commission before. They was all Victorian lace and proud shuffles and sprightly eyes. I saw more paint than shoulda been on faces so experienced, but I also smelt faint memories of sweet old ladies I had known.

Armando introduced each lady and we all clapped like we knew why we was. Then he got to their leader, Helena Troy. Now whether or not we was clapping because of her great theatrical career or because of her launching ships, I don't think I'll ever know.

Anyway, Helena clasped her hands with the sheer joy of being 'at liberty,' which I reckoned she'd been at for over thirty years. She thanked us and allowed as how they was once of the legitimate stage and sometimes took a dim view of the galloping tin types. But what the hell, work was work or words to that effect.

Marco and Chesley and Armando made big to-dos over kissing each great dame's hand and setting her down. It's amazing what ten grand will buy.

Finally we was all silent and awaiting for Marco to speak. He held up his script and began: "Children, I think what we have here is the makings for the greatest story ever told."

Now I wasn't big on religion, but I think that story had already been put down by them New Testament boys. But I kept my quiet and let him continue.

"*Birth of a Badman*, by our own Dr. Sailing Strong, is destined for greatness. If you'll turn to page two, we can go over the synopsis."

I wouldn't have ever throwed away a classic like this, so I saved the synopsis, and here it is, word for word:

In a stagecoach robbery, infant Sandy Quinlan is kidnapped from the arms of her older brother, Pastor Quirt Quinlan. In his rage, he discards his preacher's collar and takes up a life of crime and revenge.

Years pass.

Quirt rides into the peaceful town of Holygrove and enters the Singing Spur Saloon. He orders a whiskey, which Sam, the bartender, gives him. As Quirt becomes drunk, the owner of the saloon, Lupe Vacarro, listens to Quirt's tale of woe.

In comes sweet Sandy, now eighteen, carrying a basket of flowers she sells. She peddles her pedals and laughs gaily with the men. She sings a song as Sam plays the piano for her. Quirt's eyes fill with love. Lupe tells him to lay off, for Sandy is her adopted daughter, and if he comes near her she'll kill him.

Sam announces it's time for the famous nightly gypsy act and the stage fills with old gypsy women, veiled and bespangled. Alta, their leader, announces the meaning of their dance is to quiet the restless spirits. The sad song-and-dance makes Quirt sink ever deeper into the bottle. He passes out on the table.

Pastor Tex Drago comes in, looking for people to reform. Lupe tells him not to waste his time on Quirt; he's a hopeless case. Challenged, Drago carries him back to his home.

At Pastor Drago's house, two youngsters, Erik and Lyle, come to see the outlaw, who is lying drunk in bed. Drago points out this is what crime leads to. Quirt comes around and recognizes Drago as the infamous Drago Kid, gunfighter from days gone by. Drago confesses and says, if he could reform, so can Quirt.

There is a knock on the door and in comes Sandy, bring-

ing soup and comfort. There are glances all around. Sandy is attracted to the stranger, but has promised herself to Pastor Drago.

Back at the Singing Spur, Lupe and Alta sit around a table, drinking. Alta gets drunk and confesses the real reason why the band of old gypsy women came to town eighteen years ago. They had stolen the wrong baby, breaking the age-old rule to never steal from a man of the cloth. So they had brought the baby to Lupe's doorstep.

The next night, Quirt is back at the saloon drinking, and Pastor Drago comes in to reform him. Quirt stares him down and pulls a gun, which Drago goes for. In the struggle, the gun goes off and Lupe falls. Drago, unable to face his deed, takes off his preacher's collar and straps on his guns, which Sam has behind the bar. When Sandy runs to Quirt's side, Lupe whispers the truth in her last breath: Quirt and Sandy are brother and sister. Drago asks Sandy to come with him; together they will run. But it is Sam the bartender whom she loves.

In the last scene, Sam and Sandy are in wedding clothes and Quirt is dressed as a pastor. He pronounces them married. They all then turn and wave goodbye to Drago as he rides out of town and into the sunset.

Marco announced the casting, which went pretty much like I'd feared, incept he had to put in Armando and Sailing in order to keep expenses down. You will note he did leave me out. Here's how it set:

Lupe Vacarro........Rosa Montenegro (E.M.)
Sandy Quinlan........Maude Miles (Elsie)
Quirt Quinlan........Chesley Warwick (H.M.M.K.)
Pastor Tex Drago the Kid........Sailing Strong
Erik........Chick
Lyle........Tad
Sam the Bartender........Armando Cato
Alta, head gypsy........Helena Troy
Assorted roles........Assorted extras

Then E.M. and me look at each other. I was damn near busting a gut inside, and I thought she was gonna laugh too, but she put her finger to her lips like as to say I better keep my trap shut. Deep down inside she musta known we was heading for a fe-as-ko beyond description and one that she herownself had tripped us into with maybe a little help from me by insisting the P. H. of D. write the story.

Marco took a deep breath and said real serious-like, "I think *Birth of a Badman* has all the trappings of a great cinematic tragedy." To which I could only silently agree.

Then he swears alla us to secrecy, onaccounta story-stealing was getting to be the fashion, and spies was everywhere. Well, you know I wasn't gonna go talking it up.

So the actors spent the day reading through their parts, which didn't make a whole lota sense to me onaccounta it wasn't like anyone was gonna hear the lines. They talked about the characters, and Marco got all excited as he said how he was gonna film alla this tragedy. I watched him bind his spells on the actors and filming crew, and it was then, for the first time, I saw he was doing exactly what the others was: galloping full-chisel after his dream. Only his, I had to figure, was making money offa others' dreams.

On the street car heading back toward Mrs. Taylor's that same day, I couldn't wait to say to Sailing, "That's some screen story you wrote up, son. You're a real fox."

He looked at me, then asked, innocent as hell, "How do you mean?"

Now I hadn't known him nearly long enough to tell if he was serious or just funning with me. So I replied, careful and testing, "You know: like your story is all talk and no cider."

"Oh, that's rich," he says, pulling out his note pad and writing it down. Then he turns and asks me, "What does it mean?"

"Sorta like you're handing 'em the fiddle, but not the stick."

"Does that mean you do or don't like *Birth of a Badman*?"

Careful now, Royal, I was instructing myself, wondering how many times I'd told someone the best way to save face was to keep the lower part of it shut.

"'Course I ain't seen me too many movies, you know," I allowed.

"Well, I have. Say, it's a tough job writing something just corny enough to court the actors and yet still come off looking brilliant by Marco's deliciously low standards. My biggest problem was ruining Warwick and not you or your family. You will notice I left plenty of room for artistic interpretation. If Marco can direct his way out of this, great. If not, it won't be on my shoulders."

"But ain't the story on your shoulders?" I asked.

Then comes that smile of Sailing's, the one he didn't use too often but when he did it was worth the wait. He pulled off a sheet from his clipboard and handed it to me. It was the title page to his screen story. Under the warning of the title, it said

A STORY FOR THE SCREEN BY
JULES JOHNSON JOHANSEN

I looked at that, then at Sailing, and my own famous smile came acrost my face. I pointed to the Jules name and asked, "That anyone I know?"

"You don't think I'd use my *real* name on that cacography, do you?"

I passed over that word and pointed to his "J" name. "What did ol' Marco say to this?"

"What *can* he say? Everyone in that whole studio is using a *nom de film.* Besides, if the movie's a hit I'll have Marco change the name card and we'll all live happily ever after."

Happily ever after, did he say? He seemed mighty confident with that one. But he was young, smart as allget-out, and probably dreaming of two on horseback, sunsets, and sixteen-year-old girls fresh offa the rebound trail.

three

Marco set about putting up his movie and, since I'd only seen me a little of how movies is made, I thought we was commencing pretty normal, although I don't think the word 'normal' oughta go in the same sentence as the word 'acting.'

On the first day of filming we had us a scene that involved horses, so Marco took us to the outskirts of the neighborhood, where the roads was still dirt and where Marco had arranged for the rental of some saddle horses. Well, a lot he knew about horseflesh, I figured as I inspected the animals. Not to mention, the horses sported those flat postage stamp sorta English saddles and that woulda made for one funny western. So I saw me at onct a place where I could do some producing. I produced a trade with the stable man and came back with Old West-looking horses. Well, when Chesley comes out all gauchoed up in his western get-up, I think even the horses laughed, and I reckoned they was even used to such theatrics. I didn't say nothing, but held the bridle as Chesley approaches his horse.

"What do I do?" he asked me, looking like maybe he was about to climb aboard a camel and being careful that others watching him didn't hear. "You see, old boy, I've a . . . never ridden a horse."

'Course my eyes go wide and I see a opportunity for my daughter to see something she oughta, and so I said, "Nothing to it, old boy. Here. Right foot here, swing over your left, and you're up." I assisted him like 1-2-3 and he was aboard—backwards.

Everyone but him and Elsie was laughing. It was then things turned ugly. Chesley slithered down offa the horse, damn near pulling the horse over with him.

Then Chesley sneezed. Now, when I tell you he sneezed you gotta take every sneeze you ever heard and multiply it in volume, in force, and in sincerity. This sneeze was topped by another, and another, until he was almost doubled up in sneezes and wheezes and red eyes, and he topped it off by suspirating for air.

Folks made a circle 'round him, each one with a opinion. I stepped me away from the crowd and the horse followed. We was both grinning, for we knew what'd hit Chesley Warwick. There was calls for doctors and talks of letting him breathe and all, and I simply announced to the crowd that their star man had what we called on the ranch Horse Fever, and wasn't that ironic?

Chesley's hand sprang to his head like as to feel for such a fever. "Horse fever?" he asked, all concerned.

"Don't get your bowels in a uproar, Warwick," says me, thinking all this is pretty damn funny. "Think of it as Hay Fever onct removed."

"Is there a cure?" he asked, in and outa sneezes.

There was silence all about, and they all looked at me like I was a doctor, so I passed that one off to the closest thing we had: Sailing.

Sailing wrote down on a piece of paper two things: Dr. Pierce's Nasal Douche, to be taken in conjunction with Dr. Pierce's Golden Medical Discovery. They send Chick'n'Tad out to procure the cure.

Chesley gets to his feet, face all red, eyes all puffy, hair all undone, chaps all unfluffed, voice all gaspy. "Now I re-bember why I neber learned to ride. Rewrite!" and he walked off, sneezing to beat the band. Marco looked 'round at folks looking at him. He comes close to me, smiling that devil-like smile of his, and then he and me go off to the side and had us a small billingsgate.

When the dust settled, it was agreed that Chesley's scenes in and on and around horses was gonna be either changed or cut. Then we'd use a double to fill in for the riding scenes—and you're looking at him.

Well, I was there to save my money, E.M. reminds me, and each hour delay cost plenty, so I damn well better change clothes with Chesley and get myself a new paira spurs. And, she summarizes, if everyone else could apply their images to our film, then dammit, slap shut, so could I. You shoulda seen the grin on Marco's face, onaccounta he was getting his so-called 'guest-extra' after all.

Since there was damn near a whole foot difference in our heights, the wardrobe lady had to do some fast stitching and re-fitting to outfit me, but 'bout a hour later I was in the saddle, pretending to be Herman Klepelmeier who was pretending to be Chesley Warwick who was pretending to be Quirt Quinlan. That saved our premier ACK-tor for the non-horse scenes and, I hafta admit, me riding was hardly work at all. But I vowed if ever any of my boys back home ever saw me gin'n'tiddied up in those phony, fuzzed-out sheep-chaps—a whole sheep too small to boot—I'd have to kill them on the spot.

So the filming commenced. Marco yelled, coaxed, stuck his monocle in and outa his eye sockets, pulled out his hair, twirled his mustache, and agonized. He used a megaphone to inspire the troops whilst they was acting. Why, I don't know, onaccounta he was only a few feet from 'em in every scene. Maybe it was some kinda union requirement.

He'd say things like, You're raging inside! Cry, damn it, cry! More eyes, more eyes! Now go to the window, grab your heart, look to the heavens! Heave that chest! Pound that breast! Don't look at me, look at her! Now build! Not so much! Too much! Pull back! Cut! Damn it, cut!

Now I shall tell you how I thought folks was doing. First E.M.: Armando got her into a Spanish get-up, but I don't think she got into a Spanish mood till Marco put a record on the spinner, which set up a real evil kinda rhythm. It was called a tango and I reckon everyone in Los Angeles knew how to dance it incept me. Well, that music worked just fine to get E.M. 'into her character,' as Helena called it. Hell, she sure ate up the scenery with her emoting, and watching her I wondered how many times I'd myownself been taken in by her dramatical ways. I made a point to recollect this in later life, providing of course we ever did make it back home alive, safe, and improved.

Well, Chick'n'Tad did just fine as the juveniles Erik and Lyle. After all, that's what they was.

And then there was Elsie-Maude-Sandy, and I was

right about her and her actability. Oh, now I ain't saying she didn't look real minkish in that gaga-baby get-up she got her herself into, all sweetness and light, but the only memorable acting she did was when she sallied up to Sailing and flattered him some so's he'd give her some more scenes. All the while, she was still fawning over that good-for-nothing Chesley Warwick who, Sailing informed me, was a lousy actor to boot, a real ham-fat, and he thought poor Armando was gonna have a nervous collapse trying to find ways to set things up so's Chesley looked taller'n everyone else.

Now, when the day came to film the gypsy dance scene, I hafta admit I was right curious to see how Marco was gonna pull this one off. I've always done real well with little old ladies (figuring I myownself was gonna be married to one some day) but I kept having to remind myself that these ol' heifers of Gower Gulch was former theatrical ladies and, therefore, maybe not very typical. Each one was a empress, and I wondered how in hell so many monarchs could live so peaceful-like under one roof and all. Marco and Armando was smooth, I'll give 'em that. They toadied up and lickspittled the old empresses real good.

Now there ain't nothing wrong in trying to shave off a coupla years. In fact, I was thinking mighty fortyish myownself, and E.M., I think, was dawdling somewhere back in her teens. But onct a lady plants her shoes in her seventies, I kinda think they hadn't oughta time-travel too much. But when the harem presented itself to the resta the crew for their big scene, there was dead silence on the set. Each one was swaddled in silks, satins, gewgaws, and spangles, and rouged-out something fierce. Their sprightly eyes a-glowed with the thrill of one last chance.

You wanna know what? I never did see anyone work so hard at something in my whole life as them toe-tapping, tambourine-toting troopers. When at last we was done filming the gypsy scenes, the whole crew up and clapped for the ladies. They swished low and bowed deep, collected their dignities and five dollars each, and left the stage.

The lesson ol' Royal learnt that day was, age don't have nothing to do with loving your craft, and if you doubt me just look at a old person's eyes, only their eyes, whilst they're doing their craft, and try to guess their age. Betcha you'll be off by ten, fifteen, maybe twenty years.

Firinstance, lookit my eyes right now. Not bad, for a creaker.

four

You know, it's a funny thing about vanity—think it's one of them genes, you know, those things each of us has and can't get rida? 'Course, them scientists have been kicking this one 'round the lab for years, but now they say it's true—we eacha us got eye genes, hair genes, nose genes. Well, you gotta figure vanity comes in a gene too, so we're stuck with it. And like some of them other things we can't seem to evolve outa our race, like lawyers, politicians, and in-laws, vanity just seems to rise, real persistent-like, to the occasion. I don't think none of our crew was more'n two feet away from a reflective surface for the next two weeksa filming.

It was three weeks to the day that we'd been in Los Angeles and, more'n ever, I was beginning to pine for my old self, the Royal Bar L, my big beautiful chestnut, my ranch foreman, and even Ida. In that time I'd not succeeded in getting back either my money or my wife, but I had succeeded in getting myself in over my head in the damnedest flooda circumstances I think I'd ever seen. Well, after Marco Magellan told us 'CUT!' for the final time, I had no idea what I was gonna do next. He told us to stick around, onaccounta onct he put all the film pieces together he might need to redo some things.

"Ain't you been looking at the film pieces all along?" I asked him when he told us that.

"Oh, heavens no. That's not my style."

"But I thought movie men look at the pieces every day . . . yeah, in fact, that's what they even call 'em: dailies."

I think I was offending him, for he answered me back a dirty look and this: "Oh, hang the dailies! How can I work creatively when you think you know more than I do?"

Then Armando, onct someone'd started a point, was always quick to add his own two cents: "You know, Royal, Marco's never been one to follow in the footsteps of another."

Marco gave me one of his downward, arrogant glances and simply said, "Only after I've stepped away from it for a few days does the real feel for the material begin. *Birth of a Badman* will be my turning point. My shining moment! My pivotal effort!"

"Trust him, Royal," Armando said, his face real genuine and gentle. "We have a lot of film to choose from. We'll put together a wonderful film. You wait and see."

"So you actually think this moving picture is gonna be a winner, eh?" I asked.

"Oh, heavens yes," Marco and Armando said at one

and the same time. Then Marco adds, "A masterpiece with legs."

"With legs?" asks me.

"Oh yes, a real money maker!" Armando says.

Well, I'd seen that look of impending success in everyone's eyes, and hell, be honest Royal, you seen it onct or twice in your own damn eyes too . . . every time you looked at yourself in a mirror, which, as I recollect, was a helluva lot more often than any cowpoke should oughta. So what was so awful 'bout seeing it in Marco's eyes?

But it sure as hell scardt me that alla our futures, both famous and financial, was still setting in cans and not even pasted up together. Marco further assured me he'd have it all pasted up in a week or so.

"And what happens if something breaks or burns up?" asks me. "I hear that film ignites without too much outside encouragement."

"Oh, don't worry, Royal," Armando says, touching my arm with a real, genuine concern. "We had dupes made of all the master prints. We keep them hidden in the office closet. Why, we just wouldn't take a chance on losing an instant of Marco's wizardry!"

Marco smiles, but he lost it real fast when Armando added, "Of course, all that extra expense has put us. . ." He caught Marco's eyes a-blazing on him, which caught my own eye.

Marco is quick to recover with: "Well, if I'm a wizard with film, Chesley's a wizard with finances. We have God to thank for that."

Armando then takes him a stand to Marco, first ever I recollect. He puts his hands on his hips and says, "Well, your precious Chesley has put us into cost overruns. Again. *Third time this month, Marco!*"

Marco was, first time also, as I recollect, speechless. Then he looked like his own loyal dog has turned on him and he said, "This is hardly the place to. . ."

"You know, boys," I broke in, "I think my wife oughta have a look at those accounting books."

They both stopped their glares and said, unisoned, "Your *wife?*" They said it like she was the very last person on earth who oughta look at numbers.

Then I explained what a damn good number-juggler she was and if they was wondering about cost overruns, then no one knew better about that than she. I did not inform them as to why.

Now you know it ain't like me to make a long story short, but here's how that E.M. auditing event turned out. I called E.M. into the office and Armando handed her the books. I asked her if she minded giving them the onct-over for accuracy and to look for cost overruns. She wants to know where they keep their abacus, and you know how that went over. So she was reduced to mental calculations, and I could tell by the way she looked at me that she knew I was behind this idea. I knew I was gonna be in for a lecture on my untrusting nature and who was I to question someone like Chesley's honesty. I didn't say much. She hands me back the books and says as far as she was concerned everything was in order. Every expense was accounted for, including dated receipts and all the rest. Balanced to a 'T'. She ends it with a "There! You see! Wrong again, Royal!"

Marco looked pretty smug, and Armando and me exchanged glances, and I was wondering if I'd previous underestimated him. It was then the phone rings and Armando answers it.

He says, "En Englais, por favor! Englais!" He rolls his eyes to the heavens and then says, "No, Cheeesely no coma esta!" He then asks Marco, "Donde, I mean where's Chesley?"

Marco mentioned he thought he was at the bank and whoever it was to call back some other time. So back into the phone Armando says, real curt-like, "Call some other time, Miss. He's not here." And he hangs up. "Really, Marco, I wish you'd tell Chesley this is a business phone and to have his little señoritas call him at home. Really, the least all these imports can do is to learn English!"

Only one thing was clear to me and Chick'n'Tad as we rode back to our boarding house that same afternoon of the audit: we alla us needed some opposite direction. We had us two whole weeks until our showing at the Oriental Gardens and I was damned if I was gonna spend 'em fretting, anguishing, or otherwise losing weight over something I no longer had control of. And I reckon the Director General Upstairs recollected Royal wasn't no fun to watch when he was bored, so two days later I got a message that none other'n Bill Hart had called and asked for me to come up to Inceville soon as I could.

So that evening, whilst the five of us Leckners was gathered for dinner at a restaurant, I made the announcement that me and the boys was going north to reacquaint ourselfs with Bill Hart and maybe do us some ranch work for him, and would maybe E.M. and Elsie like to come along. We could play in Santa Monica, or on the beach, maybe fish, maybe hunt. I even suggested Sailing might cancel a few classes and maybe join us.

Elsie whined as how none of that was gonna improve her career, and she and Chesley had some plans.

"Damn it, Elsie," said I, "what the hell you see in that popinjay?"

"He's *not* a popinjay, Father! You don't even know him well enough to call him that!"

I just rolled my eyes and then E.M. comes in with, "You know, Royal, we left San Francisco so fast, I'm afraid I left a few ropes dangling. I better go up there and settle some things."

"Ropes dangling?" I asked, seeing thirteen turns and a loop a-swaying in the breeze. "Like what ropes?"

"Oh, get that look off your face, Royal. Nothing drastic. Just a little this and that. I ordered some items that need to be picked up, that's all."

I gave her a better-not-go-burning-down-courthouses glare and finally agreed: E.M. would go to San Francisco, Elsie could stay in Los Angeles, providing Mrs. Taylor would agree to allow a lady just onct and let Elsie take my room (so's she could be watched), and Chick'n'Tad and me was gonna head up to Inceville, where we stood a better chance reminding ourselfs who we was and where we was from. I was longing for the calla cattle and the smella horse sweat and the squish of a saddle beneath me. We'd go up and tend those Inceville cattle, for free, even if they was movie cattle. Factual, I was just as glad we was gonna stag it.

There was just one little piece of business I had to attend to before we all took our leaves of Los Angeles. I waited till no one was around and I snuck into the storage closet in the studio offices. I figured I owned 75% of those dupe films and I was gonna take 'em. I found some other old film cans and put them in the case to replace the ones I stole. And, in case you're wondering, I didn't have me one second thought or even a passing stab of guilt for stealing the whole kitchen-kaboodle of *Birth of a Badman* and packing it off with me to Inceville.

And there it was that, with a open heart, a outstretched hand, and a splint-up leg, Bill Hart welcomed our return. For he had, you see, taken a bad spill on his horse and couldn't set a saddle for a few days.

Yep, what ol' Bill Hart needed was someone just like hisownself . . . someone who could fork a horse, shoot at a gallop, and look like me. William S. Hart needed Royal R. Leckner. Just when I thought I had it up to my nosehair with 'Roll 'em and Cut it,' I just grinned him one and replied, "Why sure, Bill, I can do that."

five

"You believe in Providence, Royal?" Bill asked me whilst we was walking up into Inceville.

"Yep. Been there. Ate lobster," replies me, like I was a real wit. Well, Bill thought that was real funny and he laughs, slapping me on my back.

"Well, your coming to Los Angeles this summer is sheer dumb luck for all of us," he goes on. "We'd wrapped up this film a few weeks ago. In fact, I showed it to you: *Keno Bates, Liar*, remember? Well, we decided we needed some extra action footage to even it out. Then this happens," he stopped to thunk his bum leg and added, "and sets us even further behind schedule."

I slowed the pace some onaccounta his limp was holding him back. I still had to look twice when I realized how similar we was in just about every way. I said, "Well, if I can help you out, then I reckon I owe you the favor after you lost one of your best broncs."

He smiled at me and said, "That bronc is turning out to be one of the best saddle horses on the place." He looked down at Chick, who was trying to look a little innocent. Then Bill added, "Anytime I need an outlaw broken around here, I'll know who to call."

Then Bill led us into a big dining hall, fulla actors dressed in just about every get-up heretofore known to both man and woman and costume designers.

Well, you can be sure that when us two bookends entered and a eye or two caught us, the whole place got real quiet. All the chewing stopped which, like you know, ain't exactly normal when food is being served competitively.

Bill looked at me and said, "I suppose this is good a time as any." Then he says out to everybody, "Everybody, meet Royal Leckner, my double."

No applause, no howdy's, no chewing. Just stares.

We stayed after the other folks had left and we pretty much had the place to ourselfs. Bill told me what I'd have to do to be him in *Keno Bates, Liar.* He said the scenes left was mostly riding and looking heroic from a distance, and of course I could do that even up close. But Bill allowed as how using the camera up too close to my chin scar might be leaning up against our luck, which had been standing real straight up to then. And since he was the director as well, I didn't argue about no close-ups.

When he told me how much money I was gonna make, I saw my opportunity and I said, casting him the famous Leckner smile, "Hell, Bill, I ain't gonna take money for just horse-play."

He smiled me back and sweartagod, I think he knew he was being set up for something bigger'n money. "Oh really?" he asked me. He folded his arms acrost his chest and leant back in his chair, like I used to do when I was ranch foreman and listening to some lame excuse one of my hands was handing me for doing something stupid, like using the wrong branding iron on the entire cropa spring calfs.

I put my feet on the table and leant back myownself. I said, "I'd just as soon keep our friendships based on favors back and forth, insteada money. Hell, anybody can trade silver and gold."

"Name it," says he.

"I brought some movie film up with me. Thought maybe you and some of your boys might take a gander and tell me what you think."

Bill then put his feet up on the table and Chick'n'Tad betwixt us was mighty taken in on the doubleness of it all. Bill said, "This have anything to do with your wife? What's her name? B.M.?"

Well, that set Chick'n'Tad off to laughing so's as they almost lost their settings. I hushed 'em and corrected Bill. "*E*.M. Anyway, I brought up the dupe film we shot for that movie."

"Now let me see if I remember this right: Your wife bought the rabbit from that mountebank Marco Magellan, who promised to star her in another one of his turkeys, right?"

I said, "Well, I never looked at it from a poultry point of view, but we shot us a movie, all right. Hell, even I had to don a costume."

"You? I thought you were trying to stop it."

"Bill, ever been on a horse running with the bit in his

teeth? You might as well just set back and study the mileage, 'cause that horse ain't gonna stop till he gets home, finds a hole, or just plain drops dead."

He was looking a little concerned, so I assured him my own foreman wouldn'ta even recognized me in that Wild West get-up Armando put me in. "Don't worry, Bill, I was thinking of your career every step of the way. I ain't cashing in on you," I further reassured him.

Bill got up and said, "I'm glad to hear that. Well, how about we look at the film you brought?"

I got up too and answered, "I sure would rest easier if you experts took a look, Bill."

He told me he'd set it up whilst I was getting made up for the movie filming. Since I'd already done me some filming already, I got made up real fast.

Bill refreshed my memory about the film plot and what was happening, and why and how it was gonna all end up. (In case you was wondering, the sweet girl gets the reformed gambler.) I listened like I knew why, but mostly I was just on the anxious seat to set me a horse onct again. Then Bill introduced me to Fritz, his prized calico.

"Well, what'ya know!" says me, enjoying the velvet of the pony's warm nose. "It's ol' Pinto Bean. Glad to see you ain't dead, after all."

Well, that made Bill laugh and I could tell, just by the way he ruffled Fritz's ears, that horse was probably his closest friend. I sure knew that feeling, so I looked at Bill whilst I climbed aboard and said, "Don't worry, Bill. I'll treat him good as my own."

"This ol' snoozer doesn't generally do well under a stranger," Bill warned, standing back and admiring us both.

"Yeah, but I ain't no stranger," said I, moving him out. I followed Bill to the filming place and already I was falling in love with the heart and gaita Fritz. Normally I think twice about a pinto pony, onaccounta they can be real squirrelly. You know, sorta here, sorta there—just a real checkered critter. But ol' Bill'd trained him 'bout as fancy as I coulda, and we worked real good together for the resta the day, both just generally doing what we was born to do.

Come evening, Bill set us up in the filming tent, which, I might add, had been patched together real good. Chick'n'Tad was clinging like burrs to the seats next to me. You can be damn sure I wasn't gonna let 'em outa my sight.

In the tent with us was Cliff Smith, one of Bill's directors, Gard Sullivan, a writer, and Joe August, Bill's best cameraman. Bill called for the lights to end and for the film to begin, and we watched all the various bits, pieces, and scraps of *Birth of a Badman.*

When Chesley first made his appearance, you shoulda heard the "oh no, not that runt" comments, and someone even said, "Thought he'd be dead by now."

It went downhill from there.

When it was done, we set in the darkness. Someone lit a cigarette and, as our eyes got accustomed to the darkning, I remember the smoke snaking upwards.

Bill asked, "Cliff?"

Cliff took a deep breath and answered a long sigh.

Bill asked, "Gard?"

Gard said, "Pass the cranberry sauce."

Bill asked, "Joe?"

Joe just answered with a long, tongue-flapping razzberry.

Well, that razzberry pretty much said it all. Bill went over to a cabinet and pulled out five shot glasses and a bottle. He handed 'em 'round and poured us each a reliever.

I looked at Bill, who looked back at me. His eyes was fulla pity, like he was the jury foreman and I was the soon-to-be hung criminal.

"Magellan told me he had him a masterpiece somewheres in all them scenes," says me, taking one last grab at the straw. "What'd *you* think, Bill?"

Bill looked at his film men, then back at me. There was no use chasing him any further 'bout the bush than he'd already traveled. He was trying to be delicate and I knew that. Bill hems and haws, then answers, "I think it had . . . moments."

"Moments of what?" I ask.

"Folks said Magellan couldn't top his last chestnut," Gard Sullivan broke in, taking some of the heat offa Bill.

Bill looked over to Gard and said, "Folks were wrong."

"Cripes," woes me, "I wouldn't mind paying twenty thousand for a chestnut—one that I could ride, that is."

Well, that seemed to hit some identical chords, for they laughed some. Then Bill handed me another drink and said, "Welcome to Hollywood, Roy."

six

So now you know, in the eyes of the experts all them pieces of badmen being born wasn't gonna fit together in any way, shape, nor form into anything that resembled a movie story, let alone the masterpiece which Marco had promised. I reckon I'd been holding out hope for Marco. Now look where we were.

Factual, looking back, I think I'd musta known it all along, for I'd been spending time trying to arrange things with the Re-arranger Upstairs regarding the success of our film. Now, you gotta be awful careful when negotiating those heavenly IF/THEN bargains. You know the kind: "IF You'll arrange for me to oh, say, win a lottery, THEN I'll build a new wing on the corner orphanage." Well, ol' God, He'll grin you a big one, fold His arms, and say, "Well, OK, but you first!"

Anyhow, Bill said I hadn't oughta feel too bad, onaccounta lotsa men'd been making some pretty awful movies and at least I'd been in the hands of the best of the worst. Bill and me was alike in that way: always seeing the bright side. He set me and the boys up in a cabin and I had a helluva time thinking sleep. Things was fast going from bad to triple-worst and I was damned if I knew what I could do about it. I finally pulled off some shut-eye, but not one solution appeared during my nightmares of gallows trap doors under my bunk.

Me pretending to be William S. Hart pretending to be Keno Bates, Liar, in that movie was damn tricky the next day. Hell, by noon I didn't remember who I was, after everyone'd been calling me Bill or Keno or Hart or Bates or Royal or hey-you-on-the-horse. I tried to put the *Birth of a Badman* perplexion to the back forty of my head so's I could keep my mind on my riding.

Bill kept us all working, didn't waste a minute. He had a shooting schedule and he stuck to it. Till four o'clock, that is. At four o'clock, Bill kept the Inch fellow's rule that all action had to stop so's everyone could set and have—get this—tea. Sweartagod, just like we was still a British colony. Villains, heroes, and heroines alike, all stopping our action and sipping tea. But I liked it, I really did. Thought I'd try it up my own way if I could get my ranch hands to quit laughing long enough to get past 'one lump or two.'

I will also add that Bill found some movie work for Chick'n'Tad so's they would stay outa trouble. I reckon Bill was remembering just how scarce a good bronc was in those days. Cripes, the war in Europe was using up so many horses, it left precious few for movie-making. Anyhow, I told Bill I thought he was real smart putting the boys within lens-shot of the camera so's we all could keep a eye on 'em and even have us some proof on film if they went astray. Ain't nothing worse'n two bored younguns.

Well, we finished 'bout two on the third day, but hell, we was having so much fun Bill allowed as how we might as well stick around a few more days and see what came up. So we swam and fisht in the ocean and we watched lotsa William S. Hart and Thomas Ince movies.

Meanwhilst, Bill and me was working up a fine friendship. So, even though he was real busy with this'n'that at Inceville, he still found lotsa time to ride with us. We'd shoot at cans, show off, and move some cattle herds 'round just for the helluva it. (Like most chores, if you don't *have* to do it, it ain't bad work at all.) Most interesting of all was Chick'n'Tad, who most usually had to be threatened at gun point to do certain chores. Well, up there in Inceville not only did they smile when they was asked, they was smiling whilst they did it. I woulda gotten suspicious, incept I was smiling too.

Our days went by fast, like they do when fun is happening, and before long I decided we might be wearing out our welcome. It'd been about a dozen days, and I reckoned if we was fish we woulda been tossed out long ago and woulda worked ourselfs halfway back through the feeding chain by then. So we arranged our departure, and in honor of us Bill arranged us a beach party, complete with guitars, clams, store-bought hooch, and lotsa pretty people.

But just as we was getting ready to head on down the hill for some beach fun, Bill asks me to meet him in the screening tent. He'd found something he wanted to show me. Knowing Bill Hart so well by then, I was all set for a shenannygag or something. It would be just like him to show some film he caught of me falling off a horse or talking to a cow or something I'd done equally strange.

He hands me a drink, sets me down, and looks about as serious as I'd seen him look in real life.

"What is it, Bill?" I asked.

"My boys were taking another look at that film you brought up."

"You mean the razzberry crop?"

He smiled and said yes, the razzberry crop. Anyhow, he thought I might want to have a look at something that was on a tail piece of some film.

He had it already set up and he switched it on hisself,

then leant back against a table and watched me watch the film. It was only a few frames; that means it was short. At first I didn't see it. He rewound it and ran it again, this time stopping it on one frame so's I could see what they saw.

It was our outside set, the one with the light diffusers. I recognized our crew. It musta been one of those first days when we was alla us awaiting the costumes and the story.

What I had to look close at was some men standing sorta off to the side and almost hidden by a curtain. I walked closer to the screen and got a better look. Chesley Warwick I saw perfectly. There was only one profile like his in all the world, I reckoned. He was talking to two other men who I didn't recognize at all. I turned to Bill and shrugged my shoulders.

"I thought you'd say that." He joins me at the screen and points first to one man and then the other. "This is Juan Ortega and this is Ricardo Diaz. Were they ever a part of your operation?"

"Never seen or heard of 'em before. Why, Bill? What're you thinking?"

"They were a couple of toughs we had working for us once up here. Real bad cases. This one," he points, "better known as El Machete, specializes in loan-sharking and extortion. A real numbers man. And this one, El Diablo he goes by, runs guns to Mexico. Looks like we were right about Chesley Warwick. If he's in league with the likes of them, then you might be in deeper trouble than you think."

All I could say was, "Extortion? Guns?"

"Revolutionaries, Royal!" Bill tells me, like he needed to draw me a picture. "Bandidos. Fillibusteros. *Villistas!*"

"Pancher Villisters?" asked me.

"Correcto, mi compadre."

"You sure?" I mumbled. "The film's sorta fuzzy. And

how do you suppose they got theirselfs filmed? Ain't that sorta stupid for ones so evil?"

Then Bill informs me the card announcing this piece of film said it was a light test and that probably no one even realized they was being filmed. Camera operators often did that. Then he added he had some of his boys confirm his suspicions.

"I'm sorry, Roy, it's them. You better pack for bear. Your outfit may be in big trouble."

"You know, when ol' Pancher started out I was behind him 100%. But now, reckon he's not much more'n a hoodlum on horseback," I said, pretty much to myself.

Bill turned off the movie light and added, "Who'd stop at nothing to get guns and munitions . . . guns the U.S. will need if Woody can't keep us out of war in Europe."

How come foreign countries and their disagreements was having such a effect on poor ol' Royal, I was wondering. After all, I always had me a private policy of keeping to myownself, and now here I was maybe being connected to words like 'extortion,' 'gun-running,' and 'Villisters.' I was scardt, especially when I learnt my own Elsie mighta now been a accessory to alla this international goings on.

So when Bill offers me a prime spot at the beach party, I said no thanks, I was heading back to town at first light to investigate things.

Then I called Sailing and told him I was worried about Elsie and could he please not let her outa his sight till I returned?

Early next morning, Bill walked us down to await our ride back into town.

"I really owe you, Royal," he said.

A car came ’round from the parking lot above. It pulled up and a driver got out and opened the doors.

“What’s this?” I asked Bill.

“I won’t have three of my best pals wait for a bus when they can be driven back to town. Al was going into Los Angeles anyway. He’s happy to give you a lift.” Then Bill pulled out two fancy latigo hackamores from the car. “Here, a little memento for the top hands,” he said, handing ’em to Chick’n’Tad. I never did see more beautiful hackamores in my whole life. Braided nosebands, silver conches, and fine, oiled reins. They musta cost a bundle, but Bill added, “I made them myself. It’s a little hobby of mine.”

Then Bill pulled out a fine metal case from the car’s rumble and this he handed to me, so I asked onct again, “What’s this?”

“*Birth of a Badman* or *Death of a Movie-man*, whichever you prefer,” Bill says, grinning me big. I examined his eyes to see what he coulda meant by his reply. He had a speck of dirt on his cheek and, sweartagod, I swiped my own cheek to get rid of it, we was that alike.

“Well, me and my boys worked a little on your problem the last couple of days,” Bill goes on. He opens up the case and hands me three reels. “This is what we pieced together.” Then he shows me eight or more reels left in the case. “Those’re the cut-outs, the parts we didn’t dare use.”

My face was fulla blanks and I just said, “You mean, you got a real moving picture outa all that ham-acting?”

Then Bill put his arm on my shoulder and explained, “Well, we added a little stock footage here and there, changed the dialogue some and, you know, just generally remade the film. It’s no masterpiece, mind you, but, well . . . maybe you’ll do better with this than that. Maybe you can get a little of your investment back.” And he pointed a forlorn finger down toward the eight reels of cut-outs. "And if I'm right about your Warwick being in cahoots with those hard cases, then. . ." He hands me a small roll of film and says, "Well, in case you need some evidence."

"Gosh, Bill, I don't know what to say," says me.

"Just say you'll never mention to a living soul me or any of my boys had anything to do with this, all right?"

"You have my word." And he did. Well, up to now, that is, but he won't mind me exposing things now, twenty years later. I hope.

He said he wouldn't miss it for the world. We shook hands and, guess what: he embraced my Chick'n'Tad, and Chick'n'Tad embraced him back. It was real touching. Bill hadn't a family of his own and I think he took a real shining to mine. 'Course, he hadn't met the female side yet.

Before we pulled out, Bill said to me, "Now, don't go doing anything I wouldn't do. I have an image to maintain and I'd just as soon maintain it myownself."

I laughed, wondered if a little of 'myownself' maybe was wearing off on him, and then I told him ditto.

We was delivered right smack dab to Mrs. Taylor's with our plunder, our film, our problems, and our memories on a warmish Los Angeles day.

'Course the first thing I did upon our arrival was to ask Mrs. Taylor 'bout my daughter. I learnt that Elsie had been setting pretty much as she shoulda in her parents' absence and only went out in the afternoons.

"I don't suppose she and Sailing have been stepping out together?" I asked Mrs. Taylor.

Mrs. Taylor shot me a mean one and answered, "No.

In fact, Mr. Leckner, having those two at the same table is worse'n having your two boys."

Chick'n'Tad, upon hearing her comparison, stopped chewing their cookies and looked at me. Fortunate for them, Mrs. Taylor continued, keeping 'em outa it.

"Why, right after you left, I'd prepared a special Sunday dinner. Dr. Strong started a simple little discussion about the importance of the comma in everyday letter writing and you'd think he'd just insulted Elsie's whole entire lineage!"

"What's a comma, Pa?" Tad asked.

"Us Leckners have never been grammar-titions," I allowed.

"Well, that's obvious by the language your daughter used on poor Dr. Strong, who was only trying to help her write a letter," Mrs. Taylor went on. "Well, the next thing you know they're chasing each other all over the house, calling examples of who's stupider . . . some stuffy professor locked away in an institution or a bleached blond who thinks she can act."

Mrs. Taylor fanned herself with her napkin. "It just got worse from there. I've never seen two young people take such a dislike to each other. You'd almost think they were brother and sister, the way they fight."

So much for thinking wishful that Elsie had got off the Chesley Trail, thinks me. Well, at least she wasn't setting in Mexico.

"That Chesley Warwick been squiring her out?" I asked, feeling my cackles rise some.

"Oh, and that's the other thing. The *De-vine* Chesley Warwick calls for her every day," Mrs. Taylor replied, slapping Tad's hand as he reached for his third cookie. I too was eying my third cookie, but watching Tad rub his hand

I thought better of it. "Except the last few days. Elsie said he was out of town on business. Now she just sits around and mopes. You know," Mrs. Taylor continues, "if that was my daughter, I'd set her straight about the likes of Chesley Warwick. Just another pretty face, clawing his way to the top. That's what I hate about these moving pictures . . . takes nice-looking young folks and turns them into vainglorious cannibals!"

Since I wasn't up to discussing vainglorious cannibals, I excused myself, sprawled out on the front porch swing, and awaited the return of anybody. For, it seemed, ol' Royal still had him some flints to fix.

And I hadn't even heard nothing 'bout E.M. yet!

seven

I was setting on the front porch steps, letting my mind ruminate on all my problems. There was lotsa 'what ifs' and 'then whats' still circulating, so's I had to be real logical with my thinking.

I could see Sailing hop off the street car, and I went out to meet him halfway.

"I'm glad you're back, Royal. There's been some sort of trouble over at the studio."

I was afraid of that and I told him so. He tells me Marco and Chesley had disappeared for a few days and didn't tell anyone, even Elsie, where they was going. I was thinking the worst.

"Did they even get the film put together?"

"I guess so. Marco said they did, at least."

"Anyone miss anything?" I asked.

"Oh, so it was you who took the dupes. I figured it had to be," Sailing says, smiling at me. "What did you do, destroy them?" He looked at me like a top hand does when discussing the mercy killing of a sick cow.

"In a manner of speaking." I then confided in him Bill Hart's suspicions of Chesley and his so-called associates. I could tell he was thinking the same as me. If Chesley was a real and true blackheart and not just a ACK-tor with grand illusions, then Elsie might be in trouble deep.

It was here that Sailing goes into what looked like a real studious-like silence and I reckoned this is what Ph.D. candidates look like when they're smack dab in the midsta their oral exams. Then he says, "You know, Royal, now that I think about it, I recollect Warwick saying something that didn't quite click."

"Click with what?"

"His speech mannerisms."

"Oh, he's got hisself all sortsa heritages to call on for those," I allowed.

"Well, last week he caught Chick and Tad in some back storage room at the studio. Anyway, he blew his stack and called them a couple of renegade *waristas.* You know, I thought that was kind of odd; I've never heard the word *waristas* before. As close as I can figure, it's Mexican slang for warriors. I thought it was strange, but then it was Chesley Warwick and I didn't think anything more about it."

Well, that sparked a recollection of my own, speaking of Chick'n'Tad. I then related that the boys had come to me all in a argument. Young Tad comes up to me and tattles that ol' Chick'd been lying to him. Hell, I hardly ever listened too close when they was warring and then I was too busy 'standing in' for Chesley Warwick. Tad says, "Chick says T-N-T spells dynamite and how can that be onaccounta there's gotta be a 'm' somewheres in there?" I think I told him to look it up and I was busy, or go ask their momma, and they grumbled that she was too much 'in her character' to spell just then.

Sailing and I looked at each other. I got Chick'n'Tad outa bed and let 'em wake up some before Sailing and me starts inquisitioning 'em. They was always real sleepy and cranky upon premature wakning, but I finally got 'em dressed and awake.

"We going home, Pa?" Tad asked, sorta shivering whilst we was waiting for our taxicab.

"No, we're going to work."

"Cripes," Chick whined.

Onct we was delivered to the studio, I told the boys they was to show us the room from which they had been caught playing. Well, the boys looks at each other like they'd been caught red-handed, and Tad, the confessor, says, "Honest, Pa, we didn't know ladies undressed in there."

"Slap shut!" Chick warns him.

"You just lead the way," I says, unlocking the door and showing the boys in first.

Tad pulls his brother's sleeve and says, "I *told* you that Chees-ley would tell Pa!"

It was no less'n the ladies dressing room through which the boys led us, and I made note to set 'em straight on the issue of peeping toms usually got their peepers popped out by long, sharp manicured fingernails.

Happy was they to learn it wasn't the peep hole I was

concerned with, but the room behind, in which they'd built theirselfs a fort, they said.

Chick pushed open the small door and we walked into the darkning, cautious-like. Tad pulled the light string and there we stood, a Ph.D., two *waristas,* and me staring blank-like into a empty room. I looked at Sailing, then at my boys. Chick recognized my suspicious face. He backs up and says, "This room was fulla crates, Pa. Swear!"

Tad walks 'round the room and then just turns and growls, "Chick, somebody stole our fort!" and then grumbles hisself back into the ladies dressing room, probably to pout.

Sailing then starts inspecting the room for evidence. He kneels down and is looking at a small trace of a black sand-like substance. "Anyone got a match?" he asked.

Chick pulled one outa his pocket just like he'd maybe pull outa frog or marble or mumbly-peg, and I made a note to talk to him 'bout the dangers of smoking, too.

Sailing lit the blackish sand, watched the small flare-up, and we all knew it was traces of gunpowder on the floor. It was then Tad comes back in the room and announces, "Lookit me, Pa."

We turned to see a miniature version of a image that I'd only heretofore seen in the newspapers: a Mexican *bandido*—complete with crist-crost bullet belts over his shoulders and hanging past his knees, hand grenades a-draping from his belt, and in each hand a rifle. "Next movie, Pa, can I play Pancher Viller's son?"

We, the resta us, just froze. Ol' Tad, hell, he thought he was play-acting and all those armaments was nothing more'n movie costumes. We, of course, knew better.

"Now, Tad, darlin', you just set those rifles down,

easy-like," says me, not wanting to sound too scoldy or scardy.

"They ain't real, Pa. Chick said they was just props."

"Chick ain't told you the truth since you been born, Tad," I allows, inching toward my youngun. "Now be real easy and just let your pa help you outa your costume."

"Au reservoir, Pa!" Tad moans, undraping the arsenal offa his own body. "And I stole these special." The last to go was the hand grenades, which was what I was most worried about. He handed me first one, then another, and finally five more. He hesitated on the last, like hoping maybe I woulda changed my mind.

"Just one, Pa? Please?" he begs.

I snatched it up, and Sailing and I was quick to inspect the ordinances. My first hint something was up was seeing how light the bullet belts was, and although I hadn't tossed me too many hand grenades, I thought they was feeling a little light, too, considering the amount of damage they could do.

We stood under the swinging light bulb and made note the grenades and bullets each had a hole drilt in 'em, making 'em closer to props than armaments. Even the rifles was jammed beyond repair.

"See? I told you they was just for movies," Chick says, sounding a little too much like his momma. I apologized for my lying comment earlier.

"You boys sure this room was fulla TNT?" I asked.

"We never said that, Pa," Chick replied.

We then go 'round that one for awhile and ended up leaving not knowing much more'n before, 'cept my boys was making evil use of their spare times, which I'd always suspected anyhow.

We boxed up and hid away the so-called props and get

ourselfs outa there fast. We locked the secret door and put the women's racka costumes back infronta it so's no one could tell we'd been through.

In the cab ride back home Sailing turns to me and asks, "You think we should call the police or get an attorney or something?"

I told him I myownself probably had more experience dealing with nee-farious types than any Hollywood constables, and that nothing of this nature called for lawyers. Besides, we didn't know nothing solid yet.

After the boys had drifted off to sleep, I asked, "You spend any time with Elsie whilst I was away?"

"Hardly. She hates me. And she always wants me to know where Chesley's taking her and how it was and look, doesn't she look pretty in this white lace? Would you believe, she even had the temerity to ask me to help her write a love poem to that. . . that. . ."

I hated to see him struggle, so I offered, "Hornswoggling, blatherskiting, highbinding, pinchbecking crook. And by the way, what does 'temerity' mean?"

Sailing looked at me and said, "You took the words right out of my mouth." Then he added them to his note pad.

Then I said: "Tell me, what would you do to get her outa Chesley's clutches? If you was me, that is."

I was expecting him to say something literature-like or spout him a poem from that Byron feller or Shelley or Keats. Instead, his face growls some, like he was imagining it, and he said, "I'd like to turn the hose on them both the next time they come waltzing into the studio, arm in arm, all dressed up and looking like peaches and cream and sunshine and roses and life itself. . ." He caught hisself and looked at me and said, "I'm sorry. Was I digressing?"

Not that I'd recognize such a thing.

Then he sighs and adds, "I suppose it's too late for a convent."

Poor ol' Sailing. He had it bad.

Back at the boarding house, I found me a note in Elsie's chicken-scratching that I'd gotten me a long distance phone call, which I was to return pronto. Sailing was right—there wasn't a damn comma in her whole note.

Well, 11 p.m. or not, I quickly returned the call, reversing the charges, of course, onaccounta it was Wilton, my Walla Walla lawyer, who'd called.

"Howdy, Wilton," I said, "how'd you track me down?" I knew if ol' Wilton accepted my collect call, half asleep no less, then it had to be pretty serious or else he stood to gain a sizeable billing offa it, so I was gonna keep it brief.

He said my own wife had told him.

"E.M.?" I asked. "She back home?"

He said she'd called him from San Francisco and how the hell did that woman get me in all this *mess*?

"What'd she tell you?" (Never give a lawyer more'n he needs.)

He said, not much, you know E.M., and he needed my okay before he could un-rescind my rescinding of the power of attorney. Naturally, Wilton had to check with me first. I wondered why E.M. didn't just call Wilton's wife and arrange it through her. But I said, "She mention what for?"

He said no, but she'd talked like it was life or death.

"Was she sneezing?" I asked.

He said I was stupid to fall for that one, but I asked it again and he said, matter of fact, yes.

I told Wilton to hold the wire whilst I set back and

stared at the ceiling, like as to see written on it what ol' E.M. was up to this time. Up till now she'd done us all right equitable. What more damage could she do? I'd already locked up my cash money with my banker. Was I gonna trust my wife? And why the hell hadn't she just called *me*? I heard Wilton calling for me through the phone and then said, "I'm here, Wilton. Gotta think on this one." He reminded me all phone charges go on account.

Onaccounta that I quickly replied, "Go ahead, Wilton. Do what she asks."

He asked me if I was sure, and hoped this didn't have nothing to do with all that temper-ancing his own wife'd been dabbling in.

"You got a phone number of where she's at?" I asked Wilton, and he read it to me. I told him let her sign. I was gonna have to trust my wife.

"Again?" he asked. "Isn't that getting harder and harder to do?"

I said I wasn't gonna pay him for any more questions and told him good bye.

Then I rang the number where E.M. was. Glad was I when the voice answered was a hotel man and not the San Francisco police. I asked for E.M. and he hooked us up.

"What the hell you up to, E.M.?" I asked, trying to keep my voice down.

"Oh. Royal. Hmmm . . . hello." she says. "I take it Wilton called you."

"Look, Miss Montenegro, why the hell you cavorting 'round San Francisco when we got us a major foofaraw down here?"

"Why, what's wrong?"

"Like our own daughter is trasping after that Chesley Warwick, and wait'll you see the list I got on him."

Then I told her what I knew. She allowed as how I musta been seeing too many moving pictures. Chesley Warwick was just a little 'intense,' she called it, like 'intense' was a good trait insteada a description of pain like I'd heretofore thought of it as.

"That Marco Magellan been traveling with you?" I had to ask. After all, he'd taken off somewheres and it'd be just like the beans to go looking for the ham. E.M. laughed and said I was so adorable when I was jealous and as far as she knew, Marco was at the Hollywood Hotel just as usual. She finished off by telling me she'd be back tomorrow and not to worry, she'd explain everything when she got back. How many times had I heard that? She didn't onct ask 'bout how our movie was piecing together, but she did say, which I didn't think about till after she hung up, "The spree's almost over."

I stood there listening to the operator telling me to hang up now, my party was gone, even though I was demanding E.M. get back on the phone and tell me what the hell that was supposed to mean. The operator reminded me it wasn't nice to swear into a telephone and click, the line went blank.

Early next morning, we got us another call at the boarding house. Sailing took this one. It was Marco informing us he was done piecing together our movie and how elated he was and all he had to do now was to order him up a organist and work up the music and bang, right on schedule, we'd have our big showing this Thursday. Marco seemed to have some concern if we'd ordered our tuxedos.

"Tuxedos?" I yelped at Sailing. A tuxedo was the last thing on my mind, what with E.M. coming back, Chesley

God knows where, and maybe ol' Pancher Viller hissself somewheres in betwixt. Additional, it scart the hell outa me to think what kinda movie Marco put together, after all the scenes me and Bill and his boys had looked at. Then, thinks me, bet maybe there's no movie at all, and we'd all be setting all tuxedoed up in that theater awaiting for a movie whilst Marco and Chesley was spending Mexican pesos to beat the Mariachi Band.

So then I asked Sailing, "Did Marco say when he was gonna show the movie to us cast folk?"

Sailing looked at me and said, "That's what I was wondering. He said we'll see it opening night, with the rest of the world. He said he wants it to be a premiere for *all* of us."

"I'll just bet," I mumbled. "Ain't that sorta like loading your gun. . ."

". . . after the horse gets out?" Sailing finished for me.

I was then beginning to wonder if maybe we *had* oughta hang up our egos and call the police. But it was Sailing this time who dissuaded ol' Royal. He looked at me, sorta grinned (sweartagod), and said he had a idea and this was more fun'n handing out F's and onct a uniform entered into things it was back to day-to-day living for us.

In some ways ol' Sailing was just as much a kid as Chick'n'Tad. Boys will be boys—we was all about to prove that one—especially when there was a fair maid and a villain involved.

Hell, if I talk any more tonight, my talker will sure as hell pull up lame. Now, I know that might be a blessing to some, but since FDR's paying you by the hour, I don't reckon that would be in the best, patriotic interests of our depressed economy. So let's take a rest, son, and we'll begin again tomorrow, OK?

PART 4

one

Well, now that I got me some rest, I reckon I can get on with things. Which was where? Oh yeah . . . I left off not knowing where the hell I was in alla this fe-as-ko. And things was about to complicate. So pull up a chair, son, and hold on real tight, 'cause at this point things started moving faster'n a lawyer to a train wreck.

I guess this is good a place as any to tell you, in case you was wondering, why Sailing was so out of the ordinary enamored with Elsie. I'll tell you something about him and her that I didn't come to learn for some time. Maybe it'll better help you to understand why Sailing took so after her, and it never hurts me to be reminded of Elsie's deep-down nature and not her skin-deep play-acting that summer.

It happened whilst I was off and pretending to be someone I wasn't in Inceville, the night I'd called and asked Sailing to watch Elsie. Well, he took my request serious-like and when Elsie went out that evening for a walk unescorted, he followed her.

Elsie may have been getting a bit worried 'bout how things was progressing in her life—Chesley's vanishing on her and all—so she was walking sorta aimless-like, like maybe she didn't have no direction and was lost deep in thought on a vexing issue. Well, who knows what was going through her mind.

Anyhow, Sailing followed her clear into a foreign neighborhood, one that he hisownself wasn't familiar with, and he'd done him plenty of walking back in his impoverished college days. He was beginning to get hisself worried 'bout the directions Elsie was going and was wondering how he was gonna manage to 'bump' into her and get her back home safe-like.

Well, his fears was well-founded onaccounta, sure enough, Elsie was passing by this alley and hears a scream coming from somewheres in the darkning. Remember now, back home we don't have us back alleys and dead ends and such-like where crime and its companions sometimes set up shop. So Elsie wasn't thinking when she took herself into that alley.

Nowadays we got us alota homeless folks, being the Depression and all. But I reckon they was far and few between back in 1915, even in that parta Los Angeles. Well, in that alley, behind some old crates and whatnot, there was a woman and her daughter, without a home, poor and probably sick. And you know how jackals always pick out the weak in a herda animals? Well, there was a coupla young toughs trying to wrestle the woman outa what little she had. Now, proud am I to say that my daughter, Elsie, sixteen mind you, took on those two delinquents, which mighta not been a real smart move, but if she had to have reflexes I'm just as glad to see they was reflexes of justice. So she fights the mongrels off, and I know she come by those skills honest-like, onaccounta she could usually make mincemeat outa her two brothers.

Well, just when Sailing was about to jump into it too, the hoodlums come running outa the alleyway without even what they went in there with, and he turns to see something even more remarkable in my Elsie. And this next thing I myownself was surprised to learn.

Elsie was helping that woman and her daughter up and she brought 'em outa the alley and into the streetlight. Then she takes off her own shoes, which cost me a fortune, and gives 'em to the woman. This was followed by her jacket and a comb from her hair. Then comes the contents of her money belt. Anyone looking at that threesome probably woulda thought by then that it was my Elsie who was the indigent, and the mother and the child who was the lucky ones.

This is how Sailing summed it up: "I'm not sure if it was that left hook of your daughter's or the look on the face of that little girl when Elsie gave her the mother-of-pearl comb from her bleached blond hair. . ."

That was it. Sailing was hooked from that moment on, hooked and in love, seeing Elsie walk down that street, barefoot, without adornment and daring anyone to say anything about it.

Sailing said he just followed her home, silent, and couldn't fall asleep for dreaming.

Nextly, there's some things you oughta know about Sailing Strong. You may have noticed I gotta tendency to ramble on about how I did this and how I did that—you know, sorta me being the major player in alla this. Well, I'd just as soon you think I was the solver of all problems and the winner of all battles. But I had me some help.

On occasion.

Whilst I was setting in that boarding house, miserating over my assorted plights—you know, Marco and E.M.,

Chesley and Elsie, and what, if, when, and why that film was ever gonna premiere and really get things confused—I reckon I was steeped to the lips in my dilemma, for Sailing even asked me if I was feeling poorly. I allowed as how I'd had me better circumstances. Said I thought I'd take me down to that riding stable by the studio and maybe rent me a horse, onaccounta that's where the view was clearest: from atopt a horse. He said he'd be happy to keep a eye on the boys for me and all. Then I asked if he was gonna go out and order hisself a tuxedo.

"No," he says.

"Oh, so you don't think Marco's gonna really premiere our film either, do you?"

Sailing just replied he meant he didn't have to rent a tuxedo onaccounta he had one hanging in mothballs up in his closet. He said something about being a toastmaster for a year, which meant nothing to me incept I was reminded I hadn't eaten much breakfast that morning. Anyhow, any time anyone offers to divert Chick'n'Tad, and for free, well, you know I'm gonna take 'em up on it. So I left to find a horse and a course of action.

Here's what he was up to that same morning in Hollywood with my own two sons as accomplices, and if I sound like I was right there amidst the action, then that's because I heard this story so often from Chick'n'Tad the resta the summer that it's like I was. I shall try to tell it the way Sailing told it to me and not the way it was after Chick'n'Tad got done glorifying it and Elsie got done denying it. If ol' Sailing ever writes up his own life story, then maybe we'll get the real truth.

It all began with another phone call—Lord, that contraption sure was getting to be a bothersome noise. Maybe some day they'll figure out a way to make that ringer less irksome. Anyway, on this phone ring Elsie came flying down the stairs saying it's ten o'clock and she was expecting that call, and for the boys and even Sailing to keep their hands offa the phone. 'Course Chick picks it up anyway.

"Mrs. Taylor's Boarding House for Refined Gentlemen," he answered, like he was one. He listened, then said, "Nope. I said this here place is for *gentlemen.*"

Elsie grabbed the phone and answered, "Hello? Chesley? Oh, my idiot brother, that's all." Here, Elsie probably kicked Chick'n'Tad outa the little phone alcove. Maybe even swore—with her hand over the phone, naturally. Sailing was still setting at the dining room table, eye specs on, his nose in a book, pretending to hear not a word, but taking in every one.

Elsie said, "Well, go ahead . . . ask me. . ." (Good thing I wasn't there, I'da ripped the phone cord clean outa the wall till I reeled Chesley Warwick in on the other end.) "Well, yee gawds, Ches (*giggle*), how important can it be? Okay, noon is fine."

After a few more coos she hung up and asked Sailing, "Dr. Strong, do you know where the Oriental Gardens Theatre is? I have a date."

"The Oriental Gardens? The one the premiere is premiering at?"

She laughed at Sailing's rough dialogue and suggested he'd been spending too much time with me, her father. He tells her it's on that side of town that young ladies need to be extra careful of. She said something like she wasn't afraida anything anywhere. I can just see how she musta looked, taking those stairs regal-like, Sailing at the bottom. Him tapping his lips with his pencil in thought. Her flashing a faint smile.

Well, need I tell you that Sailing, in the 'companiment of the two best sister-trackers in the state, followed my gussied-up daughter outa that boarding house that morning?

'Course, Sailing knew Los Angeles like he knew the insida his pocket dictionary and so he cut here, tracked there, and they soon were watching Elsie, all peaches and creamy-white-laced, knock on the Oriental Gardens Theatre door. Pretty soon the door opened and they could see Chesley's shiny black hair peeking 'round to see if she was alone. Then she disappeared into the theater and my three trackers snuck to the entrance.

Chick stared into the window, which was black inside, and Tad tried the doors, which were locked tight.

"They ain't showing no movie now, Sailing," griped Chick. "Let's go find us one that's working. Elsie can handle Chees-ly herownself."

"No, wait, boys," Sailing said. "Let's go around the back and see if there's a delivery door open."

"What for?" Tad asked.

Sailing then looked at my issues and said, "You know, I hear you two are quite the hoodlums."

Chick'n'Tad glued shoulders like they always did when they thought things was commencing to a united-we-stand situation. Chick said, "Who says?"

"Oh, word gets around," said Sailing, giving a smile of respect.

At which Tad piped up with, "I onct traded my sister's horse for a jar fulla jawbreakers."

"That's nothing," Chick one-ups him. "I onct stole our teacher's grade book and gave everyone a A on that damn math test—remember, Tad, the one that everyone failed 'cept that brainer Sarah Tweves?" He was quick to inform Sailing he'd given Sarah Tweves a F. Ol' Chick, being ten, gets suspicious on how many beans he shoulda spilt infronta a brainer the likes of Sailing Strong. After all, he was also a teacher of sorts and might not take too kindly to math grades on the house.

Sailing came down to his level some, smiled, and I sure as hell wisht I coulda been witness to him when he informed the boys, "Well, I once cheated on a ethics exam."

"Ethics? Who're they?" Tad asked, a grina evil coming acrost his face.

"The Earl of Ethics? He's the one who teaches you about guilt and regret and fairness," Sailing informed 'em, sage-like.

"Wouldn't know much about the Earl," Chick admits. "Anyhow, what's that gotta do with Elsie and that creep?"

Sailing just starts walking 'round toward the back alley in search of a entrance into the theater. The boys, naturally, followed him.

It took the slimness of Tad, alla seventy pounds back then, to etch hisself through a window and then sneak 'round and open the back door to the theater.

"Easy as pie," he allows. "This here breaking and entering?" he asked Chick. Chick tells him don't worry on-accounta nothing was broke . . . not like the time he got his hands on that grade book. "Besides," he whispered to Tad, "we got us Sailing to take the blame. You know they never blame kids when there's a grownup in on it. Remember that time they blamed Ma insteada us when they found us in that bank vault a few years back?" Tad said he was too young to remember and Chick said "trust me," which Tad did all too often back in those days.

So into the dark theatrical hinterlands sneaks Sailing with my boys. I can see 'em now: single file up some stairs till into the theater itself they arrive. I can see how it musta looked: all dim-lit and dingy and fulla stale smells and forgotten images of last week's stars. I guess ol' Tad took him a spill and hurt his shin (which was always black'n'blue anyhow, till he fell outa his clumsy period.) Sailing and Chick was quick upon him, rubbing his shin, blowing on the scrape, and covering his mouth.

They found theirselfs in the backstage area. The theater, like alota film palaces in those days, was firstly used for burlesque, so it was a complete stage behind the big screen a-hanging down. And like all stages it had some peep holes drilt into the side so's the performers could look out on the audience and see if their momma or the press or the sheriff was out there.

They could see a flickera light coming from behind the balcony, and Sailing gathered up the boys close to him and said shhs, for there must be folks out there watching it, and unless he missed his guess that movie was none other'n *Birth of a Badman.* Sailing makes Chick'n'Tad swear to stay put whilst he snuck 'round the side to see him some of the movie and to find Elsie.

Now I know you're used to movies talking, but back then the only talking was coming from Chesley and Elsie, who was setting center audience and alone.

"But Chesley, sweetest, you said we'd *all* watch the movie. Where's Armando? Where's Marco?"

He had his arm around her and said, "You and me—that's 'we all.' Now, darling, please look at me. I have to ask you something."

"But my entrance is coming," Elsie said, pointing to the screen. Chesley pulled her closer and continued.

"Darling, I hate to bring up finances, but. . ."

Then Elsie said something on the order of he was rich enough for her and besides, Marco says they'll all be stars and worth oodles of money, and two could live as cheaply as one. You know, the usual female rationale. She ended with a cozy little, "So go ahead: what were you going to ask me?"

"Well, you *know* how I feel about you. But we can't just rush into anything until we're set up. Now, you know how terribly, terribly committed Marco and I are to Royal-scope and our futures. You just wouldn't know how expensive things are. Why, the rental of this theater alone is astronomical."

I can just see Sailing looking 'round that cheap theater, adding things up, a dollar here, two bits there.

Then Chesley commenced to close in on Elsie, whispering in her ear. She listened, smiled, giggled, then sat up straight and shouted, "Twenty thousand dollars! Yee Gawds, Chesley, my father . . . I mean . . . without my mother here to nudge him . . . I mean . . . twenty thousand *more*?"

"But sweet, love doesn't pay our bills," Chesley said.

"Ours and everyone else's," Elsie mumbled. Then, "You know, Chesley, if I wasn't sure you loved me I'd say. . ."

Apparently he'd heard that line before and so he swept her into his arms, sweartagod, with only that armrest betwixt 'em, and started smothering her doubts with kisses.

Sailing tiptoed hisself backstage to find the boys and to put a lid on his rising temper. 'Course, both Chick'n'Tad was fighting for the best peep hole through which to spy on their sister's interlude.

Sailing muttered into the curtain, "Why that horn-swoggling, blatherskiting, highbinding, pinchbecking crook! I'd like to rearrange that face of his."

It was then that Chick handed Sailing his slingshot, which, I am happy to report, my sons hadn't left home without. Then he handed Sailing the ammo: a coupla tar balls that the boys always collected offa hot city streets and had rolt to a perfection. But it was Tad who firstly aimed his slingshot betwixt the curtains, and you wouldn't think those skinny eight-year-old arms could shoot a sling with such power and accuracy. Well, almost accuracy.

Elsie's yelp echoed real nice amongst the empty theater. She screamed, grabbed up her eye, and started dancing 'round the aisle. Sailing rushed out thinking Chesley had accosted her, Chesley jumps up not knowing what was going on, and Chick'n'Tad rolt theirselfs up in the curtain to hide.

So there's Chesley and Sailing squaring off, there's Elsie hopping 'round swearing a blue streak and trying to pull bits of sticky tar offa her face and outa her hair.

'Course, Sailing is still hanging onto Chick's slingshot, so you know who Elsie was swearing at. She issued the standard lines: "who the hell do you think you are, anyway?" and "well, I didn't need any help!" and "I've never been so insulted in all my life!" and she ended with "if I wasn't a lady I'd rearrange your face!" which of course is where it all started. So they had 'em one of them completed circles which alota sabbatarians preached about back then.

The movie ground to a halt, and the projector man came down and added his opinion, which was pretty much that they can all get out of the theater at onct and these movie people was gonna be the deatha him yet and he was nuts to switch to flickers and why the hell hadn't he stayed with strippers and nasty jokesters, who was by far a better classa people than movie ACK-tors?

Well, by that time, Chick'n'Tad had got theirselfs all twisted 'round in the curtain and from now on when you hear the expression "Bring the curtain down," thinka my boys in red velvet and gold fringe, a-bundled and a-squirming about on a empty burlesque stage.

The projector man tells Chesley that was the last favor he'd ever do for him. He musta been outa his mind letting a ACK-tor in for a private showing.

Elsie and Chesley left in a huff to find a steak for Elsie's black eye and other first aids. Chick'n'Tad was gathered up. And Sailing assured the projector man that Marco Magellan would pay for all damages.

Then Sailing turned to the projector man and asked, "Say, were you watching the movie from up there?"

"Yeah. What about it?" he asked back, not feeling too friendly at that point.

"What did you think?"

"I only get paid to run 'em, not critique 'em."

Then the P. H. of D. asked, "Well, if you were Caesar, say, and that movie was a gladiator . . . would it be this. . ." he pointed his thumb up, "or this?" and his thumb pointed hell's direction. The movie man looked at him and not only did he point one thumb down, he added another to it, and his face looked like he mighta wanted to add a few more, if he had 'em.

Wisht to hell I'd been there.

two

So, whilst alla this is going on, ol' Royal is setting him a rented nag, who turned out to be right sympathetic. I was never partial to lighter-colored horses—you know, grays, whites, palominos and all—onaccounta they're hell to keep clean on a ranch in Washington State. But this one, whitish with dapples of gray, was all shiny and clean, and I don't think this interfered with his opinion of hisself. Well, you know Royal wasn't gonna stick to the bridle trail. You know I ended up taking that clean horse into the dirty parta town where Royalscope was located. I told the horse I'd clean him up for free if he'd just keep his head low and not get squirrelly 'round the buses and trucks and noises. Last thing I needed was a skiddish horse bolting ninety to nothing down the streets of Los Angeles.

But he did just fine, and if he noticed folks staring at us a little, outa our element as we was, he didn't say nothing. I reckon it was 'bout two o'clock by the time I'd rode us up to Royalscope Studios. I unmounted and tied my horse up to a fire hydrant. Ain't that a picture combining last century with this? Anyhow, I was gonna corner Marco and lay my cards on the table.

Surprised was I to learn that Royalscope Productions had a sign planted over the door that advised the world that we was all

I didn't know if I was more surprised to learn we'd moved or that there actually was such a place. The studio was closed up tighter'n a bank come three p.m.

I walked to the side where Marco kept his office. Now, you know I ain't never been above hearing 'round corners, and that's what I did, for like hell Marco was in Bagdanistan . . . he was in his office, lights off, shades drawn, and on the phone. And since he was speaking in the heat of a vehement situation, I heard every word from where I crouched. This is his halfa the conversation:

"I told you we'll have it! I'm meeting with Mr. Warwick this very evening and he assures me our financial picture is wonderful . . . Yes! Yes! Just a few more days, please! These things take time! . . . I swear, this isn't anything like *Russian Roulette.* This new film will be. . . But the premiere is just three. . . three more days, for God's sake! Surely he can wait three short days! Yes, I'm listening. . ."

And here he took a long pause. I wisht to hell I could see his face so's I could get a idea of just what kinda trouble he was in. He ended the conversation this way:

"Thank you, thank you, thank you . . . No, you won't be sorry . . . Yes, bless you."

Well, it musta been pretty damn awful if a man like Marco had to bless someone, and over phone lines to boot. I grabbed up my horse and headed back. Now I had me even harder thinking to do.

Even the easy clip clop of my horse's hooves couldn't unclog my brain now. I turned him in, thanked him, paid the stable man, and wandered back toward Mrs. Taylor's. Pretty soon I was cornering in on my own little parta Hollywood.

I was coming close to a park and could recognize my boys' water-play voices a whole block away. I consulted my pocket watch and wondered how in hell so many hours had passed without me noticing. I found me a swing the same time some four-year-old did, and for some reason the kid takes one look at me and runs off crying, so I got me the swing.

Not far away I see me a familiar-looking lady, and she's in a heated discussion with a familiar-looking gentleman. It was Elsie and Sailing. Damn, wonder what them two younguns is discussing, wonders me. She was using her arms this way and that and I recognized that parta her discussion. She was hanging onto some sorta paper or letter or something and Sailing was getting some words in edgewise, that I could tell. When she stomped off, he'd pull her around, she'd pull outa his pull, and he'd follow her, and then they'd do it all over again.

I'd of given anything to hear what they was saying. Pretty soon, Sailing stomps off and it looked for a minute like she was gonna follow him. Then she stamped her foot—a spoilt little girl action her momma and me'd never been able to break her of. Then she walks off opposite.

I set in my swing, ticklish on the horns of alla my dilemmas. I stretched my legs out and leant my head back. Ever play Clouds when you was a kid? You know, where you look up and make things outa the puffs, then try to guess what the other kid was making outa his cloud? Well, after a bit, from behind comes, "I see a big ship on my cloud. What do you see on yours?"

It was Elsie. I looked at her, and I have to tell you this, even upside-down she looked like my ol' Elsie—complete with black eye. (Chick'n'Tad had given her lots over the years.) Oh, her hair was still a maze of curls and

I think even a little of her black roots was making it look somewhat on the piebald side, not to mention she had a trace of tar gracing her temple. But she comes 'round and stands there in fronta me, dressed in summer whites, the shade of the trees on her face and a breeze pulling her hair a little—well, I thought she was the most beautiful thing in the world.

"Howdy, sweetheart," said I, setting up and looking at her eye. "You been cuffin' fists with the boys?"

"Sorta," said she, her voice soft like it was back home. She was holding that letter.

"What'cha got there besides a shiner?" I asked.

I thought that was a simple question, but it was difficult enough for Elsie, for she said a tearful, "Oh, Daddy!" and flung herself into my arms, making us two on a swing, just like when she was a baby.

And so there you have why I was born, why I was in Los Angeles, and why I was in such a bewildered state. Well, she cried and cried and I just held her tight and said it was gonna be all right, no matter what the problem was. She stopped whimpering, I offered her my tear-duster, and I helped her pull herself back together.

"You wanna tell your pa about it?" I asked.

"It's just that I've been so stupid," she sniffed.

Well, she wasn't gonna get a argument outa me, so I kept shut and let her continue. She fluttered her tearful eyes skyward like as to keep the new crop from falling out and said, "I love Chesley so."

Well, that wasn't what I wanted to hear, so all I did was tell her, to each her own, said the old maid kissing her cat. I waited for that to sink in, and it ain't as though she'd never heard me say it before.

So she takes a pause, then continues, "Or at least I thought I did. . ." She crunched the letter in her hands. "But this. . ." Well, it musta been too much to continue, for the tears recommenced.

I think she was on the right trail, so I took the letter and asked if I could read it. Whilst I read, she dissolved, mumbling lovelorn words like 'flusticated,' 'rat,' and 'never.'

Sailing earned his Ph.D. in the right area, thinks me. What was strange about the letter was, it musta been that *billet d'amour* he'd written for her to give Chesley, for Sailing'd crost out the "My Darling Chesley" and wrote in "Dear Elsie," and at the end it was signed not, "Your truest love, Elsie," but "Your Most Ardent Admirer, S. Strong." At the bottom of the letter, in a different color ink I made note, was a P.S. It read, "P.S. If it makes you feel better, I'm truly sorry for what happened at the theater today. But believe me, Warwick is no gentleman and if it's the last thing I ever do, I'll prove that to you."

I handed the letter back. She finally blew her nose, which, like her momma, generally meant the worst was over, and I asked her what she was gonna do about it.

Chick'n'Tad had come within earshot. I gave 'em my most dangerous glare and they turned right 'round and found other swings.

"I don't know, Daddy. What do you think I should do?"

Now there was a tough one. No matter what I advised, chances were big she would do the opposite. So I just said, "I think you should follow your heart and not let your head get in the way."

I thought that was safe and sage. She said nothing, but tried to get her breathing more even. So I took another chance and added, "Something else I don't think you should let get in the way, Elsie."

She took a long, shaky suspiration and asked, "What?"

I lifted a strand of her bleached, spuzzed-out hair and simply answered, "This." Well, either she'll get my meaning or she won't, I figured.

She started to cry for a third time and I just held her and rocked her, right there, still in the swing, like daddies are supposed to. Then the words just fell outa me, but I think she was ready to hear 'em. I said to my sixteen-year-old daughter, "I think I agree with Sailing's P.S. here, incept the theater part, whatever that is. Warwick ain't what he seems. Now I never onct forbid you nothing and I sure as hell ain't gonna tell you who to love. But I'd be proud to think you'd be like your Ma and keep a feller guessing. And darlin', nowhere does it say you can't break a few hearts along the way."

And she informs me it was *her* heart that was broken. I lifted her chin and said, "Then I reckon you know how Sailing's been feeling these last coupla weeks. Maybe it's him you oughta be talking to."

She nodded and for the first time smiled a little. I saw alota E.M. in her face. She blew her nose onct again, rose, and said real solid-like, "I will! I'm going to tell him to . . . to go to hell!" On that she turned and assumed a pace like she was going to town for a new cook.

What hath God wrought? I asked myself. I watched her determined clip and there I set, all wrung out, holding my wet hankie and wondering what the hell had just transpired.

"Where she off to?" Chick asked me, watching his sister disappear.

"I don't know for sure, but I think she's off to tell Sailing she's taken a shiner to him."

To which Tad puts his head to the heavens and howls a perhaps very appropriate, "Run, Sailing! Run!"

three

'Course I already had the opinion of Bill Hart and his experts on the sorta film *Birth of a Badman* was probably gonna be made into. But when Sailing told me the projector man at the Oriental Gardens had suggested a Caesar-like slaying, I reckoned I saw what a hopeless affair it really was. Sailing wanted me to pull the plug on the whole shebang altogether, but I told him to set tight: there was forces at work that we wasn't yet sure of. Hell, for all I knew we mighta still been working off the effects of that curse ol' Countess Arellia had slapped on us.

Then E.M. returns to Los Angeles exactly two weeks after she'd left, which was one day before the big showdown premiere. As though I didn't have enough problems. But she was fulla grins and contracts, and she said she'd done herself proud on all the land dealing she'd dealt. I will admit, her nose looked a bit on the pinkish side from all her dealings.

But I wasn't listening to all her talk onaccounta I was still in a quandary about *Birth of a Badman* and I didn't know quite how to break it to her she had herself a big, fat Columbus on her hands.

You see, I looked at it two ways: I could tell E.M., down and dirty, that Marco's movie was a pitiful excuse for entertainment. Then I could also tell her that Bill Hart and his friends put us together a more suitable movie to display to the world the next day. But just when I thought I had the right answer, I'd stop and think again. If the movie was a flop, which Marco's was bound to be, then maybe Elsie and E.M. would give up this movie foofaraw and get on home where they belonged. Then again, how was I gonna get any portion of my so-called 'investment' back if we had us a flop? And Marco was up to his monocle in some kind of problems, probably too evil to even think about. Somewhere betwixt alla this was Chesley Warwick and his ilks, rumored to be nee-farious and maybe even so to be permanently attached to my own daughter.

So I'd go back and forth, from one to the other, pushing and pulling and in a general state of tug-o-war with myownself. And there wasn't one damn soul in that whole town that I could get a unbiased opinion from or, for that matter, who'd even set and listen to my problem.

Elsie moved back in with her momma at the ladies place and, I gotta be honest, I was just as glad. You see, I was getting a little weary of her tears and plots and all. It was just too painful watching her and Dr. Sailing Strong decide whether it was hate or love, war or peace.

So then comes Thursday, the day of the big showing. And I think I'm beginning to get a rash from all my galley-west fretting back and forth. But ol' Elsie and E.M., they was all a-twitter and looking forward to their dazzling screen debuts. They spent the day at a place where ladies get all gussied up, blissful as hell and not knowing the chalk from the cheese.

Chick'n'Tad both took baths, and me? well, I did what any normal cow waddie would do in the midst of a curious quagmire: I had me two fingers of rye and set thinking. E.M. had sent over this tuxedo for me to dress up in and, sweartagod, I hate those things. Oh, sure I'd been pressed into wearing fair winds before, but that didn't mean I liked it much. But looking at myself in the mirror, I guess I cut a pretty good figure, for someone my age. Chick'n'Tad got all dressed up too. Sailing looked like a ad for a tuxedo seller. We all looked too good for a streetcar, so I ordered a taxi cab and we drove on over to pick up Elsie and E.M.

Well, E.M. always cleaned up real good, and she looked just beautiful in all her new fur-trimmed get-up, which she said was a Lady Duff Gordon, whatever that was. Well, I sure would know when the bill arrived. Her dress had what she called a hobble-skirt, and even though hobbles was outlawed on the Royal Bar-L, I allowed 'em in E.M.'s case. Elsie looked wonderful too, but she almost always did, incept the makeup didn't cover up her black eye too well. But I noticed the black roots on her shingled hair had disappeared and I knew I'd be getting the bill for that too. She wore this beaded thing acrost her forehead, which reminded me of a headstall on a bridle, but she was quick to tell me it was a Castle Band and don't touch it onaccounta it falls down on her nose real easy.

I noticed Sailing and Elsie didn't have too much to say to each other, but they was stealing glances when one thought the other wasn't looking.

So there we was, us five Leckners and Sailing Strong, looking about as highenmighty as we ever did. But even though our get-ups was a fine distraction, I was still working things around the front-forty of my mind. I'd tossed

Bill's movie case up with the driver, and I was thinking all the while, which one? Marco's or Bill's?

We was told to get to the Oriental Gardens early so's we could greet the viewers as they came in, I guess onaccounta we was all new talents and nobody was gonna line up early to see folks they'd never hearda make a entrance.

I, of course, found producer-reasons to stay outa view; I just thought and watched.

Well, don't for a minute think ol' Marco and Armando left out a single detail to that evening: The marquee warned:

BIRTH OF A BADMAN
Bringing To The World
A Cluster of Shining New Stars!

Well, E.M. and Elsie took that in and gushed all over each other. Sailing looked at me and I had to shrug my shoulders. Hell, I had a good hour before I had to make my move. No use rushing things.

Marco also rented two searchlights, and of course I thought, Ohh great, now the Director Upstairs would know exactly where Royal was and would be watching his every move.

And Marco had hired some girls to gypsy-dance 'round the outside of the theater, and then they was to become the ones that leads people to their seats. I hoped none of 'em was gonna get knocked down as people stampeded outa the theater.

I sunk deeper and deeper into my despair, watching all our movie crew. A more excited buncha eccentrics I never saw. At first, Sailing didn't leave my side and he was commencing to pace until I told him, dang it! would he just set down! He'd know when I was making my move.

People kept streaming in and they was all taking this here showing right serious. They all seemed to know each other, and Marco and Armando was at their theatrical best, welcoming folks like they knew who they was.

Then, when the whole theater is practically filled with witnesses, Marco stands on the stage, looks around, and then claps his hands for silence. He points (and someone with a spotlight follows his point) and we alla us is treated to Chesley Warwick walking down the aisle. Hell, even *my* heart skipped a beat, he looked so damn perfect in that spotlight. I read about shoe lifts in catalogs and such, and I was now witnessing 'em in action. Chesley was maybe alla 5 foot 6 that night, but he was strutting 6 foot 4. He was wearing a tuxedo that put the resta us to shame, and he had his hair all macassared back and shiny, and he had this white silk scarf 'round his neck. Folks clapped his arrival, and even if they didn't know who he was, sure as shootin' they clapped his appearance.

He waves a kiss toward Elsie and damn near every woman close by threw him one back. I looked over to Sailing a coupla rows away and watched. Funny thing, I thought he'd gotten taller too.

Chesley takes a seat next to Elsie, then looks 'round to see who's maybe looking back. Then I see him go all concerned, like maybe he'd spotted a few critics. He then rises and walks hisself backstage, leaving my family there seated alone all by theirownselfs to suffer the slings and arrows of what was to come.

I slunk further and further away . . . not wanting any of my Bill Hart-ness to spread around.

In fact, Bill was the only one I was wanting to see. So there I was, hiding behind some curtains, looking like a opera singer with stage fright about to be cattle-prodded onto stage.

Finally, from behind me a hand taps my shoulder and there he stood, Bill, dressed just like me. We scorned each other's taste, then shook hands.

"I'm laying real low, Bill. No use showing the whole world what we look like."

"I appreciate that, Royal. I owe you one. So, tonight's the big night. Say, who are all these jokers?" he asks me.

I looked 'round at all the folks and said, "Don't you know? Ain't they actors, directors and such?"

"Don't recognize any of them," he said, smiling some. Then he adds, "Although it looks like your Magellan has papered the house and hired some lookalikes."

"Lookalikes?" asks me.

"Yup. Right out of the bullpen," says Bill.

"Bullpen?" asks me.

"The bushwa," says Bill.

Hell, it was getting worse. "*Bush*wa?"

"You know, bourgeois," says Bill, funning me some.

I knew what a bourgeois was, so I looked out over the crowd and nodded whilst I said, "Oh, Frenchmen."

So Bill laughs hearty, no doubt remembering where my turnip truck came from. He thunked my back and clarified, "Off-herd, grub-line riders!"

Now *that* made some sense and so I said, and wisely, I thought, "Oh, extras!"

Then I spotted my own two bushwas, Elsie and E.M., at the pinnacle of their careers, a-glowing and all fulla life. How'd they get to be so gracious, I was wondering.

Then Bill mentioned he'd be interested to see which movie was gonna play that night, and I muttered back, "So will I." I was hanging tight onto the Inceville version.

Before taking his seat he wisht me luck and shook my hand, and we looked at each other. I couldn't help but grinning whilst we adjusted each other's ties.

I looked up at the projection room. Then I looked down at my family, all the crew: Marco, Sailing, even Armando. The theater was overflowing with one-upsmanships and I knew I had to decide. But you know, it wasn't till all them great dames from the Curtain Call Home came sashaying in did I make my decision. They was greeted by many who musta known them from their theatrical hey days. They bowed, waved their hands, and generally spread their old-time elegance upon everyone. Especially Helena, looking like she had one more ship to launch in her yet.

Hell, thinks me, we alla us get old eventually and we alla us want a chance to keep on showing to others we still got what it takes. That did it! Royal was gonna do the handsome thing!

So I spring upstairs, four at a time, clutching the good film under my arm, tuxedo tails a-flapping in the breeze. I burst into the room, scaring the projection man half outa his wits. "Here," says me, "you got the wrong film set up. String this one in."

The projection man says I'm not supposed to be there, but I didn't listen and started to undo the film he was ready to show. Downstairs on the stage, Marco was making his pre-film speech to the crowd and I had no time to discuss rules with the projector man.

"Stop that! You can't do that!"

Well, you know how much I hate admitting it, but I pulled that man clear offa his feet, held him to my nose, and said, "Do you know who I am?"

"Yes, you're William S. Hart, but you're still not supposed to be in here! I'll have to call. . ."

I unbuttoned my tuxedo coat so the man could plainly see ol' Smitty and Wes tucked into my encumber-bun. But still he didn't budge. In a lick of desperation then, I pulled out a fifty-dollar bill from my pants and handed it to him, and you shoulda seen how fast that man changed the film.

I set in the projector room looking down on the whole scene below. Marco was introducing the resta the cast: I saw Elsie rise and take her bow, throwing kisses to the crowd. Then came E.M., who also rose. Some man, a stranger to my eyes, setting next to her seized her hand and kissed it passionately. My life scorched past my mind, like they say happens when you're drowning . . . my ranch, my mode'o' life, my happy home, my E.M., my everything. Life as I knew it was never gonna be the same if that good movie showed. I'd sooner walk through hell on a hat fulla water than hurt my kin intentional, but a man's gotta preserve his mode'o'life.

So that did it! To hell with old-lady last-chances, vanities, and careers, and to hell with my twenty thousand clams! I turned and glared at the projector man.

"Now what?" he asked.

"Switch 'em back!" I commands.

"Look, I've seen this turkey," he says of the first one. "Whatever this one is, go with it."

I onct again starting to unwind the film. This time, he holds out his palm. I greased it and he re-switched the films in nothing flat, but grumbling that no one knew nothing in Hollywood.

That was it. I'd made the right decision. I'd ruin everyone's movie careers but I knew I was saving their lifes. Proud I'd done the right thing, I headed for the door.

"You sure?" the projector man asked me just as I was opening the door.

I turned and looked at him and said, "Reckon so."

I left and then set on the back stairs to wait for the horror to unravel itself and the chips to fall.

Setting on the stairs, I listened to Marco wind up his spiel. He then said the dancing usherettes was gonna do us a warm-up dance to get us all in the mood of the movie, and the organ began to play.

Well, the rug on the stairs was tacked down good but it was still pulled out from under me. For you see, a few moments later, on the landing below, I heard some men talking. I looked 'round the corner and saw Marco up against the wall, being propped there by the threat of two men, one holding a gun.

"Ju have some 'splaining to do, Mahellan!" says one.

"We want our money back," continues the other. "The merchandise was no good. Warwick said ju were the brains behind this operation and ju would make good on the whole deel."

"Gentlemen, I have no idea what you're talking about. Chesley Warwick, he's the money manager. He arranges the investments, I just sign the papers. I swear . . . he made all the arrangements." Then his face goes awry and he asks, "What merchandise? I make movies, not merchandise. See? You have the wrong man. I thought you boys were . . . investors."

"Some people they think of us as that," says the first.

"Well, whatever money you've put into my picture, you'll get it back with interest, I swear." Marco indicates the movie exposing itself on the other side of the hall curtain. "Just wait until my movie is over. You'll see what a smash it'll be. Just wait for the reviews," Marco added, the sweat glistning offa his forehead. "Just look at all those names out there! Do you think they'd all come to a movie that wasn't going to be a hit? Why, there's Mary Pickford, you can tell by her hair. And there's D.W. Griffith, that hat is famous, and oh, look, there's Charlie. Everyone knows Chaplin." I looked toward his point and saw the lookalikes.

"All right, Mahellan, never mind about all the beeg names. Tell you what we're gonna do: we will sit through your movie, then you and your Warwick friend better make good on that shipment or hand the whole ten thousand back."

"Oh," said Marco, like maybe he was trying to charm the badsters, "then you're film *distributors.* Oh, that's better. Now I understand."

Then the man with the gun turned to the other and said, "He must be telling the truth, Ric. No one is *this* loco."

"No," Marco agreed, now looking panicked.

They crunched Marco up tighter on the wall and said, "Ju better pray that movie of jours is a—what is they call it?"

"El smasho," the other offered him.

"El smasho," he laughed, sorta evil-like. Then he added, "Jour signature on a lot of papers means ju owe us a lot of money, Mahellan. And the people we deal with do not really care where it comes from."

"The money," finished the other, "or the merchandise."

And they left him in a crumpled heapa confusion.

Cripes, now things was getting serious! I bolt back up the stairs with the good film and burst open the door. The projector man was looking out his window, and when he saw me he gave me a sad look, a thumbs down, and asked, "Where've you been? We're fifteen minutes into this fiasco and boy did *you* goof, Mr. Hart! Can't say I didn't warn you."

I looked down at the sight below: Marco's masterpiece had mouths wide open. Already seats was beginning to empty on the great cinematic tragedy.

And I'd come this close to preventing it.

I joined the projector man at the viewing window and together we looked down on the screen. We watched, silent. Believe it or not, what I saw was even *worse*'n those bits'n'jagged edges I'd already witnessed. Marco had done it. He really overcooked this turkey.

Naturally, all I could do was pull the plug on the whole thing. Whilst I switched off the electricity, I recollected how I felt having to put down a two-headed, three-legged calf back in '97. I always felt bad about that, thinking, hell, the critter might learn to walk on three posts.

The projector man came over to me, put his hand on my shoulder, and said I'd done the right thing.

And the theater went dark.

four

I, of course, was not surprised to see mosta the audience was gone. Only the cast and crew, a few polite, paid bushwas (three of 'em asleep), and Bill Hart was there when we flicked the lights back on. But I was surprised to see that Marco and Armando was also nowhere to be seen. Either was Warwick.

I ran into the lobby, not caring who saw me now. Those who'd helped put such a monster into the can was all screaming, swearing, and grabbing for my attention. I worked my way over to Bill and took him by the arm. "Bill, you got a car here?"

"Yes, but too bad you didn't use. . ."

"Not now, Bill. Marco's sloped off and he's got a coupla Mexican roughnecks after him," I said quietly, trying not to alarm anyone around me.

Sailing found me, and when his eyes land on Bill his face goes first blank, then astonished. "It's you," he says, forgetting all about our assorted plights. "It's really William S. Hart." He plunged his hand into Bill's and shakes it like he was priming a old, wore-out hand pump.

I gave a quick introduction, then E.M. finds me and says, "Wait till I get my hands on that no-good, chiseling bascadero! Making me look like a saloon floozie! How dare he!" Hell, she was madder'n a meat axe!

"But you was *supposed* to be a saloon floozie," I reminded her outa the corner of my mouth. But E.M. was staring face to face with Bill Hart.

"Holy cow, you really *do* look alike," she said, grabbing his hand just like Sailing'd done. "How do you do, Mr. Hart, I'm. . ."

"Later, E.M. Marco's made off and I'm following him. You and Elsie go back. . ." And I stopped to look around. "Where's Elsie?" I asked. Everyone looked around, especially Sailing.

E.M. said, "Why, I don't know. Chesley came and got her after the movie started."

Me and Sailing found the same conclusion at the same time. Bill was way aheada us. He says to hang tight whilst he got his automobile.

"You take the boys and go back to your place," I ordered toward E.M. "You do know where the *boys* are, don't you?" She pointed to a taxicab and I recognized their two heads jumping up and down in the front seat. "Okay, then get outa our way, E.M." I shoulda knew better.

"You with us, Sailing?" I asked, and all he said was can Dan Patch run? Which he sure as hell could, and so could we.

We three piled into Bill's car. I looked behind just in time to see E.M. pull the taxi driver outa his cab, followed by a toss of money. Then after her comes Helena Troy and foura her old-lady comrades from the Curtain Call Home. (Don't worry, they had them a driver.) I turned my head 'round and warned alla 'em to head on home, but no matter how much I yelled they proceeded to weave right along with us through all the traffic.

I told Bill where the Royalscope studio was, thinking maybe Marco would go there, for I knew first-hand he had a wall safe.

Bill floors it and mumbles, "And me without a film crew!"

Ol' Bill knew his clutch from his brakes, I'll tell you that. He shunpiked that car of his in and outa more short cuts than I ever imagined coulda been in that town. In no time flat we'd arrived at Royalscope and had almost succeeded in losing the two cars a-following us.

I leapt outa the car and found not only was the front door wide open, so was the wall safe in Marco's office. Bill honked out front and I ran back out.

All our guesses was correct so far, for there in the road aheada us was Marco and Armando's car speeding away, followed by the two desperados. Setting in the back seat, with his white silk scarf a-flapping in the breeze, was Chesley, and next to him who could mistake Elsie's fuzzed-out hair?

So now we made us a fine parade, only we was going mighty fast, faster'n this ol' hand had ever gone in a automobile before. None of us stopped for nothing, and every onct in a while I'd look back at E.M. in the car behind us and warn her to go back! Alota good that did. She just agitated the communicator at me, and I doubt that horn was ever gonna be the same.

We was heading north, like toward Santa Monica. I recognized the road all right. Bill pushed ahead, and when I looked at him he was grinning like the devil. I braced myself with my leg and held onto the granny handle. Sailing in the back seat was trying to sign language with E.M. in the car behind, but you gotta figure that was pretty hopeless.

"I'll bet he's heading into the hills," Bill shouted over to me, pointing to the cars ahead. "But we'll get him if he doesn't know where he's going. Pretty soon the road runs out."

That was good to know. I set back and wondered why Marco was taking flight. If he had the money, then why didn't he just give it to them two highbinders and call it a lesson? What the hell was those slicks up to? And Chesley? Most troubling was, did my Elsie go on her own accord or was it gonna be one of those kidnapping affairs?

Now, you may wonder why my face ain't going all red like it usually does when I'm reliving a riling situation. Fact is, getting one of my womenfolk picked up and placed elsewhere ain't nothing new to ol' Royal. I've spent me some time on the delivery end of a ransom note. And most times, any man who has the spuzz to take off with any Leckner-associated female oughta number one, have thought twice, and number two, be prepared for quite a ruckus. And I never onct had to pay to get anyone back, either. I even made a little profit on one such occasion, I recollect. Anyhow, seeing ol' Elsie's chiffon swosh away right infronta me didn't scare me none. Sailing in the back seat, though, was looking right concerned, and I had to tell him more'n onct to let me to the talking.

I reckon we coulda caught 'em, had it not been for us having to wait for a train. Sweartagod, the two cars slipped by that train with maybe a coata paint to spare, and Bill was barely able to stop in time. E.M.'s car wasn't so lucky, and she dang near bumped us into the train. The little ol' ladies screeched and bumped E.M. in turn. Nowadays, we call it a chain-reaction event, but then I just called it lucky.

By now, darkning was coming all 'round us and Bill's headlights didn't do much good to light the road ahead. Like he'd foretold, the road ran out some ten miles later, became dirt and then just a trail. By the time we caught up to 'em, the two cars we was chasing was setting next to the trail, empty of course.

We got out and examined the situation.

"Too dark to track 'em now," Bill said.

"And I ain't exactly fit up to do any tracking," I allowed, noticing my encumber-bun was collapsed under the weight of my gun.

"Look, Inceville is just over that hill. My idea is we go back around, drive up there, and pack some horses. We'll ride back over that direction and pick up their trail at first light."

Now he was talking.

"I'm going, too," Sailing said, his hands on his hips.

Bill and I looked at each other, thinking the same thing.

"You ever been on a horse?"

"Does polo count?" he asked back. Bill and I looked at each other and allowed as how that qualified. Polo? Hell, he could probably outride botha us seasoned cowpokes and swing a mallet all at the same time.

Just as we was turning the car 'round, in follows the two others, a-jogging their contents with the bumpiness of the road.

"E.M.!" I hollered. "You take yourself right on back, you hear?"

But she's outa the car and running toward me, her Lady Duff hobble skirt not working worth a damn. The boys piled out with her.

"Royal, I demand to know what you're going to do!" she said, hands on hips and looking more'n'more like the E.M. of the Range and not the Rosa of the Screen.

"They got Elsie?" Chick asked.

"How much these boys askin'?" Tad followed.

"Now, E.M., this here's man's work. . ." and I regretted it soon as I said it. "I mean. . ."

"I know what you mean," E.M. finished for me. "You're afraid of what I'll do if I get my hands on those low-down sonsa. . ."

"Now, E.M., not infronta the boys. Why don't you and the ladies all circle on back? Take the boys to your place and wait it out."

"Ah, Pa, that's a *ladies* house," Tad growls. But Chick smiled in a way I don't recollect seeing before. He advised Tad to slap shut, and I knew we'd be ordering pimple cream before too long.

E.M. kissed me good luck and whispered in my ear, "Remember that time in Wichita?"

Well, I sure as hell did, and I said, "E.M., we promised we wasn't gonna ever bring that up again."

"Well I am, and I just want you to do to Marco Magellan what I did to. . ."

"Shhshh, E.M.," says me, looking around. "That one's still on the books."

She smiled up at me, and I could tell I had her carte blanche to handle things anyway I saw fit.

I smiled back at her and asked if I'd ever let her down before. She smiled back 'no.' She also confessed she had some cash hidden under her bed, in case we was gonna hafta pay for Elsie's return this time. I said that was a comfort, onaccounta she was now driving a stolen car and one with a crumpled front to boot, and with her criminal record maybe she oughta make good on that first. E.M. called for me to be careful and, just this onct, don't bother thinking before shooting. She got in the hijacked taxi and turned it 'round. The old ladies' car followed suit, but not without some 'go get 'ems' from the girls. They all left and we got on with our plan.

Onct we got up to Inceville, Bill offered us some clothes, and we packed all we thought we'd need for the next coupla days, should we find ourselfs in a wait-'em-out situation. We put up late that night, but who could sleep anyhow?

It'd been a long time since I'd stalked me a trail. But I knew how, you can guara-damn-tee that. What jigswiggered the hell outa me was, ol' Bill Hart knew how to stalk him one too.

five

'Course there's lots I didn't know in those days, even though I probably thought I knew just about everything. After all, I was damn near forty and there I was heading out with a cowboy-actor on one side, a Ph.D.-polo player on the other side, trying to chase us down a coupla slick ones who was theirselfs being chased by a coupla hard cases, and somewheres betwixt 'em a daughter in chiffon, a Chesley Warwick, and the memory of Tad's empty arsenal.

Huh? Oh, all right, forty-five.

Well, it might seem like cheating to you, but we chugged the horses along in a truck trailer for the first leg of the journey, I'd say about ten miles or so. But hell, it was all uphill and still dark, and trucking it put us pretty far into the schedule. When the trail got too rough for the truck, we pulled over and saddled up.

The sun was not yet blessing our mission, and I can still feel the damp of the morning in my bones. I looked down the road we'd just come up and noticed two more sets of headlights a-winding their ways upwards.

"You call the police?" I asked Bill, pointing down the side hill.

He didn't even look down, but kept on cinching the saddle on Fritz. "Nope," says he. "just a few of the boys, in case we get into trouble."

"I'd hate to think of 'em spoiling our little surprise," I said, plopping some horse luggage fulla provisions over the back of my horse.

"I told them we'd fire for help if we need it. Don't worry, Roy," Bill continues, giving me that same smile of confidence I'd seen in his movies when he was sure he was finally doing right by some pure young thing. "No one's going to wreck our fun."

I nodded like I knew just what I was gonna do up there in those hills I knew nothing about.

Bill brought out three scabbards from the truck and handed me one. I took it, strapped it to my saddle, then said, pulling out ol' Smitty and Wes from my saddlebag, "Hope you don't mind if I hold up my paunch some." I strapped my unconverted friends on. They felt mighty equalizing. Fact is, I felt like I was a kid again. I knew what E.M. would say if she coulda seen me then: "Shoot Marco, not your foot!"

Sailing took his rifle, inspected the chamber, and looked down the barrel, expert-like. He looked at me, tossed that roan hair outa his eye, and winked. "Rifle Team," he explained, which woulda been my guess.

Bill took the lead and we rode in silence till the sun was bringing some pinkning to the Eastern sky. We took a moment high up and looked out over the darkning that musta been the Pacific Ocean. Then bang! comes the dawn.

If someone had picked that moment to shoot me dead, then I reckoned my last view would be pretty close to paradise itsownself. Lord, what a view! The pink of the new day was meeting up with the emerald green of the ocean below. I thought maybe we could see all the way to Frisco from there.

We rode some more and before long we was on a hill looking down on where we'd been the night before. The two cars was still parked there, so we knew they'd continued on foot up into the hills. Now I just didn't see where Marco and Armando was built for much hill climbing; then again, even though I'd only glimpsed 'em, the two hoods didn't look like they was track stars either. And then there was Elsie. Near as I recollected, she hadn't worn her hiking boots under her pale yeller chiffon. Chesley? Who cared!

"Where do those trails all lead?" I asked Bill as our horses picked their ways downward.

"Hunting cabins mostly. This is Los Angeles's back yard, don't forget. People come here to camp, hunt, fish, just be in the wilderness. My guess is they've got a hide-out up there and will just sit until the heat wears off. Or until we get a ransom note."

"Or a I.O.U.," I mumbled down to my horse.

We rode some more down, then we crost trails and started to follow theirs. Bill looked down and I did too. Reading the footprints was easy as aging. We didn't even have to get each other's opinion about it.

The woods was beginning to get deeper, but the trail was good, worn and wide. Like Bill said, some major recreating went on in these parts real regular.

I came up next to Bill and asked, "You learn trail signing when you was a farm boy?"

"From the Sioux Indians. Learned to speak their language, too."

"No kidding? You speak Sioux?"

He smiled me good and added, "I speak Shakespeare, too."

I could tell he was smiling on carefree days of youth. You know that look. We alla us get it from time to time when we gets a reminder of something past by.

"I spent half my life in New York in the legitimate theater."

I looked at him setting his pony, which he fit about as good as I did on my chestnut back home. I said, "Do tell? You're quite a conglomeration, you know that, Bill?"

He looked over to me and laughed. Then he said, "I doubt my conglomeration could beat yours, Royal. After all, I've never been married, nor have I had children."

Well, that made me laugh too. I said, "Handsome eagle like you musta had plenty of offers."

Then his smile faded some and he sorta sad-like allowed as how his life had been too cluttered. But then Bill started fidgeting with the horn of his saddle and said, "I'd trade every good review, every autograph, every bank account for two sons like your Chick'n'Tad."

"How many bank accounts?" I asked, knowing when to turn a mood. He laughed and I continued, "Fact is, Bill, I just don't think you can afford the likes of Chick'n'Tad. If you think that bustin' bronc episode was a rocker, you oughta hear some of my Chick'n'Tad stories. Scary part is, they're only ten and eight. Maybe we could work out a exchange program or something."

We laughed, then we silenced for a while. I knew what Bill was saying, even though it was in a joke. We alla us choose our trails and there ain't no going back. Best we can do is enjoy the scenery and laugh at every chance.

The trail we was on just then was getting less hilly, and I reckoned we was gonna change scenery soon. The trees was thinning out and we was heading for some meadowlands. Bill suggested we canter through the meadow, saying Fritz'd been fighting him for some real exercise. I looked back at Sailing and asked if he had enough glue on his pants to stick through some faster paces. He said he was game and I told Bill okay, but for a different reason. Meandering through a meadow means a clear shot at a slow-moving target and I never did enjoy the feeling of some yap spying on me from betwixt crosshairs. So we let the horses have their heads.

Now, let me tell you something 'bout horses and what they're generally thinking when they're let go side by side. Each one of 'em thinks not only is he faster, but he's a damn sight smarter than the other. I've never seen it fail. Now, two horses let go is a race, and three is a stampede. So neither Bill nor me was surprised when we found ourselfs hitting the flat in a neck'n'neck'n'neck race. Being two old cowpokes, me and Bill fell right natural-like into the spirit of the competition. And I have to admit, I forgot all about Sailing, who soon was swallering our dust. Bill and me was running so close we coulda swapped saddles. My horse had longer legs than Fritz, but Bill had the advantage of worshiping his horse and vice versa, whereas my mount and me was practically strangers.

The meadow flew by faster than a canter, for we was damn near in a out-and-out dead run, horse-n-horse together . . . riding like we was packing the mail through hostile territory. A fine buncha trackers we was, I remember thinking.

Bill and I was almost to the other side of the meadow and I'd all but forgot about ol' Sailing, trying to earn his name. By the time we heard him and looked around, he was low and flat as a jockey on his horse's neck and he overtook us by a whisker. I always sorta felt bad ol' Fritz didn't win that one. Anyway, Fritz was a real gentleman about losing, and Sailing was a real gentleman about beating his elders.

We let our horses catch their breaths and we shook hands all 'round on a good race.

"Racing horses is a capital offense on my Royal Bar-L," I said, catching some breath myownself.

"Yeah, we don't allow it at Inceville, either," Bill agreed. We all promised to keep it our secret, horses included. Then we cooled the boys down and struck up the track onct again.

Outa the silence, Bill starts to snigger. Pretty soon he's out and out doubled over. When he finally got control of hisself, he began to talk. "People ask why I love horses so much," he said. "I usually just dodge the question because I don't think very many could ever understand."

"Loving horses is a personal thing, Bill," I returned, patting my horse's neck.

"Ever read *Ben Hur?*" he asked us, right outa nowhere. 'Course, I think he's just doing some dodging.

"Sure. Ain't everyone?" said me, and Sailing said he'd even taught it in one of his classes.

"Well, did you know it was a Broadway hit for years?"

I told him I even did hear that onct. Though sweartagod, how they'd ever put up that sea battle and that chariot race on a stage I could never figure.

"Well, I played Messala for years in that show."

I look over to him, recollected what a villain that Messala was, and I said, "Say it ain't so, Bill. Not you."

"Yes, me. For I don't know how many hundreds of nights. Mean and wicked to the core and dying quite nicely each night because of it, I'll have you know."

I thought that was interesting, but waited for him to tell me why he found that so damn funny up here in the middle of nowhere. Then, from atopt his horse, he orates like the fine actor he was, and with his words he held me and Sailing in a transport of delight. What a voice. Anyway, this is what he told us:

"Ben Hur's four chariot horses were all bays . . . about as beautiful a team as you could imagine. My team, Messala's team, was two whites and two blacks, almost symbolic of the good and evil racing in that chariot race. Two white and two blacks . . . Rosie and Topsy, Tom and Jerry. I'll never forget them.

"The stage was fitted up with a treadmill, which ran its entire length. Each night Ben Hur and Messala would race their chariots along that stage and the horses would run, faster than lightning, but not really going anywhere because of the treadmill. The boys off stage knew just when to let Ben Hur's bays pull ahead, and no matter how much heart Messala's team put into it, they always lost. Night after night, week after week, for nearly four hundred performances, they lost the race.

"'Course a horse doesn't know much about theatrical plots and mechanics. I fully believe my team knew they could, and would, someday, beat the bays.

"We were someplace in Maine, touring the show. We'd been everywhere with it, but no matter where we were the race was always won by the bays. That night, as fate or perhaps as the God of Horses would have it, something failed in the treadmill mechanics and the section that had always allowed the bay team to pull ahead and win didn't work. There we were, our chariots neck and neck, hooves pounding, sweat flying, nostrils pulling in life for one last, wonderful sprint ahead.

"I pulled back, I screamed, I begged, but my team couldn't, wouldn't hear me above the roar of the audience. I was helpless. There was nothing in heaven or earth or in those machines that was going to stop my team of black and whites. That night, with no apologies to anyone, the plot of *Ben Hur* altered slightly. Messala had won the race! For one night, Rosie and Topsy, Tom and Jerry were the victors. You know, I don't even remember how we covered the mistake. All I remember was standing offstage with my steaming horses, hugging them while the audience damn near screamed the roof off. Hell, plot be damned! It was the best damn horse race of all time!"

He took a pause, and I knew he was back in that theater somewhere in Maine. Then he added, "It's funny. I always knew my team could beat the bays. And by God my team knew it, too."

I was all grins, three by nine. And Bill added, "And that's why I love horses the way I do. I don't tell that story to very many people. It's too close to my heart."

All I could do was agree. I had me plenty of horse stories, but I couldn'ta matched that ring-tailed snorter.

Sailing, who was riding within our earshot, pulled up and waited for Bill to catch up with him. He leant over and said, "Sir, you really ought to write that down. That story is poetry. Sheer poetry."

Bill looked genuinely flattered, which, like maybe you know, is a real feat for some artists. "Well, maybe I will someday."

"I'd be happy to help you in any way I could," Sailing says.

"I hafta agree, Bill. That's the. . ." But I didn't finish, for somewhere ahead of us a shot rang out.

We was closing in on our villains.

six

The shots was coming from a clearing ahead. We dismounted, tied our horses off, and crept toward the sound. 'Course I expected to see maybe a old miner's cabin, a shacka some sorts or, hell, maybe even a cave. But what I saw was a big log lodge sticking on the side hill, taking in a view of paradise.

"How'd that get up here?" I asked Bill, as we crouched down low in some brush.

He pointed to a dirt road from the opposite direction and said, "I have a feeling Marco Magellan knew perfectly well where he was going last night. You don't just stumble onto a place like this in the middle of nowhere."

"Well, why didn't they just drive up here?" I asked, pointing to the road.

"That comes from a different direction." Then he seemed to get his bearings as he talked. "Say, I know whose place this is. This is Griffith's hunting lodge. Sure, I didn't recognize it from the back."

"D.W. Griffith?" Sailing asked, setting up higher'n he oughta when there was gunfire.

I pulled him back down and asked Bill, "How'd you suppose ol' Marco knew about this place?"

Bill shrugged his shoulders, and then another shot rang out. It came from the barn acrost from the lodge and it musta struck a window, for we heard glass a-shattering. I remember Bill saying that if anyone had the gall to bleed on D.W.'s oriental carpets, better do it to death or else they'd be hung at dawn, no witnesses. That sounded a little callous to me. But I kept my quiet, crept forward some, and unhooked my side arm from its holster.

Slowly we crept 'round so's we could get a better viewa the action. The fronta the lodge was fulla bullet holes, but other'n that it just looked like alota pot-shotting, and not much else, had gone on.

Then one of the bruisers shouts out with, "Hey, Mahellan! We have some men coming up to help pry you out of there!"

I turned to Bill and said, "Say, Bill, that reminds me. Those boysa yours gonna show up to help *us* out some?"

He looked from whenct we'd come and said, vague-like, "Maybe."

Then Marco hollers out from the lodge, "It's that Chesley Warwick you need to be talking to!"

'Course Marco didn't know Chesley was right there on the premises. 'Course we didn't know if Chesley was holding a gun or had one held on him.

I looked at Bill and he looked back at me. I don't think either of us had a plan. Sailing came up from behind and asked, "What about Elsie and Warwick? Which side are they on?"

Well now, that was a good question. It was one I thought I'd just flash a white hankie long enough to stand up and ask the crowd. But it was answered before I asked anything. For from the car stable between the barn and the house comes a odd sound, one that I got to know all too well whilst city-dwelling. It came again, and you know what it was? One of them hi-UUUUU-ga horns offa a automobile a-tootning.

I turned to Sailing and said, "Elsie's in the garage. She could never onct pass by one of them tooter horns and not give it a few squeezes." I could tell he was gonna stand up and shout out her name, but I pulled him back down in time.

Bill flashed me his ivory and he says, "Tell you what, let's get your daughter out safe, then start some fireworks."

"Tell you a better what," I says back to Bill. "Let's let 'em know we're here. See if we can get 'em all out in the open and talking." Royal the diplomat.

"Well, I didn't come up here to air my vocabulary," Bill said. "But go ahead. It's your party."

"What do you think, Sailing?" I ask. "Sailing?" I turn 'round and he's vanished. I look at Bill and he looks at me. "Now where do you suppose that kid went?"

Bill had no idea, but looked 'round, nervous-like.

Then we see the doors of the garage crash open, and out comes a real nice white Stutz Bearcat going like hell through the clearing. We damn near had to run for additional cover, for the car swept right past our bushes and then came to a stop, well, actually, came to a crash on the corner of the lodge. Up pops a head and it's Elsie's, her Castle Band a-draped acrost her nose. Then, slowly, in the back seat, up pops Sailing's head. Everyone, including the absconders, was taken by surprise.

Bill saw the crushed front end and said, "Oh my God! Not Jesse Laskey's Bearcat!" And he shook his head, tragic-like.

Sailing pulled Elsie outa the car and swooshed her along to us.

The first thing my daughter says to me, fresh outa her escape is, "It wasn't my fault, Daddy. I couldn't see where I was going." And she adds, "This damn Castle Band!" And she rips it offa her face and tosses it to the ground. Kids and excuses, all the same. Anyhow, I gave her a huga welcome back safe and asked where Chesley was.

"Ooooh, that Chesley Warwick! Do you believe he had the nerve to pull a gun on me? Well, I changed his mind about that," she growled, handing me the gun. "I should of given him the mitten weeks ago!"

"You didn't shoot him, did you?" asked me, swallering a little uneasy.

"Oh no, but I had my chance. Sailing probably saved that polecat's life. When he broke into the garage, Chesley took off into the woods. I was gonna shoot, Daddy, but then I remembered what you always told us about back-shooting. That Chesley Warwick's a coward to boot! Wouldn't even face me!"

"Why was he taking you along with them?" I asked, ducking under more gun fire from the barn to the house. "Was you being kidnapped?"

"Daddy, after careful reconsideration I don't think that Chesley is really an actor at all. He and those other two in the barn—yee Gawds, I think they were *foreigners* to boot—

were talking about Mexico and the revolt down there and Paco Somebody and empty guns. Ugh," she says, taking inventory of her get-up, "the last thing I want anything to do with is *politics.*" She looked down, frowned, and said, "Oh damn, I ran my hose."

Bill gives me a exasperated look and said something to the effect that he had to be to work by next Tuesday, so maybe we oughta settle some hashes. So he calls out, voice fulla authority, "All right, we got the place surrounded! Everybody throw your guns out!"

Not that we was expecting 'em to, but it was a powerful announcement, one that, I have noticed, has been used in alota good versus evil films ever since. Anyhow, we was then plastered with gunfire from both the lodge and the barn.

Bill and me ducked for deeper cover and then looked at each other. Bill says, "Well, so much for that. What now?"

It was then I got me another idea. I filled Bill in and he looked a little like 'oh what the hell, why not?' So Bill and me quietly began to make our way toward the barn. Now, in a situation like that, you always look behind you, just to cover your rear, but I gotta tell you, although I didn't see nothing, I sure did get the feeling we was being followed. And I don't mean by Sailing or Elsie or our horses, either. But since I didn't see or smell nothing, I just tried to keep my eyes on the mission ahead.

Onct we get to the back of the barn, we put my plan into action. Bill crept through the paddock and then held his gun infronta him whilst he slowly pushed aside the door to a horse stall. Meanwhilst I went 'round the side of the barn and stuck real close to the shingles, awaiting for Bill to make his move.

When I heard him call out, "Drop 'em!" I whipped 'round the front and held my gun out. It worked just the way I planned. For there was Bill Hart coming at 'em from behind and there was Bill Hart coming at 'em from the front. The toughs did their double-takes like they'd rehearsed 'em.

I aimed my gun at 'em and said, evil-like, "Don't even break wind."

Slowly they dropped their guns, and Bill, keeping his eye and his gun on 'em, picked up their pieces. Both the mugs was real shocked as they raised their hands.

Then one said to me, "So, the great Beel Hart to the rescue."

Then the other thug says, pointing to Bill, "No, *theese* eez Beel Hart."

Then Bill introduced me to Juan Ortega (better known as El Machete) and Ricardo Diaz (better known as El Diablo) whilst we tied up them two jelly beans. When our thugs was hogtied, Bill asked 'em what was going on. The machete one says something about the fifth amendment and Bill reminds him he ain't even an Americano and he could tell that to the judge, who sure as hell wasn't gonna be no Mexican.

Then Bill and me looked cautious-like toward the lodge, which'd been pretty silent of late. So Bill did what I thought was a odd thing. He steps out into the clearing and looks from whenct we'd come. He raised his hand, like as to signal someone. When he came back in, I said, "You outa your mind? Marco coulda picked you off cleaner'n a rabbit in a corncrib!"

Bill said, "I was just seeing the direction the wind was coming."

"What for?" I asked.

Bill looked at me like I was a greenhorn idiot and replied, "I always check the wind when setting up for precision shooting."

"Look, Bill, you can be shooting in the middle of a tornado and it ain't gonna affect your aim real significant."

Well, I coulda argued that point some more, but it was then that Marco called out from acrost the yard, "Hey! What's going on out there?"

I said to Bill, "Look, I don't think he'll shoot at me. I'll just let him know I'm here to save his hash. It might work."

Bill said, "Be my guest, but be sure to pause out front and look around first."

So I stepped out from the shadow. I put my gun in my holster and called out, "Howdy, Marco. It's me. Royal."

"Royal! What are you doing here?" Marco calls back.

Bill whispers out to me, "Take a few more steps out. I'll cover you."

I did, but I don't know why. Then Marco calls out, "Don't come any closer, Royal!"

"Aw, come on, Marco. Give it up, will you? All we want's our money back."

"It is?" he called back.

"Sure. Now, why don't you and Armando give it up and we'll work things out?"

But Bill calls to me, "No, Roy! Rush the place!"

I turned 'round and said, "Cut it out, Bill. The gun play's over. This ain't no movie, this is real life, and I'd like to keep it that way for a bit longer, if you don't mind."

Then Marco calls out, "Who's that with you?"

"Bill Hart," I replied.

Then Armando calls out, "Hi, Bill! Love your work!"

All this chit chat and no problem-solving was making me restless. After all, it was ol' Royal duck-setting in the middle of the yard. So I took a few more steps toward the lodge and said, "Come on, Marco. You know you gotta settle things up sooner or later."

"Why?" he calls back.

"Because you got a name to clear up back in Hollywood," I said, figuring it was worth a try.

"Not after *Birth of a Badman* I don't!"

"Well, there'll be other films. You just gotta find someone else's money to do 'em with, that's all. So come on now, Marco. Dance is over. Come on out!" I waited, then suggested we alla us just face things. I ended up telling Marco, "You give me back my money and I won't press charges."

"What if I don't have it?"

Well, that was a whole other problem, but all I said was I wasn't gonna take it outa their hides like our two finger-poppers was. I ended with, "The way I see it, since we got these two goofs offa your backs, you owe us a whole lota explanations."

I could hear Armando and Marco discussing things some.

Then Bill calls out to me, "You better at least hold a gun on 'em!"

A little exasperated, I yelled back, "Do you mind?"

Then slowly the bullet-laden front door opened and out comes Armando and Marco. Their hands was held up and Marco carried a small satchel.

I said nice'n'easy, so's not to spook 'em, "Howdy, boys. Now, you can put your hands down. I. . ."

But Bill said, "No, I think you better keep 'em up." He was standing behind me, gun drawn and face hard.

seven

I slowly looked 'round and said, "What the hell you doing, Bill?"

"You too, Royal. Stick 'em up."

Well, you gotta know I was more mad than I was surprised. You watching this, Sailing, I remember thinking. Elsie, you remember your pa, don't you? I sized up my back friend and looked him hard in the eyes.

"Or what!" I growled.

"Or I'll blast you!" he growled back, giving me a snarl.

"The hell you will!" says me, leaping for his gun and shoving it upwards. It went off as I sailed into him and we fell to the ground in a life or death struggle. I was madder'n I ever been at anything in my whole life!

We hit and rolled and cursed and socked. Finally, when I had him straddled with my legs and was going in for the face-kill, he starts to laugh. Oh, he was coughing and spitting out blood, but he was laughing. It made me even madder. Finally, he spit out some words. All I caught was something about a cut. Well, he was cut all right and I was gonna make some more.

He caught his breath and issued a stronger, "Cut!" and he managed to motion behind me. I stole me a glance and then doubled it. There, smack dab in the middle of the yard, was a man cranking a camera and Gard Sullivan, Bill's writer, jotting down notes to beat the band.

They stopped doing their stuff and then stood there applauding us. Bill was laughing and I was in a state of roiled-up confusion. He got to his feet and wiped the blood from his face. For a man just took a beating down to his spurs, he was mighty jovial.

"I'm sorry, Royal," he begins, "I guess I owe you an explanation."

"With interest!" barks me.

"The boys have been filming us all along," he said.

"You mean this here's just another damn movie you been making?"

"No, no, this is real life, like you call it. I knew there'd be some drama and maybe even some shooting and well, you can't blame me going for authenticity." To which his cameraman commends us on some good work.

I took all this in and my heart was still raging. I looked at the barn, then at Marco and Armando, who seemed as spun about as me. Then I looked to Bill and said, "So that's why you wanted me to rush the place! Why, you dirty sonuvabitch, I coulda gotten kilt!"

"Now, now Royal," Bill says, trying to settle me down some, "you yourownself said Marco wouldn't shoot at you."

"That was just a lucky guess!" I yelped.

"Look at it my way," Bill continued. "I'm up here helping you out, losing time filming my own pictures. I'm just killing two birds with one stone."

"Yeah, at the risk of my life!"

Pretty soon all witnesses was all laughing, including I think some smirks from our two tied-up Mexicalies in the barn. So I myownself started to chuckle some. No harm done, I allowed.

But it was too bad the cameras wasn't rolling when, just as Bill slapped me on the back, I turned 'round and landed a full-loaded, side-winding buncha fives to his jaw. Well, he looked real stunned, reeled back, lost his balance, and landed flat on his afterpiece.

"Nope, I reckon no *real* harm done, Bill," I said, rubbing my fist and feeling much better.

I reckon the whole scene musta looked like a movie set, alla us counting our coups, when outa the woods comes none other'n Chesley Herman Manuel Mendoza Klepelmeier Warwick being escorted at gun point by Sailing O'Sullivan Strong, P. H. of D. He pokes him into the clearing to add to the explanations. 'Course, he was immediately beset upon by everyone, the loudest being my own Elsie.

I watched Elsie watch Chesley as he tried to worm his way outa his badger game. He finished off his spiel, which contained phrases like 'outa control,' 'too big for the botha us,' 'betrayed compatriots.' We even heard some Spanish to the hard cases, and I reckoned ol' Pancher Viller's ears was burning with alla the times Chesley tossed his name 'round. The more he talked, the more I knew we was alla us heading for a court of law and probably lawyers, to boot.

Then Chesley goes over to Elsie, takes her hand in his, and asks, "Elsie *sweetest*, you believe me, don't you? You know I never meant you any harm. Just think of the publicity if we play this right!"

She wasn't gonna let her face betray what was going on betwixt her eyes. She smiled sweet-like. Lordy, how I come to respect that sly smile. Then she picks up a heavy metal film box by the handles, heaves it 'round with both hands and all the spuzz that was in her, and lands it — SLAM! — right under Chesley's chiseled, etched-glass jaw. "Think of *that* publicity, sweetest!" she said, dusting her hands off for a job well done.

Chesley was out cold and never looked better.

We alla us packed outa the hills and back to the two automobiles, with the intentiona taking our five villains straight to the police in Los Angeles.

Bill ponied off our two horses with Gard and the cameraman, and they went from there back to Inceville. I thanked my horse for his good work, noticed Sailing was doing the same, and I remembered to give Fritz a pat, too. What a horse!

Sailing drove one car, with Elsie setting close next to him, and with me, Marco, Armando, ol' Smitty and Wes in the back seat (just in case). Bill drove the other car, with Juan, Ricardo, and Chesley all tied up in back.

We deposited the five characters and their car with the police, and since it was getting late and on the word of two William S. Harts, they locked 'em up till we could figure out what we was gonna do with the whole predicament.

Nextly, we took Elsie to Aunt Audie's, then Bill dropped me and Sailing off at the boarding house and then left for the Alexandria Hotel. Bill thanked me for providing him with one of the best damn days of his life, including that day Messala's horses had won the chariot race.

Sailing, being a youngun, headed for the kitchen, but I was fagged out and head to toe with dirt and blood, so I said good night. The lights in the house was dim and I figured it musta been later than I thought. Everyone musta been in bed. Good, thinks me. All for the best. I felt like I was hanging by one eyelash and too beat to even talk about it. I'd thought about ringing up E.M. at her place to let her know I was almost alive, but I was even too tired for that and reckoned Elsie would fill her in on my condition.

The stairs seemed double to me that night, but I finally worked my way to the top. I opened the door on my

Chick'n'Tad and eased my way in. The light from the bathroom shined on 'em and I softly kissed each cool forehead. Boy, was they gonna be mad when they learnt what fun I'd had without 'em, thinks me whilst I snuck on out.

I wearied my way into my room and went straight for the bathroom. I turned on the light, closed the door, and ran the sink water. I looked at myself in the harsh light and did I look a sight. I didn't even look like Royal Leckner, let alone Bill Hart. And my only consolation was Bill probably didn't look like hisself that night either. I cleaned my face up and assessed the damage. It was a good thing my acting career was over, for I think I was gonna have me another chin scar, meaner looking than the first.

With the water running I didn't hear the door open. So when I looked back into the steamed-up mirror, I almost dropped dead at E.M.'s reflection next to mine. All she said was, "Here, let me help you. Set down." She took the washcloth, soaked it in water, and repeated, "Stop staring, Royal. Set down and let me look at your chin." Her voice was all soft and kind and not like it was when she started one of her curtain lectures.

I did like I was told. I winced some whilst she dabbed my wounds. After each dab comes a kiss.

Finally I asked, "How'd you get in here? Buy yourself a ladder, E.M.?"

"No, Royal, I told Mrs. Taylor I was your wife, proud and legal, and I was moving in with my husband, providing of course he ever came back alive."

"I almost didn't," I said, maybe pulling the long bow a little.

"I've suffered tortures not knowing if you were alive or dead," she allows.

So I asked, a little sly-like, "What about Rosa Montenegro? She suffered tortures, too?"

"I think all that can wait until tomorrow."

"Ain't you even a little curious 'bout Elsie or what happened?" I asked.

E.M. wrung out the wash cloth and said, "I already know. She called me from our place."

"She did us proud, Ma," I said. I only ever called her 'Ma' when I was exceptional boastful of our offsprings.

"*You* do us all proud, Pa," E.M. returned. "Now hush. No more Hollywood. Tonight or ever. It's the furthest thing from my mind."

She stepped back and I noticed how playful the light was through her gown. "It is?" I asked, feeling some strength return.

"It is," she whispered. Then she set on my lap and kissed me, being real gentle 'round my wounds. Don't ask me where I got all my strength, but I picked her up and took her to my bed, where we didn't onct mention the words money, movie, or Marco.

eight

You staying with me thorough alla this, son? Need a review of the situation? Good, 'cause I don't think I could backtrack now, not when we was alla us heading to a court of law to settle this whole Royalscope fe-as-ko.

Now, courts in those days was a lot more relaxed than nowadays, where you gotta wait your turn, what with the Depression making crime a little more necessary to some folks. Anyhow, back then in Los Angeles they was able to find us a judge who had the clear grit to set and listen to all our gripes and accusations. Well, the one that marched into that courtroom was a real peach: he couldn'ta been more'n five feet tall and he was so rotund inside that gown of his, I swore there mighta been a coupla him inside. But I allowed as how round folks is generally a happy sort, and I knew a sensa humor might be a real asset that day.

He introduced hisself as Judge Henry Thorpe and allowed as this was just a hearing and for alla us to set down and don't be nervous and he'd get around to hearing eacha our pieces. Present was alla us principle players, including Miss Helena Troy and four of her great dames from the Curtain Call Home. And present also was the two ugly customers, the Machete and the Devil. Chesley was setting off to the side, all done up with a jaw-wrapper. His face was swolt and black-and-blue clear up to his eyes—a mere blur of his former beauty. He had him a jail guard next to him. Bill Hart set in the back with another man, who I reckoned was his lawyer.

Now, I ain't gonna tell you what everyone said, but you can be damn sure everyone had something to say about things. Somewheres 'round here I even have a whole typed-up transcription of the entire affair, but it gives me a headache to read through it. So I'll give you the general rundown, and like Judge Thorpe you can start drawing some conclusions of your own.

The first person, wouldn't you know, to toss in his two cents' worth (which was mostly his total value) was that Chesley Warwick. He comes up to the judge and starts mumbling words that no one could understand even if they coulda heard 'em. Judge Thorpe finally hands him some paper and a pencil, and Chesley commences to write up what he's saying. The judge reads it first to hisself, then to alla us.

"'I demand to be taken to the Mexican Embassy.' What for?" the judge asked. Chesley wrote some more things down and the judge read, "'Asylum. I operate in the United States under full protection.' From who?" asked the judge.

To which Chesley scribbled, "I can say nothing more except I am innocent of all charges."

The judge looked almost a little reliefed, then ordered his bailiff, "Harry, take this man to the Federal Courthouse. He wants protection; let the Federal boys do it. They're always gripping I get all the interesting cases; let's see what they do with this one. One less problem for me. There. That was easy." Then he looks out over the resta us and asks, "Anyone else here too good for my humble little court?"

So they begin to escort Chesley Warwick outa the court and outa our lifes. But just so's he knew I knew there wasn't gonna be no sanctuary or asylum or anything, I took Chesley aside and showed him a small roll of film. I held a few frames up to the light. I could tell by the redning in his eyes he needed no further explanation. I handed the film to the bailiff, suggesting he and them federal boys watch theirselves a little moving picture show. Ol' Chesley mumbles him some expletives in God knows what languages and is escorted out, bringing Chick'n'Tad to their feets with hoops and hollers, like they was booing him off a stage.

With him gone, the judge then said as how ladies oughta go first and, of course, I didn't think E.M. would have had it any other way. She provided him with the Royalscope Productions contract and he just set it aside and said, "Why don't you tell me in your own words, Mrs. Leckner, just what all this is about."

Well, I ain't seen E.M. pull up short in the vocabulary department too many times in our lifes, but she just looked at me, blank-like, then turned back to the judge. I reckon she finally figured out she'd been milking the wrong pigeon. She said, "I'm not sure what all this is about."

"You're not?" he asked back.

"No, that's why we're here in court. To sift things through. Of course, it's your court, sir, but if I were you the first thing I'd do is narrow down the population." Then she ticked her head toward the two thugs.

The judge looked at 'em, who was both handcuffed and standing before a policeman. Then he asked E.M., "Oh? How do you propose I do that?"

"Well, these two men are obviously just ordinary extortionists. Why don't you send them off to jail? My husband told me they're just common juice dealers."

"Juice dealers?" asked the judge, like he ain't never heard that before. Folks was beginning to laugh.

I don't think the judge wanted to lose control so early in the game, so he rapped his gavel and then asked the policeman, "Anything on these two . . . juice dealers?"

His reply was yes, they was known arms smugglers Juan Ortega and Ricardo Diaz. They both had a long lista outstanding things that they could be put away for, up to and including rustling some horses from Tommy Ince back in '13.

E.M. says, "There. You see? Put 'em away!"

And the judge came back with, "Madam, do you mind? Anybody here see any need to take up any more of Señor Ortega's or Señor Diaz's valuable time?" No one said nothing and Judge Thorpe was looking mighty prouda hisself when they handed two more over to the Federal boys.

As the policeman escorted 'em out, Ricardo—El Diablo—said to Marco, "You are in beeg trouble, Mahellan! No one crosses El Diablo!"

Marco here looked all innocent and wounded onaccounta he held his heart like he'd been hit with a hard one. He replied, "Mr. Diablo, I assure you, I never crossed anyone. I'm just a poor film maker." Which, looking back, was the whole truth and nothing but. They led our two bascaderos away.

The judge picked that one up and said, "Well, let's start with that point, Mr. . . . what'd he call you . . . ?" he looked down at his notes and then said, "Ma*hell*an?"

Marco stepped up and said, "Ma*gell*an. I swear, Your Honor, I was just borrowing money. Chesley Warwick, he set it all up. He secured investors and then handled all our money. Look," and he starts to pull out several folded-up contracts to show how many times Chesley had him sign on the dotted line. The judge takes a quick look at the papers and said, "Gee, I wish you hadn't shown me these."

"Why?" Marco asked, real righteous-like.

"Because now I have to admit them as evidence."

"But there's no law against borrowing money from. . . a. . . private enterprise."

"No, that's true, Mr. Magellan. The 'law against' part comes when you don't pay it back. Or when you don't deliver on your product."

"Well, I *will* pay it back! " Marco barks, real regal-like. "As soon as my movie starts to make money. These things take time!"

"How does fifteen years to life sound?" I asked, outa turn, but not caring.

"And which one are you?" the judge asked, pointing his gavel at me.

I stood up, all patched up hither and yon, and replied, "Royal Leckner, Your Honor. The 'Royal' parta 'Royal-scope.' Marco here owes me close to twenty thousand dollars that my wife—that's her—invested in his moving picture."

"Look, Mr. Leckner, an investment is just that . . . a risk. You should have realized you might have lost your money if this movie . . . what was it. . . ?"

We alla us answered, "*Birth of a Badman.*"

"Your Honor," I continued, approaching the bench and trying not to appear too much taller'n him, even though he was setting on a platform. "I know about risks and all. But Marco's a shyster, plain and simple. He took alla our money and then ran out to leave us high'n'dry. Hell—I mean heck—he's *famous* for it."

"Famous?" Marco asked, a tiny smile on his lips like he'd long awaited association with that word.

"Sure. Ask anyone," I said.

It was here Armando came to Marco's side and said, "Your Honor, we ran because once we saw the sort of creature that Chesley Warwick was, we were afraid we'd get muscled. And just how can Marco make another film to secure the investments if he has two broken legs?"

"Or no eyes, heaven forbid!" Marco added, crossing hisself, Catholic-style, for luck.

Then the Artistic Interpretator added to his Director-General, "If you'd only listened to *me*, Marco. I warned you not to trust that philistine Warwick."

Then I said to Marco, "You know, I was willing to believe you was upright and above board. A little eccentric, maybe, but not on the beat and out to chisel us. But then you took for the hills. It don't matter who you was running from or why, you was running!"

It was then Miss Helena Troy stood up and corroborated my case and added her own which was another ten thousand's worth.

She handed the judge their contract, which he skimmed over.

"Let's see now," the judge said, "that's twenty thousand to you (me) and ten thousand to you (the ladies)." Then he looked at the bailiff and asked, "Are there any seized assets?"

The bailiff put a money bag and three cans of film on the desk and handed the judge a slip of paper, which he announces to us, "Says here total assets are: $9,623.29 cash and one movie, *Birth of a Badman*."

"Mr. Leckner," the judge goes on. "Would you retire the debt for, well, let's just call it an even ten thousand? That's fifty cents on the dollar. You wouldn't get half that in a bankruptcy, even being first on the payoff list," the judge said, trying to move things along. I think he knew what a pickle the whole thing was and just wanted alla us outa his court and his life.

Don't be a stubborn sonuvagun, Royal, I was saying to myself. Take the money and your family back home where you all belong. I looked at E.M., then at Elsie, then at Chick'n'Tad, who was being real quiet. No doubt the boys was wondering if maybe some cases of their own was gonna be next on the docket.

I said, "I reckon I best take what I can."

The judge handed me the money sack and I thanked him, thinking to myself, That wasn't so bad, and we'd be on a train home by four o'clock. He told his bailiff man to write up a receipt.

Well, soon as I touched that bag, the five ladies from the Curtain Call took their cues and commenced to weep and put hankies to their noses and 'there-there, they'd muddle through somehow' back and forth.

I again took a look around. No one said nothing, not even His Honor Upstairs Who'd always been right insistent in kicking me in the right direction.

I took a sigh, knowing myself better'n that. I handed the ladies the money bag and, by the way they took it I had the feeling it was all being filmed. I got bless yous and kisses and I reckoned I'd done the Golden Thing. But, of course, that left me outa the settlement and still a 75% owner of a big, fat zero. Unless, of course, I counted those three cans of film setting on the judge's desk.

nine

It was at this point that Sailing approached the bench and said, "Your Honor, I've been following all these events quite closely and I think I can shed some light on things."

He told the court who he was and what his role was in alla this. This is how his IQ summed things up:

Chesley Warwick, also known as Herman Manuel Mendoza Klepelmeier, had strong ties to the Mexican Revolution. He was funneling Royalscope money into a shady dealing outfit which supplied guns for the revolution. As near as he could tell, Warwick sliced two sets of books, one for the movie productions and one for the arms purchases. Money being invested into the company was being diverted, plain and simple. Folks thought they were investing in films, but it was the *Villistas* who were seeing the dividends. The two hoodlums were the go-betweens. Somewhere along the line, they bought a shipment of arms which had been rendered useless, and when I heard the words 'rendered useless' I knew where Sailing was going. But Sailing was a step aheada me, for he then produced the so-called movie props which my own Tad had stole. The judge then accepted the dismantled armaments as evidence, and even though ol' Tad set up a fuss 'bout having his stolen goods get in turn stole, they was sent over to the Federal Courthouse. Sailing ended his spiel by telling the judge that in his opinion it was all just as well, because wasn't the whole point to keep arms, any arms, away from the German sympathizers, who were known to be gun shopping all over the West Coast? And wasn't it strange that part of Warwick's original name was pretty damn German?

The judge took a long look at Sailing, sighed him a deep one like he didn't want nothing to do with Germans now on topa everything else, and said Dr. Strong's opinion would be noted in the court records but don't bring it up again, and now could they get on with the case at hand?

'Course, by that time all I wanted to do was escape the tentacles of Hollywood. "Look," says me to the judge and anyone else who was interested, "I dismiss all the charges and. . ."

"There aren't any charges," the judge interrupts, resting his head on his hands and looking a little low in the chops.

"There ain't?" I barked. "Then what the hell we doing here?"

It was then the judge glared at me, and I thought he looked like he was all fogged up. He said, "I don't know. Somebody requested a hearing and so here I am, hearing."

It was then Bill Hart rose and spoke up. "Your Honor, *I* requested a hearing." Those who hadn't noticed his shiner-eyed, luminary presence was now all smiles that a *real* ACK-tor was amongst us.

Bill came over to stand next to me. We shook hands and compared facial wounds.

The judge said, leafing through his desk papers, "Let's see now, that would make you William S. Hart." He wasn't impressed by the name, but he sure as hell was when he saw us standing side by side infronta him, identical down to the swolt right eyes. "Say, anyone ever mention you two look alike?"

"Yes. In fact, Your Honor, that's one reason why I asked for this hearing," Bill says. "What I have to get done here today has to be clean and legal."

"Well, don't stop there, Mr. Hart," the judge recommends, leaning back in his chair.

Then Bill began to pull some legal papers outa his pockets. "This," he says, "is a distribution contract for the Royalscope production of *Birth of a Badman*."

Now, I wasn't first-hand sure what that meant, but I think it meant ol' Marco was stepping down off the gallows. There was gasps abounding in that room. But it was E.M. that gasped the loudest. She trumped up with, "Oh no you don't, William S. Hart! Nothing you can say will allow me—my husband—to let the lousiest, most stinking, rotten thirty-five minutes of film history be shown to anyone!"

And she seizes up the three cans of film and holds 'em to her breast like they was Chick'n'Tad 'bout to be snatched up by kidnappers. Let me rephrase that: she grabbed the film like it was a life jacket and she was on the Titanic.

Well, now we was alla us confused. But Bill barreled her down like I'd done a million times and she barreled him right back up. Sweartagod, it was like watching a movie of one of our own battles.

Bill said for me, "But Miss Montenegro, I thought you wanted to be a. . ."

"That movie will make me and my entire family the laughing stock of the entire nation! We own 75% of this movie and I'm going to destroy 75% of it! Anyone got a match?" And she looks 'round, her eyes a little wild-like. I glowered at Chick in case he was thinking 'bout supplying the arson.

The judge broke in and said, "You put that movie right back down, Mrs. Leckanegro or whatever your name is! Now if this man, known far and wide as a fine film maker, says he's going to give that movie a chance, then you've got no right to complain if you lose money on your investment."

Just about everyone in that courtroom agreed, and E.M. said, "But Your Honor, it's awful! Just watch it yourself and you'll know what a mistake it is to. . ."

Well, I'd been watching her wheels turning. She stopped mid-sentence and turned to Bill, smiled her I-talian smile, and asked how much for distribution rights. That's my E.M.—fastest grab on a dollar in the West.

He showed her a check for five thousand dollars. I looked over his shoulder, and E.M. and me looked at each other. Maybe our prides wasn't as big as first she thought.

So we agreed to take the money, thinking two bits on the dollar was better'n a kick in the teeth.

"There is one proviso," E.M. said, before handing over the dotted line: "That movie is not to be shown in either Washington State or Oregon State. Agreed?"

Bill agreed. 'Course ol' E.M. didn't know it then, but that was one of the biggest favors she ever did for me.

Bill went on. "Now then, we have the problem of Royal Leckner." He looked me over like I was Exhibit B. He walked around me like he was the highest nabob and I was the lowest hoi polloi. "What to do about Royal Leckner?" Well, he onct again pulled out some papers from his pocket and handed 'em to the judge.

"Now what?" the judge asked, looking up and down the paper.

"I am willing to offer Mr. Leckner the sum of five thousand dollars in exchange for his signature agreeing to stay out of films for as long as I am appearing in them."

What a fox.

"Bill," I says, "You can have that for free."

E.M. sidled over to me, pinched my arm, and sneezed me three big ones, which I recognized as a sign to sign. I grinned at Bill as I did. That made two agreements the judge had to notarize, and now we was back up to fifty cents on the dollar.

"Let's see," Bill said, patting his pockets. "Is that everything?" But he found a third set of papers and these also he handed to our judge, who was looking mighty tired by then. "Oh yes, one last thing." Which the judge allowed onaccounta Bill'd been doing all right so far.

"This last check," Bill says to me, "also for five thousand dollars, is a quit claim to your . . . a . . . somewhat 'volunteer' performance in the film we shot up in the mountains." His eyes gleamed and I could tell he was sure enjoying hisself.

When I asked him what I had to do for that, he tells me nothing I hadn't already done, and he figured five thousand dollars was right equitable for a few days' working as myownself.

"Right equitable?" I asked, recognizing some of my favorite words. Sign I did, and the judge looked at his watch and asked Bill if he was done.

"Yes, Your Honor. I shall now take my exit."

The judge looked out over everybody and asked, "Does anybody . . . *anybody* . . . have anything else to add to this. . . this fiasco?"

We looked about and just when I thought we'd made it through the hearing with our dignities and some money to boot, up pops the man Bill had been setting with in the back of the room.

"I do, Your Honor," he states.

"I knew it," His Honor grumbled to his bailiff. "Approach the bench."

He comes forward and takes his floppy hat offa his head and he told the judge his name. Everyone, even the little old ladies, recognized the name David Wark Griffith . . . the grand sachem of the movie business.

He comes over, shakes my hand, and says, "Well, well, well. If it isn't the owner of the famous Royal Bar-L. Nice to see you again, sir."

'Course, I was enjoying E.M.'s face, which was pretty damn much wide open. And you shoulda seen Marco when he saw him. You'd think that God Hisownself had come to give His Judgment on the whole situation.

Griffith had one of those faces that always seems to be hiding a joke. Kinda a half-smile, like he knew the outcome and wasn't gonna tell anyone.

"Now, what do you have to do with all this?" the judge asked.

He said real elegant, "Well, Your Honor, it seems it was *my* hunting lodge that got shot up during the fiasco, as you called it. Not to mention the damage done to my friend's Stutz Bearcat."

"Oh, no. A Stutz Bearcat was damaged?" the judge asked.

Mr. Griffith nodded tragic-like.

"I've always wanted a Stutz Bearcat," Judge Thorpe added, and I wondered if we was gonna lose everything back we'd so far gained.

The judge looked to his bailiff, then through all the papers on his desk, and said, "All right. What got shot up?"

Hell, I thought, bringing up the shoot-out would just most likely bring the two thugs back into it and that would start us all over again. So I said, "It was for the movie, Your Honor. Nothing too serious." Then I turned to D.W. Griffith and said, "How much damage was done? I'll pay for it outa my own pocket."

E.M. comes over to me and says, "Royal, *we* shouldn't have to shell out money for. . ."

But I shished her and reminded her it don't do to get too greedy when we'd been dodging bullets all summer, and wasn't it she who always said "pigs get fed, but hogs get butchered?" So I onct again asked Mr. Griffith how much.

He turned to the judge and said, "I don't want money."

"Well, Dave, I ain't got nothing else," I said, getting wearier'n poor Judge Thorpe.

D.W. turned to me and said, "Royalscope currently holds some contracts that I'd like to take in exchange for all damages."

I had to think 'bout what he was talking 'bout. "What contracts?"

D.W. continued, "It so happens Mr. Hart here ran *Birth of a Badman* for me this morning and, although I'm not fond of the title, I think there's some moderately potential talent on the Royalscope lot."

"There is?" I asked. You can imagine my expression, and there went all the ears in the room, perked up like horses' ears hearing the can in the oat bin.

Then it was Mr. Griffith's turn to pull out some contracts. He handed 'em to me and I called out the names of Sailing Strong and Marco Magellan. I had one left and I was afraid to look at the name on it, onaccounta both E.M. and Elsie was now looking at me like hungry wolfs. "Miss

Helena Troy," I said, and the great dame rose like she was accepting the Royal Order of the Garter or something. I looked at my undiscovered two womenfolk. E.M. just gave me a what-the-hell shoulder shrug and Elsie, I'm proud to say, was busy sharing Sailing's good fortune with him. I knew things was gonna be all right with their prides.

Bill leant next to me and whispered, "Naturally, Mr. Griffith need never know about Marco's version of *Birth of a Badman.*"

We both looked like we was mighty fulla ourselfs. I replied, "Naturally." We shook hands and then just enjoyed the dreams that was coming true right there before our eyes.

"By the way," ol' D.W. said, looking stern-like over at Armando, "the next time you use my lodge, young man, I'd appreciate your leaving the weapons at home."

We was all quiet and just gawked at Armando. He grinned a little meek-like and just said, "Yes, Uncle David."

You shoulda seen the expressions on Marco's face whilst he stared, plumb speechless, at Armando Cato, Artistic Interpretator. How do you like that? All along, that friendly little Armando had him the best entree into the whole movie world and he never onct let on. Like I say, I always did like ol' Armando. And I liked him even more for blazing his own trail.

Let's you and me move on out to the porch. There's clouds in the west and that always makes for a fine and fitting sunset. Yeah, bring the bottle.

The Final Reel

Now tell me that ain't a beautiful sunset. The view up here is mighty powerful and it can surely take my breath away. One of these days I reckon it'll take my breath away and it won't come back. Well, that'll be okay with me. Can't think of a prettier sight to be my last.

You know, lots came outa our summer in California in 1915. One of the best outcomes was Bill Hart and me to this very day being best friends. Hell, he's a whole team and a horse to spare, in my book. He used to visit us at the Royal Bar-L real regular. We'd ride, fish, play with Chick'n'Tad, shoot cans, mend fence, and swap lies.

Now there's something else betwixt Bill and me other'n friendship. Seems outa our association and such, one of his writer men hatched him a movie plot a coupla years later that had Bill playing twins. I think he got the idea whilst watching the filma Bill and me duking it out that day. Now, I ain't saying I did and I ain't saying I didn't—but it just could be that in Bill's movie *Three Word Brand,* maybe when he sets down to have a Hart to Hart talk with hisself, well, maybe halfa it wasn't trick photography. I reckon it's one of those things I've seen fit to forget for a price.

Now, none of us coulda seen what the E-motion pictures was gonna become—that they'd just get grander and grander. Hell, now that they got that sound added and with all this talk about color, no telling what they'll become. Well, none of us knew much that summer.

Oh, speaking of not knowing much, it might interest you to know that Armando Cato, Marco Magellan, and Sailing Strong all changed their names shortly thereafter, like movie folks is inclined to do. Changed their names and changed their callings. Sailing Strong got him a *nom de plume* and commenced to be a founding father of screen stories. Marco, looking as interesting as he did, hung up his director's outfit and became one of filmdom's finest—I love the term—*character* ACK-tors. Think he mighta even invented the term, and what a character he was.

Speaking of characters, ol' Armando was one original character hisownself. I always did like that feller. He's nowadays considered one of the finest artistic boys in the business. He travels all over filmdom opinionating 'bout colors and costumes and makeups and lighting and you name it. If it needs an opinion, Armando's the one to ask.

Now here's a little hint on who those three became: Up to now, 1935, they have, betwixt the three of 'em, five of them Academy Award nominations in various categories. So that oughta keep you guessing.

And that Chesley Warwick? Or Herman Klepelmeier as he is known nowadays? Well, remember that day in the courtroom when Sailing expounded his theory of Germans and guns and such? Well, turns out ol' Chesley Warwick was deep-connected to all sortsa gun smugglers and runners and such, and when we finally did enter the War to End All Wars, Chesley was in the thicka things—only this time he was working undercover and, you guessed it, according to his just published memoirs he became a real handy U.S. spy. Turns out that smash Elsie delivered to him in his face went a long way to build him some of that credibility he always says his good looks kept him from getting. See? Everything most usually happens for the best, including stitches and espionage. Maybe someday Sailing will write a movie 'bout ol' Herman Mendoza Chesley Manuel Warwick Klepelmeier. Hope he includes that part about Chesley's momma being a Mexican spy and his daddy being a German spy, which I think might explain all Chesley's fretting over not having him any credibility.

Oh, I almost forgot! It might interest you to know that there was a good reason why E.M.'s nose would commence to itching and sneezing so much 'round Marco Magellan. Turns out she was having a nasal reaction to the Macassar oil he used to slick back his hair. Well, I knew all along it was allergies, but I held in my I-told-you-sos. For, as it turns out, she had a even bigger I-told-you-so to hang over my head and here's why:

You might think we lost five thousand dollars that summer . . . fact is, we did real good, thanks to E.M.'s nose and her little trip up to San Francisco. Seems that she traded half-interests for half-profits in our vineyards to two little I-talian brothers, fresh offa the boat, who hardly spoke any English. Well, E.M. reckoned they didn't know we was cruising for prohibition in the United States, but he put up one helluva glassa grape. I know, you're thinking what a mean-spirit my wife was, right? Nip-cheesing poor ol' immigrants for failure? Nope. Put away your fears. Never mind 'bout them little I-talian men. With our land and their talents, we alla us made out real equitable. Chances are, when you hoist a domestic glass, you're putting one of their grandkids through college. Ours too. And we survived Prohibition all right, thanks to them Catholics and their sacramental wine needs.

Now, remember I said E.M.'s insisting on not having *Birth of a Badman* ever be shown in Oregon or Washington proved to be real good for me? Here's why: E.M. never knew Bill Hart released the good version, the one he had his own crew put together. She never saw how passable she was in that movie. So, never again did E.M. have the chance to get screen-struck. In fact, onct she got her hair to grow back out, we hardly ever mentioned it. Well, every onct in a while E.M.'d get a little fulla herself or lathered up about something. You know, just in a general state of distraction. And I'd pull out the three tin cans fulla that awful Magellan film asking if she'd like to become a film star in Walla Walla Wash. Usually she'd laugh and I'd laugh, then we'd glare at each other a I-dare-you. So I always kept those cans hidden, just in case.

Ah yes, so's I don't keep you in suspenders: Elsie and Sailing finally got married. 'Course, theirs was a rocky courtship . . . after all, Elsie *is* E.M.'s daughter. Well, don't get me started down that trail. I don't think either of us is up to their love story just now. Anyhow, Elsie had her schooling to finish and Sailing had some hard-work years aheada him under ol' D.W. Griffith's wings. But whenever they came for a visit, Sailing and me'd saddle up and ride and we'd end up talking 'bout that summera 1915. Too bad Sailing turned out to be such a good adjective-jerker. I always thought I coulda made a damn good cowboy outa him. Hell, he could fork a horse, shoot a gun, and he even knew the language. But no matter what, he's ace-high in my book and a good provider to my daughter.

Now, about Chick'n'Tad, God love 'em. No two boys was ever happier to get back on their ponies. Don't think they got off 'em for the resta the summer. Well, they grew up real fine, strong and straight like me and fulla piss'n'vinegar like their momma and sister. Since I still legally owned 75% of that place called Royalscope Productions and since all those other eccentrics made good with their dreams, you'll be interested to know that Chick'n'Tad both returned one day to Hollywood to reopen the studio. But that's a whole other episode and maybe even one which you oughta get straight from their mouths; but I will warn you now: talk to each one separate, onaccounta they'll never see things the same.

You know, when I set back and look out over my summer fields, I thinka that time in Hollywood. In a way, our lifes was kinda like Hollywood itsownself: up-starting and arrogant. Hell, we lived through just about every kinda picture on the marquee: We laughed our way through a few Mack Sennett slapsticks, we shot our way through some William S. Hart westerns, ham-acted our way through some Thomas Ince mellerdramers, and we even mushed our way through some D.W. Griffith romances. We had us some Cyrano and Roxanne, some Svengali and Trilby. Even had us some Phantom of the Horse Opera, just to keep us laughing.

Moral? What moral? Hell, all this has been is a story 'bout being who you ain't and becoming what you are. Simple as that. And if that don't make any sense to you, then I guess you've never gotten too fulla yourself or seen your face bigger'n life on a screen, or taken yourself too serious, like we alla us did that eccentric summer of 1915.

That's it. Everything. All swell that end swell and. . .

Ah, reservoir!